I0731289

A MATCH (NOT) MADE IN HEAVEN

The Match Girls, Book 1

By Michelle L. Levigne

Zion Ridge Press LLC

Mt Zion Ridge Press LLC
295 Gum Springs Rd, NW
Georgetown, TN 37366

https://www.mtzionridgepress.com

ISBN 13: 978-1-949564-74-7

Published in the United States of America
Publication Date: February 1, 2020

Editor-In-Chief: Michelle Levigne
Executive Editor: Tamera Lynn Kraft

Chapter One

By 11:30pm, December 23rd, despite mistletoe hanging from every light and in both doorways of the church parlor, I was kiss-less.

What did I get wrong?

Thad and I had been "officially" dating for more than a month. It was nearly Christmas. We were alone. There was mistletoe all over the place. Reggie (my best friend and his cousin) had hung all that mistletoe when we decorated for the Singles Christmas party. Thad knew it was there, because he teased her about how much she had put up. He also joined in teasing the three couples who had gotten engaged since Halloween, warning them not to park under the mistletoe and block traffic.

He didn't kiss me under the mistletoe.

Granted, cleaning up after a big party, late at night, wasn't the most romantic setting. Thad wasn't the most romantic guy, either. He was president of the Singles, and I was the Jane-of-all-Trades for the Singles, just like I was for our church office. It was up to us to clean up. Just the two of us thanks to Reggie's conniving. She certainly had more hopes for my relationship with her cousin than I did right about then.

Approaching midnight of the day before Christmas Eve, I was kiss-less and exhausted, and loaded down with all the leftovers. (But not the mistletoe -- that went into the trash.)

Thad drove me home, because Reggie and I had come to church together and she had abandoned me. He helped me carry the food into the house. I should have had him leave it on the front porch. It was cold enough to use as a walk-out freezer. With the bushes to hide the porch contents from view, it had served that purpose often enough.

He put the stack of aluminum trays on the counter, turned, and saw his Christmas present. I had left it out, to give him when he dropped me off after the party.

Granted, I had mapped out a different sequence of events. He was supposed to kiss me in the church parlor, then drive me home, and we'd exchange Christmas presents.

The deluxe car care products were visible through the green cellophane wrapping the aluminum wash bucket, so Thad had to know it was for him. A man and his car. Obviously, his BMW meant more to him than I did. His eyes lit up. He grinned at me. I thought he would lick his lips in another moment.

"Merry Christmas, Thad." Exhausted, I was moving on autopilot. I picked up that bucket, gave it to him, and *then* my brain kicked into gear. No kiss for me, no present for me, should have equaled no present for him. Too late.

"Wow -- that's incredible. Oh." That glow left his eyes. I thought maybe he would be sick, right there in my kitchen. *Not* the present I was looking for. "Sorry. Forgot." He dug in his pocket and pulled out an envelope. "Merry Christmas, Dinah."

He leaned forward, and I thought he would try to kiss me. Better late than never, right? Then he yawned. He was falling *over* from exhaustion, not *into* the spirit of the season.

"See you in the morning." Then he was out the door with that gift I shouldn't have given him.

Reggie and I had spent *four hours* finding all the brands he preferred. She insisted this and the holidays would boost our relationship higher. More proof she was better at selling cosmetics than dating advice. What had we missed from the checklist of warning signs we had developed from watching other relationships bomb?

I couldn't feel a gift card in that #10 envelope. What could be in it? Too late for tickets to the ***Nutcracker*** at Playhouse Square, or the Radio City Rockettes. Both shows had closed, and Thad hadn't reacted when I mentioned wanting to see them. Several times. I had learned from living with Dad that men needed hints and nudges. Often.

Not too exhausted to be curious, I opened the envelope. Get the pain over with quickly.

A paper certificate.

From the Galactic Bookshelf. Thad's favorite store.

The scenario was too familiar. I spent eight years after Mom died, nagging Dad to remember things like doctor appointments and church meetings and groceries. When he had to buy a present, Dad's routine was to "forget" until he had no time to shop. Then he'd ask me to do it. When he forgot to ask me, or I didn't have time, he always bought what he would want, not what would please the other person. It just never occurred to him, despite constant reminders (or the embarrassment of giving a gift that was dead wrong) that maybe other people didn't have the exact same taste and interests as him.

The Galactic Bookshelf was just around the corner from the computer services company Thad ran with three of his many cousins. He probably ran out to the store on his lunch hour on Friday, when something or someone reminded him that since he had a girlfriend now -- *moi* -- he had to buy a Christmas present.

I'd been to that store once. Other than three shelves of fantasy books, there was nothing among all those gaming manuals and cards and figurines and computer software I would want.

"He's going to dump me," I whispered. What else was I to think, after he ignored all that mistletoe and came up with a Christmas present so very obviously last-minute? Which he didn't give me until *after* he got a present from me.

I laughed. Exhaustion was definitely setting in and causing brain damage. Shouldn't I be upset? What did tonight say about his idea of our relationship? Maybe he didn't even know we *had* a relationship?

My next thought? *Relief.* That revealed a lot I didn't have the energy or alertness to contemplate. After all, it was officially Sunday, Christmas Eve day, and I had a ton of things to do at church in the morning.

Church in the morning.

That thought woke me up like getting dragged out of my tent, in my sleeping bag, and into the lake at church camp.

In eight hours, Reggie would want a full report on how things went after the party, when Thad and I had been alone.

I was doomed.

<><><>

"So?"

Reggie caught my arm as I went down the hall at the T-intersection in front of the church parlor doors, and pulled me out of the current of people leaving after the first service. Despite being my closest friend since being dumped in adjoining cells (cribs) in the overcrowded church nursery, she was the last person

I wanted to see. Especially not after last night's epiphany.

"So what?" I offered my biggest cheesy grin and tried to yank free, to head to the left where the main hallway led to the fellowship hall and the coat racks. The only alternative was to make a U-turn and out the big double doors, back out into the Christmas Eve morning snowstorm.

Reggie wasn't having any of my pretend obtuseness. She took the third option, yanking me along behind her hard enough I had to follow or else go to my knees and get dragged. We landed in the short hallway that ran between the little kitchen (as opposed to the main kitchen at the other end of the church) and the second door into the church parlor.

"So, what did Thad get you for Christmas?"

"Besides the glorious news he's getting ready to dump me?"

"He isn't going to dump you."

"Not until after the New Year's bash. He needs me to take care of all the food while he handles the games and music."

"He messed up the gift, didn't he? I told the big dope --" She stopped, her eyes wide and stricken, and pressed one long-nailed hand over her mouth.

In honor of Christmas, her nails were painted to look like light bulbs, alternating in red and green, with gold bases. As a beauty consultant, she was paid to play with all that goop. One benefit of having Reggie for best pal was that she could run all the analyses and get me the perfect makeup for my coloring and skin type -- as presents or on employee discount.

"You *told* him to get me a gift? Don't you know that ruins everything? It totally skews the factors that indicate if a guy is serious or when he's going to break up with you!"

"That's a stupid theory."

"It's *your* theory!"

"Yeah." She looked down at the floor, then up at me, remorse making her eyes go Bambi-wide and dark. "Sorry. I didn't even think of that. I just didn't want him to get you something totally lame. Especially after we spent so much time putting together that present for him."

"If he didn't get me a Christmas present, I could have gotten my money back." Part of me wanted to laugh, but there was the agony of time that was always in short supply, spent on a guy who clearly didn't care about me.

I didn't have much time or money to waste. Being the Jane-of-all-Trades for our church provided me with just enough sense of having a ministry to augment my salary. That and a major dose of guilt kept me from quitting my job every time someone used the "but we're family here" line as a club to get their way.

The little tokens of appreciation I received nearly made up for the salary that hadn't seen an increase in the last three years. Most came from the silver-haired iron ladies who ran the church behind the scenes -- often without the knowledge of their husbands, who thought *they* did, because they were deacons and trustees and the chairmen of various committees. We women knew better.

"Just how lame was the idiot's gift?" Reggie asked, cringing.

"Gift certificate to the Galactic Bookshelf."

"I'm going to pound him at the family party on Friday," she growled. "I told him if he couldn't remember all those hints we've been dropping, he should play it safe and get you a gift card ... Well, it doesn't matter now. You gave him that kit we put together for him, didn't you?"

"I was too tired to think straight. He saw it when he drove me home. Which is partly your fault. You stranded me there."

"You let me! You didn't argue when I suggested carpooling for the last-minute errands."

"True. It was still a dirty trick."

"Was supposed to be a nice trick," she muttered.

I could only sigh. At least she hadn't asked how well all that mistletoe had worked. That thought made me panic and I hurried on before she asked. "What was I going to do when he saw his gift sitting there? Pretend there was *another* guy in my life who would get it? I don't even have Dad around to blame."

"I was hoping he might ask Grammy for a ring for you."

"Why? We've only gone on six dates." I managed an almost-but-not-quite rusty laugh.

"Yeah, but you two have been together, a pair, running everything for the Singles, like ... forever," she said with a shrug.

"Even forever has to end. I love you like a sister, but that's not enough reason to marry Thad. But it doesn't matter because he will never get around to asking."

"I didn't know the two of you were dating," a woman said

from behind us. That rich, elegant voice that always made me think of spicy-soft dusting powder sent me into a panic, even before I identified it.

Reggie looked over my shoulder. Her eyes got big and stunned. Which confirmed what my gut instinct was telling me.

I should have just stayed home that morning. Except I had to help with announcements and get the leftovers from my car for refreshments for class, which was starting in fifteen minutes.

Why was I always so responsible?

"Grammy," Reggie managed to say with minimal shattering in her voice.

Thus died my last hope. Victoria Grant, the leader of all the silver-haired iron ladies who ran the church.

Well, that answered one question. I had wondered when I would get lectured by her about dating one of her grandsons. She had twenty-some grandchildren. A widow with two children, Victoria had married Archibald Grant, a widower with three children. Then they had two sons of their own. The Grants helped build our church. I knew that for a fact, because I had been compiling all the dusty, musty historical documents for the church's seventy-fifth birthday. The Grants were there from the beginning of time.

If Reggie's grandmother didn't know I was dating Thad, that proved he was dumping me soon. He kept our relationship, whatever it was, secret from his grandmother. He was just keeping me around until he could coerce another hard worker to take over my duties on the social committee.

Maybe I could get Reggie to break into Thad's apartment and get back that present before he used it?

"They only went out a couple times, Grammy," Reggie said, while I was still turning around to face her. "Thad and Dinah run everything in Singles, so they're always together. Sometimes the only ones working, you know?" She choked. "I mean, I help, but you know, I have my job and now the kids' theater production coming up and ... You know?"

"I know the feeling quite well." Mrs. Grant stepped out of the shadowy little kitchen as I met her dark, assessing, don't-try-to-hide-the-fact-you-skated-down-the-Sunday-School-hallway-in-your-socks-during-the-starve-for-hunger-fundraiser-sleepover look. Then she patted my upper arm. "Dinah Clydesdale. A very good match."

"They're not a match, Grammy." Reggie raised her voice a little as Mrs. Grant glided around us and tucked the Longaberger basket under one arm as she tugged on her gloves.

Reggie was one brave chick, contradicting her grandmother. I was so glad she was my best friend.

"Thad got her a lame Christmas present," she continued. "It's a typical dump warning sign."

"Maybe he did it as a stopgap measure." Those thin, pale rose lips quirked up. "We were talking about family jewelry the other day, and he mentioned my grandmother's diamonds ..." That sparkle in her eye was enough to scare me. Especially since it was aimed at me. "I quite approve of you, Dinah."

"Umm ... thanks," I managed to say. She brushed my cheek with the tips of her soft old leather gloves. She patted Reggie's cheek a lot harder. I had the feeling it was partly in reproof. Nobody crossed Mrs. Victoria Grant. Not even her favorite granddaughter.

Then she was gone.

"I bet you get an engagement ring for New Year's," Reggie whispered. We stood there like terrified deer, listening to the staccato sound of her grandmother's heels among the slaps and splats when people hit the sodden rug in front of the doors leading outside.

"I'll have to quit the church when I say no."

"Why would -- oh, yeah." She met my gaze and swallowed hard. "A marriage proposal somebody forced him to make isn't worth any more than a Christmas present somebody made him give you. Rule eight." Then she nudged me with her elbow. "But Grammy said he was asking her about Great-great-granny Theresa's diamonds. That has to mean something."

"Uh huh. Desperation measures." I turned to go, pretty sure the coast was clear.

Unless Mrs. Grant caught up with Thad somewhere in the crowded hallways as people went to classes or came in for the next service. I could easily see her grabbing hold of his big arm with her bony little hand that could bring a Sumo wrestler to his knees in agony. Yanking Thad down to her level and pouring a lecture into his ear.

"What's that 'uh huh' mean?" Reggie scurried to catch up with me as we wove our way down the hall to the coat racks. It was something like doing the slalom, but with moving obstacles. Why did church people have to stand exactly in the middle of the hallways to have conversations?

"Doesn't she sit each of you down, regular as clockwork, and ask how come you're not married yet? I bet it was his time, and he asked about the diamond just to get her off his back."

"But he could have been -- no." Her momentary hopeful look faded. "Grammy didn't know you were dating. He didn't tell her the diamond was for you." She sighed and sagged and ran into me, pushing me sideways into the coats, just like we had been doing since we were five years old. It was our code for, *I've been more stupid than usual, huh? You still love me like a sister, huh?*

One of our rules was that when one of us had been especially oblivious and tending toward a single-digit I.Q., she had to perform a helpful chore for the other. I proposed my plan for her to break into her idiot cousin's apartment and take back that present so I could get my money back. Easy enough, since her father owned the apartment building where Thad and some of the other grandsons lived. Reggie liked it, and we were both feeling much better as we headed for class, plotting. Of course, we were so distracted with impending doom and trying to avert it that I forgot all about the food in my car until we had hung up our coats and walked into class.

Well, I consoled myself, after such a disastrous, frustrating start, the day could only get better. *Please, Lord?*

We didn't get much plotting done, either before class started, or during the service, or after church. It was Christmas Eve. I had to be back at church at three to make the final preparations for our three Christmas Eve services and the cookie socials after each one. It would be standing-room-only, don't-tell-the-Fire-Marshall numbers jammed in as our regular attendance tripled. Central Avenue Christian Church had a reputation to keep up, after all. Besides, we were right across the street from the mall. Between all our decorations and the lighted sign proclaiming our Christmas Eve services, all that visibility guaranteed a lot of walk-in attendees at the holidays. It was our biggest outreach of the year, although our eight-months-new senior pastor had plans to change that. He had been saying for some time now that *outreach* implied something active, rather than passively sitting and waiting.

All that could wait until the new year started. I had to get through Christmas Eve. As church secretary, I had to make sure the custodians had enough tables set up, and all the people who volunteered to bake cookies came through. Someone had to wait in the big kitchen to check off the last-minute deliveries. Me. And run out to the grocery store at the mall across the street to replace the eight or nine dozen that didn't show up as promised. Me, as well. It was a good thing there were three Christmas Eve services, or I'd never see the candle-lighting service or hear the kindergarten choir lisp *Silent Night.*

Reggie helped me with the last-minute work, but she had to make a command appearance in the Grant family pews (yes, plural) for the first service. Mrs. Grant required all her children and grandchildren and their spouses and/or significant others to join her. The grandchildren without significant others and prospective in-laws to visit came back to her house for dinner and board games.

Amid that chaos, that little detail hit me like an icicle falling off the roof. Thad hadn't arranged to spend Christmas Eve with me, or me with his family. Another sign of our impending split? Or more evidence I read more into our relationship than he did?

Funny thing: I was even *more* relieved now. I hadn't really thought about the implications of being Thad Grant's significant other -- as in command appearances at family get-togethers -- until I ran into Mrs. Grant that morning. She was pretty cool, and some of Reggie and Thad's cousins were okay, but there were the Three Witches, to be avoided at all costs. I should have thought of them when Thad and I started dating. Reason enough not to want to marry into that family.

Definitely, breaking up with Thad would be a good thing. Equivalent with having a fender-bender on the way to the airport, so I missed a flight that crashed on takeoff.

<><><>

Christmas day for the last five years had been quiet for me since Dad moved to Arizona for work. I hosted the single girls without families or prospective in-laws, or abandoned by siblings and widowed/divorced parents to spend the day with their significant others. This Christmas, thanks to the depredations of romance, we had three fewer girls than last year, bringing us down to seven.

First there was Reggie. Then Brenda Daniels. She had a semi-regular job at the Green Rooster, a restaurant on the corner of the mall closest to the far end of the church parking lot. Her other job had been as a secret shopper, until someone at corporate got mean and started sending her into lingerie shops and sex toy stores. She got enough harassment from the busybodies in her apartment building and the town where she lived (think Mayberry in need of mood-altering herbal supplements), she had to quit. Yes, the town was the tiny kind where everyone knew everyone else's business, commented on it, and tried to control it.

Then there was Anita Sanders, one of the steady and reliable members of Singles, who came to every social function because she had nowhere else to be. In the words of some of the guys who escaped Singles by no longer attending our church, she was a founding member of Bachelors-'til-the-Rapture. Anita was all right, despite desperation flaring every once in a while. She was a night shift stocker for Rockaway and ran a used bookstore with her great-uncle who was not that great.

Toni Gilbert was sort of in the same position as Brenda. Her grandfather, who raised her, used to be our senior minister. Rev. Gilbert was one of those wonderful old men everyone hoped would be around forever. One day he turned the service over to Pastor Greg, said he had a headache, went to his office for aspirin, and never walked out. More than three dozen elderly members of the congregation resided at Briar Hill Assisted Living, and they had adopted Toni. Meaning they were constantly checking up on her. Trying to find her a better job. Trying to find her a husband. The current job and boyfriend never met the standards of the interfering old ... ahem ... darlings, so they got her fired and drove away the boyfriends on a regular basis. If her life were a revolving door, the wind from the constant movement could provide enough electricity for Cuyahoga County.

Beth Conrad worked for an IT company. Her job kept her moving, either traveling out of state or answering emergency calls from clients, so she rarely got to attend church or Singles events.

She was also one of those unfairly fit girls who could spend all day sitting at her desk and look like she spent five hours a day working out. The new guys always hit on her whenever she did show up at a game night or Bible study. One of these days, she would get enough seniority for a regular schedule, we would see more of her, and some guy who treated her right would sweep her away to the Young Marrieds class.

Melanie Porter rounded out our dwindling, comfortable, slightly griping social circle. She was a trainer at the fitness club on the far corner from the mall and knew how to dress modestly while still showing off her physique. Only the totally clueless, or aging-and-desperate guys weren't intimidated the first time they laid eyes on her. The Oblivious Squad went running for their lives soon enough.

Not that these were the only girls in our Singles class who didn't have other commitments on Christmas day. There were a few who thought they were too good for us, and yes, I must confess, a few I had had one too many nasty encounters with as church secretary. They never got an invitation. Then there were the husband sharks. We didn't want the guys to know we associated with them, because that would just hang a "run for your life" sign over our heads.

I had plenty of room, since I was living alone in the bungalow where I had grown up. Dad worked for the Cleveland Indians, and he escaped the Northeast Ohio weather scene to join the staff at the training facilities in Arizona. He would have taken a transfer a lot sooner if he had been aware of the matchmaking schemes focused on him, starting one year to the day after Mom died. Dad had a tendency to be King Oblivious. Not when it came to his job. Just his personal life. And me.

Come to think of it, I joined the social committee for the Singles after I used my 'in' with the Tribe to get us all great seats in the all-you-can-eat section one season. What if Thad had only moved our relationship from co-workers to dating so he could have access to good tickets?

I told Reggie my theory when we were alone in my kitchen, and she was taste-testing Melanie's cranberry ginger ale punch. She choked and giggled and a few drops came out her nose.

"You're horrid." Then she hurried out into the living room to share the joke with the others.

She went on to explain all the back story, about the lame Christmas present and Thad asking about their great-great-grandmother's diamonds but not mentioning me. Everyone agreed Thad was not participating in our relationship anymore.

"You need to be the dumper, rather than the dumpee," Anita offered, after Reggie shared her rules for predicting for commitment or breakup.

I took her words with a grain of salt. The "sharing" grapevine in Singles (good Christian girls don't gossip, they "share" their concerns and theories) believed she was interested in Thad, but didn't act on it for two reasons. First, no good Christian girl would steal a man who already belonged to another girl, especially not in the same church and social group. And second, Anita agreed with Reggie's rule that the only way to have a lasting relationship was for the man to do all the chasing. The slightest hint that a girl was on the hunt would have him turning tail and running.

Maybe Anita hoped that once I had dumped Thad and he was lost and hurting (as if he would notice I wasn't in his life anymore if he didn't need my help?) he would be vulnerable to a proper, demure, available Christian girl.

I wished them both luck.

"Dinah can't dump him," Brenda offered. "At least, not until the New Year's overnighter is done. It'd bomb without her."

"What does that have to do with getting rid of a guy who obviously wants out of the relationship?" Anita frowned hard enough to get wrinkles between her eyebrows -- and she tried to avoid them whenever possible.

"If Thad and Dinah break up, one of them can't be there on New Year's. He's just oblivious enough to show up and run everything, without any concern for her feelings."

"Because he hasn't had any to date," Reggie offered. Melanie and Beth raised their glasses in gestures of agreement.

"So that means Dinah can't show up. And without her to coordinate everything, the whole party is a mess. Which proves that even though Thad is president of Singles, Dinah actually makes things happen, and she is far more valuable than all the officers put together." She got up and bowed, and we applauded her brilliance.

"Which is just more proof that Thad will never pop the question," Beth offered, when we were quiet and reaching for the munchies spread on the coffee table. She grinned when she got general looks of "huh?" from the rest of us. "Thad likes being in charge, and if he marries Dinah, they have to leave Singles and join Young Marrieds."

"So? Thad will just try to take over there, too," Reggie said.

"Yeah, ordinarily, but Pastor Marcus won't allow it."

I understood what she referred to before the others did. After all, I was responsible for taking our senior minister's brainstorms, deciphering his handwriting, and straightening out his twisted syntax for the sermon notes in the church bulletin.

What Beth referred to was from the Old Testament, where a newly married man was prohibited from serving in the army of Israel for a year after getting married. Focusing on his wife's happiness and solidifying their marriage relationship was more important, according to Pastor Marcus. Newly married couples were forbidden to participate in any committees, ministries, outreach programs, any kind of service to the church, for a full year after marriage. That meant holding office in a class.

That sounded good to me, but Thad would be miserable. Reggie said so, when Beth explained what she was talking about. The others laughed.

"Face it, Dinah, you're condemned to eternal membership in Singles," Melanie said. "What would we do without you?"

"We'd be condemned to cookouts with nothing but raw hot dogs, that's what," Reggie said. Our gazes locked and we slouched on the couch together and laughed.

Anita and Melanie weren't members of our church at the time of the infamous cookout, so we took turns with Beth, Brenda and Toni, giving all the horrendous details of the time some guys put together a Singles outing. They chose to go rock climbing in the local Metroparks and charged us $20 each for equipment rental and food rather than everybody bringing food.

Church singles groups being the same the world over, no one commits to anything too far in advance. Always leave your options open for a better offer. When the day arrived, twenty-two people showed up, fifteen people had signed up ahead of time, only eight of those who showed up were on that list, and only six of us had paid ahead of time. All girls, by the way. Most of the money went to the rental equipment. The rest of the money, collected at the last minute, necessitating a last-minute shopping trip, went toward a new cooler on wheels. One of the guys decided the battered old coolers belonging to the Singles just weren't good enough anymore. They kept the food cool, didn't they? By some miracle, the guys charged with getting the supplies did remember to buy some food, despite the argument they were still having over the cooler when they met us at the pavilion in the park. What did they buy? Six packs of hot dogs, five bags of off-brand chips, and a pack of paper plates. No buns. No condiments. No utensils. No foil to cover the cruddy, rusty grids of the grill next to the pavilion. No toasting forks to hold the hot dogs over the flames. And no flames, because no one bought charcoal or lighter fluid.

"Face it, girls. Church guys -- especially our guys -- can't get anything right," Reggie said, gesturing with a limp, cold, breaded cheese stick.

The others agreed. We did not, however, spend the majority of our Christmas day bashing the oblivious, clueless, who'd-want-to-marry-those-losers-anyway guys in our church. We had more important things to discuss, such as finding new jobs for Brenda and Toni. There was a new job matching service on the corner of the mall farthest from the church. This one claimed to be faith-based, which sounded interesting. And promising. No more secret shopper jobs, for instance, sending workers into questionable locations.

I must admit, the raw hot dog incident just illustrated one of many reasons why I didn't invite the guys who were at loose ends on Christmas day. We needed a chance to be without them and let off some steam.

Besides, if word got out there was an open house at my place, we would be inundated, and none of them would bring any food.

Chapter Two

Tuesday morning came as a relief. Back to normal schedule. At least, as normal as possible with only four days to do the work I could barely cram into five days of the normal duties of the average church secretary.

I came back to the church office around 10:30, after conferring with the custodians (an under-appreciated group of hard-working, good-hearted men who got to wear jeans and sweatshirts to work, lucky dogs) about the arrangements for the holiday activities for the remainder of the week and year. Nearly every room that wasn't a children's Sunday school room was scheduled for a committee meeting or social event. I maintained the floor diagrams for the tables and chairs, movable white boards, and freestanding dividers. I had to run down to the big kitchen five times already that morning to meet the people in charge of food for different parties and give them access to their assigned refrigerators.

Yes, plural. We had eight refrigerator-freezers donated by people who had upgraded to newer models. Except for the one assigned to the church staff, the others were kept chained and padlocked shut. Only the people authorized to use them were given the keys.

Why? Let's just say some people took the idea of the church being a *family* a little too far. These were the people who would normally be the irritating middle brother with the attitude that "what's yours is mine." And never reciprocates with, "And what's mine is yours."

(The guy who routinely ransacks your room to find out if you have anything you're hiding from him, in case he would want it, and takes it without permission. You have no right to violate his right to know every detail in your life so he can confiscate, condemn, or mock it. The guy who whines to Mom that you won't share when you take back your rightful property. The one who doesn't realize that sharing is voluntary, and when it's involuntary, it's stealing.)

(Let me say I am eternally grateful to my parents for making me an only child. I had heard enough horror stories from my friends and classmates about their siblings from h-e-double-hockey-sticks to have fond feelings for China's one-child rule.)

Yeah, those people. The ones who ignored the sticky notes on food containers that said, "For the Son-seekers Sunday school class potluck," appropriating the goodies for their own class. Or they cut into the sheet cake that said, "Happy Retirement, Pastor Ed," two hours before the party started.

Hence the need for padlocks to protect supplies bought for specific events. I had to get the keys back when the social events were finished and ensure someone cleaned out the refrigerators. That last was important. I went to Arizona last spring and spent two weeks looking after Dad. He got pushed out of the bleachers by a drunk fan and broke his left leg and three ribs. When I got back, the people filling in for me had forgotten about that last step, and the fact that very old refrigerators sometimes died. A dead refrigerator loaded with abandoned food made an interesting science project.

When I came back to the office that morning after Christmas, there were six women sitting or standing by the front counter. Silently, they watched Mrs. Babcock separate the used candles from the plastic cup candleholders used during the candle-lighting service, in between answering phones. She glanced up and that big smile of relief on her thin, pointy face warned me, even before she called out, "There she is," and all six women turned to look at me.

I was hoping for five minutes to sit down with a cup of hot chocolate and check my to-do list for the rest of the day.

"What can I help you ladies with?" A longer look helped me match them up with, if not names, at least the social groups they belonged in. Most were my mother's age or slightly younger, if she were still alive. Basically, they were the ones with children in high school, college, and grad school. Their children were in (allegedly) self-maintenance mode. Granted, some had grandchildren who might get dumped on their front doorsteps with no warning, but they had a lot of freedom, and were old enough to be retired or working part-time. These women could volunteer for needs in the church if they didn't have jobs or elderly parents to look after.

I took a second look and revised my estimate. Some had been making noise over the last few months about how good Christians should be able to get along on one salary. Married women had no right to work outside the home, according to them. If I remembered rightly, several of them had gotten a little nasty, criticizing a few men who couldn't find jobs and depended on their wives' jobs to keep them in their homes.

These were not the silver-haired iron ladies who kept company with Mrs. Grant, no matter how valuable their volunteer service might be to the church.

"We're here to help you, Dinah," Mrs. Rizetti said, tipping her head sideways and wearing that sweet Shirley Temple puckered lips look. "Sweet" did not apply to the conniving Pharisee who blamed me when Dad evaded her attempts to drag him to the altar.

Why was it that widows were allowed to live their lives without any interference from the rest of the church, but widowers were considered unable to breathe on their own? Mrs. Rizetti had decided Dad was her mission project for the rest of her life, or his, whoever kicked off first. She claimed he was too busy trying to get me through high school and then college, and then marry me off, and couldn't see the God-sent woman right in front of him. Her theory was trashed when Dad moved to Arizona, leaving me behind, still single. Somehow that was my fault, too.

Then again, she hated me because of Mom, who had "stolen" Dad from her -- before she trapped Mr. Rizetti.

If she was here to help me, I knew it wouldn't be helpful at all. Except maybe to "help" me find the nearest cliff to fall over.

"Help me." I forced the smile I saved for people who wandered in from the mall. The ones who couldn't find their car in our parking lot. Or they really had parked in our lot and wanted a shuttle to get across the street to the mall. "Help me with what? Things are kind of slow in the week between Christmas and New Year's."

Yes, I lied. A self-defense reaction.

Slow for everyone but me, of course. Still, I would never have dreamed that anyone would notice.

"That's why this is such good timing," Pastor Marcus said,

stepping into the front of the office area.

Pastor Marcus had been called by the congregation in late April. I still wasn't sure where to classify him, because he kept showing new facets when I least expected them. How could I work with and for and around the staff unless I could file them into some standard categories? When one person said "emergency," did I put his emergency ahead of or behind someone else's emergency? Only by knowing these people, what they considered vital, how long they let chores slide before handling them, and what their boiling point was, could I efficiently organize their work and my schedule.

Pastor Marcus was still a cipher. I had to accept he was a good man, a true minister, devoted to the ministry and to God, because Rev. Gilbert had recommended him as his successor. He believed strongly enough in Pastor Marcus to put it in writing. However, I had seen Pastor Marcus in action enough, trying to revitalize our congregation, to feel a shiver of apprehension now when he smiled at me. He was always in action, rather than being mostly inaction, like un-missed Pastor Neil.

"Good timing?" I hated being reduced to echoing what someone had just said, to prompt them to fill in details.

Missing details requiring prompts were always a bad sign. Kind of like the movie soundtrack that shifted to a minor key just before something vicious, slimy, and suffering hormonal imbalance dropped onto Earth from another dimension.

"These ladies are here to learn all the aspects of your job. To fill in when you're not here." He nodded to everyone, looking like my Dad's vintage Carlos Baerga bobblehead that used to sit in the back window of his Mustang. Then he beat a hasty retreat.

Six people were expected to learn all my jobs? Well, that might be enough to fill in for me when I took another vacation. If I was ever allowed to take another one. Sure, I always took a trip to Arizona to spend the last week of spring training with Dad, but I lived with the unspoken threat that my vacations could be cancelled for the sake of the needs of the congregation.

Still, it was nice to see someone around our church was at least partially conscious of the wide variety of my duties.

That nice feeling of being appreciated -- of being visible -- lasted about twenty minutes. Long enough for me to get the women situated in the big workroom with the three eight-foot tables set up in a horseshoe, where I did a lot of the assembly work and handled the copying. This room was the only way I managed to keep anything organized. I could lock the door and keep out the people who believed they could just walk in and take over equipment, rooms, tables and chairs without asking. I had three tack board/dry erase board combinations, one each on the walls without a door, where I kept track of who had reserved what equipment or room and on what date for what function, and who was the contact person for the group requesting them. This room was where I safely kept the keys, signup sheets, insurance forms, and any other necessary paperwork.

I gave the ladies a general introduction to the setup of the room. They then divided into teams of two each and claimed the different duties I had outlined. That was a little scary. I should have known something was up when they all whipped out notebooks and pens and wrote down most of what I told them.

"What is your day-to-day schedule?" Mrs. Rizetti unfolded a big sheet of paper on the far end of the worktable from me.

It turned out to be one of those month-at-a-glance desk pad calendars that I had learned long ago were totally useless. Just when you filled it up with notes to organize your life for the next few weeks, someone would spill coffee on it. Or write a shopping list in the margin, then tear half the month off and take it with them. Or park their child at that spot with crayons, to keep her busy while they took up the copier and printed something for their class -- usually in the middle of the rush to get the bulletins printed for Sunday morning. Said child would color all over the calendar, and then take the entire page with her.

No thanks.

An automatic ripple of revulsion worked through me when Mrs. Rizetti pulled out that page to make notes.

Long experience had taught me not to ask her questions, not to protest. Just play along and make no commitments, no matter how much she pressed me and tried to use guilt-inducing tactics. She had an amazing talent for turning every question I asked into an attack on *her* competence -- even when it was obvious she had no idea what she was talking about.

So I excused myself and got that cup of hot chocolate I

desperately needed now. Then I sat down to walk through my usual routine with the ladies. About halfway through the Tuesday schedule, they started whispering among themselves and exchanging glances and nods. All taking notes. By the time I was done with Wednesday, they were again dividing up my tasks.

Right about then, I grew certain they weren't there to "help" me with anything. "Help" implied that I had some choice in the matter, and some control. Since when did volunteers come in and take over a job entirely?

It smelled more and more strongly of Dinah being edged out of her job, with Mrs. Rizetti as ringleader in the endeavor. My imagination -- and more experience -- envisioned the scenario clearly. The tactic had been tried before, at various times, usually fizzling out completely before anyone entered my work area.

Here was how it usually went: Someone on the church staff brought up the subject of how overworked I was. Maybe they could ask some people to volunteer to come in during the really heavy workload days, to help out? Someone else was utterly surprised that anyone thought I needed help, because I never asked. (I had given up asking years ago.) Someone else sat down and made a list of all the work I did, to prove that not only didn't I need help, but I had so little to do, they could justify cutting back my hours. Maybe make my job part-time, and remove the need to provide me health insurance?

Then when they had the list of all the work I did, someone had a hissy fit over how much work one person was expected to do. Someone else insisted there was no way I could handle it by myself. Therefore, essential church functions were not being carried out to properly serve our congregation. Someone else demanded volunteers, to raise the standards in the church office. The same person who wanted to cut my salary brought up the bright idea that instead of having people come in a few hours a week to help me, they should have *all* my tasks handled entirely by *volunteers*, and let me go completely.

Usually these efforts failed when people realized just how much work would be left in *their* hands when volunteers put their own lives ahead of the church chores. Suddenly the "unnecessary expense" of a church secretary wasn't so unnecessary. With all these women in the office, someone (Mrs. Rizetti was the most likely suspect) had finally done their homework and put together an effective campaign. Or at the very least brainwashed enough people in power into believing that all my duties could be handled by a handful of volunteers with a few days of training. With no reduction in service to the church body.

Despite that knowledge growing more solid every second in the back of my brain, I got through my list of duties by days of the week. When I excused myself and left the room, pretending to replenish my hot chocolate, the whispers rose to full volume. I heard one person say she was astonished at all the work I did.

Mrs. Rizetti immediately shot back that I was exaggerating, and I depended on the pastoral staff and the custodians to "pick up the slack" for me. Before I was entirely out of earshot, someone else retorted that she had been in the church office enough times to see me at work. She knew I filled in for the rotating staff of grandmothers who answered the phone and I got the custodians to do last-minute jobs when no one else could. It was nice to know someone noticed what I did, but I knew it was too late. The guillotine blade was already falling. Did someone think they were being merciful by blindfolding the victim?

Mr. Stephen Phillips was a contemporary of my dad, head trustee, head deacon, and on the finance board. No, our church wasn't that small, that people had to cover multiple jobs. It was more along the lines of ninety-five percent of the work being handled by five percent of the membership.

He was in the office that day, and if anyone would know the truth behind the volunteers, he would. I was pretty sure he was one of the few who knew just how much work I did, and he would have defended my job in those budget meetings.

"Got a minute?" I tapped on the door of his office. It was one of the larger offices in the church office complex, but it was so full of ledger books and manuals and filing cabinets, the actual floor space was equal with a closet.

"Dinah." His welcoming smile faded into something tired and resigned. He gestured at the single empty chair in front of his desk. "You took a little longer than I anticipated when I saw Joyce Rizetti walk in the door. How many ladies showed up?"

"So, it's true." I shook my head and stayed in the doorway, leaning against the frame. If I sat down and then needed to make a hasty exit, I would probably trip over something on my way out. "I'm getting the heave-ho."

He winced and offered me that same crooked grin of sympathy he gave Dad when Mrs. Rizetti's matrimonial campaign had grown painfully obvious. Her idea of capturing a man's heart was equivalent with bashing him over the head, then dragging him into her lair. I always envisioned it looking like the caves where Frodo fought free of Shelob, in *The Return of the King.*

"How many ladies? We had fifteen on the roster who were interested in filling in," he added, when I just looked at him.

"Six showed up."

"Uh huh. That should make things pretty interesting, when the ones who didn't get trained this week show up and contradict the ones who were here."

"All week?" I swallowed hard and consciously forced my voice into a civilized volume before it rose to a horrified shriek. "Is that all the time I'm allowed to train them?"

"Of course not. That would be foolish." Pastor Marcus rested his big, clay-damp hand on my shoulder. I swear, I felt the dampness through my sweater and the turtleneck underneath it.

I was in no mood to be polite, so I shifted sideways and broke that unwanted contact as soon as possible.

"We want things to run as smoothly in this office in the coming year as they did under your capable stewardship," he continued, not even blinking at my reaction.

Funny, but using spiritual words like *stewardship* didn't make the concept any easier to swallow. I was being let go, and I had to train a gaggle of women my mother's age -- led by someone who hated my mother -- to take over all my work.

"Why are you firing me?" I took refuge in the office, putting my back to a filing cabinet. Pastor Marcus stayed in the doorway.

"It has nothing to do with the quality of your work. Our church is in a transition period. We're crystallizing and clarifying our philosophies, our viewpoint, our image. One of our goals is being a family-oriented church. We want to get the entire family involved, every member taking responsibility. Mothers and fathers bring their children with them when they volunteer around the church, displaying service and stewardship in action."

So help me, he offered me the same cheesy smile I saw a

politician paste on his face. Just before he swore he hadn't sexually harassed three teenage interns, it was all a big misunderstanding. The videos currently running on YouTube weren't him at all, but someone who just sounded like him and had the same tattoo on his lower back.

"So ..." I did take a few seconds to organize my words, "you're saying I'm being fired because I don't have children to bring to work with me?"

Yeah, it sounded just as stupid when I said it aloud as it did in my head. I glanced at Mr. Phillips. He had his head bowed. Probably so we couldn't see him fight not to grin or roll his eyes.

"Of course not. But that brings up another concern. Our young Christian men are in desperate need of strong, capable, spiritually mature women in their lives. We need to encourage those women to take their eyes off worldly success and focus back to the basic values that made our country great -- home, hearth, and children. We need to encourage women to make themselves available to the men who seek helpmeets to complete them."

"What about finding men who will complete *us*? It's a two-way street."

Where was this stuff coming from? It was like someone was sitting in another room, typing the words just fast enough for them to spill off my tongue.

"Well, you must admit," Pastor Marcus said with a chuckle that didn't fool me for a minute, "we men certainly need a great deal more help than women do."

"What about what Paul said, that remaining single made it possible for men and women to serve the church more fully? No distractions. No competition for their time and energy and devotion. I have always considered my job here a ministry."

"Well -- yes -- of course -- for those who are called to singleness -- certainly those who have experienced marriage and are on their own again." His face darkened, and I wondered if he was choking. The question was, on what -- his tongue, his size fourteen Oxfords, or realizing he was a hypocrite? "It all comes back to stewardship."

Mr. Phillips sighed.

"We are benefiting the church on two fronts," Pastor Marcus continued, his brows lowering a little and those creases appearing around eyes and mouth. No more happy politician. "It is our duty to make it possible for people to grow spiritually, emotionally, by serving in the church, and to provide a fine Christian example to their children. And, we have a duty to save as much of the church budget as possible for more important matters. If a job can be handled by a volunteer, then it is bad stewardship to pay someone to do the same work."

"So essentially I'm out because I'm not married and I want to make a living? Is that the bottom line?" My voice cracked. Something tightened inside me. I wanted to run back to my workroom and make sure those women, preparing to take over my job, hadn't rearranged everything already.

No, that was just a need to escape, not protect my workspace. But the job and workspace weren't mine anymore.

I needed to look for a new job. The sooner the better.

"We realize that your skills and your training and your years of experience are invaluable. It will take quite a long time for our volunteers to learn to keep our office running as smoothly as you have. Of course, when you are married, if you would like to come back and volunteer, we would be delighted to use your invaluable skills once again."

"Basically, you want me to work for you, but you don't want to have to *pay* for it."

"Come now, Dinah, that's not a very Christian attitude. I expected better of you." He stepped into the office and reached out a hand to rest on my shoulder again. He was going to hug me. I had seen him do it. I had no idea what cheesy interpersonal conflict training his seminary offered, but grabbing hurting, angry, stunned people into hugs for unwelcome personal contact was not the way to resolve conflicts. It was the way to get him slapped with a sexual harassment lawsuit.

Tell me again why Rev. Gilbert thought he was such a great choice?

"It's going to be really hard to give time as a volunteer." I sidestepped past him, to take his place in the doorway.

Maybe that reflected my position in the church now?

"See, I'm going to be busy making a living. Paying bills is good stewardship."

"But your husband will be responsible for the bills. If a family has a decent income, there is no need for the wife to work outside the home. And if there aren't any children, there's plenty of time for church service. It all works out wonderfully for everyone."

"I'm not married. I have no plans for getting married."

"But I thought you and Thad Grant --"

"My personal life is none of your business!" I bit my tongue to keep from admitting Thad and I were probably going to be ancient history as of 6 a.m., New Year's Day.

"Come, come, Dinah, we're all a family here."

"Really? You could have fooled me. Just *when* were you planning on letting me know I was fired? How much warning were you going to give me, so I could start looking for a new job?"

"We have a fine severance package set up that should carry you for a few weeks --"

"Does that mean you *weren't* planning on giving me a warning?" I looked at Mr. Phillips, who stared at Pastor Marcus from under lowered brows, lips pressed flat together. Was this news for him, too? "So Friday afternoon, you were just going to hand me an envelope and say Happy New Year, don't come back to work on Tuesday?"

"Don't be silly." Pastor Marcus snorted and gestured with his hand as if waving away a minor distraction, like an insect. I had the feeling I was the insect. The question was whether I would be a ladybug, to be cooed over, or a mosquito to be squashed to destroy the irritation I created. "We would wait until we were sure all your volunteers were fully trained. It could take two weeks. Maybe three."

Three weeks of working with Mrs. Rizetti and her cronies? Repeating myself endlessly when they refused to follow procedures that had been proven efficient and logical? No thanks.

Instead of being a mosquito, how about a bee? A wasp? A dragonfly that buzzed around everybody's head and got out of there at Warp Factor 10?

"Turnabout is fair play, don't you think?" I glanced at my watch.

My lunch hour was near. I had no compunctions about leaving those untrained, interfering old biddies alone to take my full lunch hour. For a change. First stop, that Christian job matching service Toni had mentioned. I would hit it before I got something to eat.

"Turnabout?"

"Since we were going to let her go at a moment's notice, Dinah does have the right to leave as soon as she finds a new job. Without the standard two weeks warning," Mr. Phillips said. "Since she wouldn't get any from us."

"But -- but -- that would leave us in the lurch!"

"And firing me without giving me adequate warning isn't leaving *me* in the lurch?" I said, my voice cracking.

"But you know about it now," Pastor Marcus retorted.

"Just when were you planning on telling me?"

His mouth opened and closed a few times with no answer coming out. That was all the answer I needed. I had to be fair and give them proper warning, but they didn't owe it to me. Why? Because I was single, or because I was a woman, or both? Despite all his sermons about respect and equality and "the ground is level at the foot of the cross," Pastor Marcus didn't mean it. He sided with the people gaining volume in the church who insisted women were created to serve men, rather than to be partners, as dear, thoughtful Rev. Gilbert always interpreted "helpmeet."

I nodded my thanks to Mr. Phillips. He gave me a grave nod in return. It was nice to know Dad's friends would stand up for me. As much as they were able. He hadn't been able to talk some sense into the people who only cared about saving money.

"Pastor, you're so concerned about the church's image." Mr. Phillips stood up and stepped around his overloaded desk and reached for the coat rack tucked in between two filing cabinets.

I had to muffle a chuckle when his action resulted in Pastor Marcus walking backwards out of the office, unconsciously taking the cue to leave.

"Yes. What does that have to do with Miss Clydesdale thinking only about her convenience?" He sounded like a pouty little boy. I couldn't see his face -- was his lower lip sticking out?

Somewhere in there, I had stepped outside (maybe more accurately, I had been shoved out?) of the "we're all family here" circle, and I was *Miss Clydesdale*, not *Dinah*.

"What kind of image will this present in the community? Every place where Dinah applies, they will ask how soon she can start work. When she says 'immediately,' they'll ask why. And she'll tell them she was let go without any warning, as a cost-cutting measure. How do you think that will look?"

Pastor Marcus's mouth dropped open slowly as he turned and looked at me with wide, horrified eyes. He managed to close his mouth after a moment and swallowed hard.

"Miss Clydesdale -- Dinah -- several members of our congregation work in human resources. I will ask them -- wait -- let's start over. I'm sure all of this was presented badly."

"I'm very sure of that, too," I said. Kudos to me for holding my tongue and not spilling all the things going through my head for the last ten minutes. "Thanks, but no. I've been living in this town all my life, and I certainly know a lot more people than you do. Excuse me, but I have to get back to my trainees."

I turned and walked away, back down the long hallway lined with offices and storage closets -- and offices that had been turned into storage closets, or vice versa. Maybe that had something to say about changes in our church over the years?

Fortunately, that hallway was long enough that even when our voices were raised, the women in my workroom wouldn't have heard anything. The last thing I needed was to get smirks from the Rizetti gang. I wondered about the other women who had signed up to learn my duties. Had they given up when they realized they had to work with Mrs. Rizetti?

It hit me for the first time that maybe I *would* have to leave the church. Not just because of Thad. Church politics generally contradicted the ideal Christ set up for us, that we should be one united body, caring for each other, supporting each other, loving each other. Church politics meant power struggles. No matter how much of the truth came out, everyone would have their own side of the story.

Someone would feel duty-bound to "counsel" me on this loss. Someone else would be delighted that I had been toppled from my position of power. I had heard the grumbling from people who thought I didn't have a servant's heart, meaning I wouldn't let them walk all over me or break the rules for them. Then there were the people who would take my job loss, the reasons behind it, and the way it was handled as ammunition for their ongoing battles in the congregation. Another excuse for another fight. Another rehash of all the things people didn't like about Pastor Marcus, his policies, and the changes he had instituted.

We were family, all right. All the ugly aspects of being family, as well as the good ones. Sometimes I wondered if God looked down on our church and shook His head, laughing with tears in His eyes.

"Dinah." Mr. Phillips caught up with me two doors down from my workroom. Pastor Marcus had retreated to his office and we were alone in the hallway. I heard the phone ring in the front office. Mrs. Hooper answered with her sweet, dusty voice.

She was single, but she wouldn't be fired. She was a volunteer, a widow, and nearly ninety years old. Widows had it made in our church -- no one interfered with their lives. Maybe the answer to my problem was to trick Thad into marrying me and then hope he died on the honeymoon? Then I could come back to church, safely ensconced in the do-not-interfere position of a widow, and use sympathy to get my job back?

Why would I want to come back and work with those people?

I had to find a new church. Maybe I could use my breakup with Thad as an excuse to leave before everyone found out about losing my job?

"Dinah?" Mr. Phillips waved his hand in front of my eyes. I had totally zoned out on him.

Chapter Three

"Sorry. Lots to think about."

"I should have warned you, but I thought it wouldn't start until after New Year's." He sighed and reached into his coat pocket and pulled out a few business cards. "I had hoped to have more ready to give you when we talked. Here's a good place to start." He tapped the card on top.

I took the business cards. The stack seemed pitifully small, yet I cringed at the thought of needing to use any of them.

"A Match Made in Heaven?" I read aloud.

Seriously? Either the guy who owned the service had a giant ego, a lot of faith, or he didn't know the difference between a job match and a matchmaking service.

"No, that's *for*. A Match Made *For* Heaven. Zach has been in business maybe three, four months now -- over in the old Dog House building."

"Oh. Right." I nodded and slid the business cards into the folded cuff of my sweater for safekeeping.

Just a coincidence this was the same place Toni had mentioned? The Dog House had been a fast food stand, selling mostly hot dogs, fries and fry pies. The owner died when I was in high school, and it seemed like there was a new business in the building every year, on the corner opposite the mall. It would be easy enough for me to walk up there on my lunch hour, get registered and start the job search.

I hoped nobody would ask me to go to the Green Rooster to pick up lunch, because Brenda had mentioned a couple times that the manager was a crony of Mrs. Rizetti. I did not want to have to look at that woman's smirking face. From now on, my lunch hour was mine. No more sacrificing. This job wasn't my ministry anymore. Every single girl for herself.

"It'll be okay." Mr. Phillips patted my shoulder as he stepped past me. "Man proposes, but God disposes."

I managed a smile and nod and watched him head for the door to the parking lot. Then I checked my watch -- fifteen minutes until I could call a halt for lunch and get out of there.

<><><>

"Welcome!" A little silvery, wrinkly lady dressed all in neon orange popped up from behind the tall counter when I stepped inside the old Dog House building.

I had to stop calling it that, because it no longer looked like the hot dog stand. The counter in the middle of the room cut it in half, with a half-dozen chairs and a low coffee table on one side and two desks on the other. I saw two doors behind where the grill used to be. One was marked "restroom" and the other hung open enough to see a table and several folding chairs -- I assumed it was a conference room.

"Welcome to A Match Made in Heaven!" She clapped her hands and beamed at me. "Oh, sweetie, I know it's hard finding the love of your life, but with our help --"

"Aunt Gertie," a man said, stepping out of the restroom. He dried his hands on a paper towel. From the restrained frustration in his voice, I had the feeling he had hurried out to stop her. "We're not a dating service."

Whew! I was on the verge of panic, considering the thoughts I had when Mr. Phillips gave me that card.

"Yes we are. You let me set up my program and you said I could give all the romance help I wanted," Aunt Gertie retorted, sticking her bottom lip out. On her it looked cute.

"We haven't started advertising your matchmaking services yet, so how could this nice young lady be here for that?" He offered me a lopsided grin, stuck the towel in his back pocket, and held out his big, still slightly damp hand to shake mine. "Sorry about that. I'm Zach Foster. This is my Aunt Gertrude."

"Dinah Clydesdale. And I'm sorry, Mrs. Foster, but I really am here to find a new job. Thanks anyway."

"Dinah. Right. Steve Phillips said he'd send you by."

"Oh, great." Worse than the entire church knowing I had been tossed out like a used Vacation Bible School manual, this total stranger knew I needed help before I could tell him.

"No, don't worry. We're completely confidential here." He kept hold of my hand and tugged, gesturing toward the conference room. "Steve and my dad were in college together, and he helped me get set up when I moved to town last year." Zach paused in the doorway. "Aunt Gertie, could you --"

"Get you the introductory packet. I know the procedure. Somebody would think you don't trust me." She sighed but ruined the hurt feelings image by winking at me.

"And somebody would think I was very rude to my favorite aunt if I expected you to know what I was thinking." He gestured at a chair pulled out from the table.

"Favorite aunt, my foot," she huffed, and slapped a green hanging folder down on the table in front of him. "I happen to be this hotshot's only aunt."

"And if I had a dozen, you'd still be my favorite." He grinned, mouth flat, until Gertie snickered and skipped out of the room, pulling the door closed behind her. Then he laughed, rubbed his face with both hands, and sat back in the chair. "Sorry. Despite our fooling around, we really are professionals."

"If Mr. Phillips recommended you, I don't mind." I opened up my coat, took off my hat and put it down on my purse. "What do I need to do first?"

"Well, he already laid the groundwork. I know about your job history at the church, your responsibilities. Quite impressive. You could be in demand at any number of churches or Christian organizations around the country."

"Excuse me?"

"He did tell you we cater to the Christian employment field? We match your skills and goals with churches, mission groups, Christian schools and service organizations. Your skill sets, training, experience, and spiritual standing all factor into the matching process."

It took about ten minutes to get my basic information. Then he flipped open the folder and pulled out a stack of documents held together with a medium-sized bulldog clip. I estimated twenty pages in that stack.

"First step is to fill out a questionnaire to build your profile." He handed me the stack and reached across the table to one of those desk organizers made up of tubes of various sizes, holding pens, pencils, clips, erasers, and correction pens.

"Questionnaire." I slid my coat off my shoulders. "How long does this usually take?"

"Half an hour. Forty-five minutes, max."

Honestly, my first thought was that I couldn't get anything to eat on my way back to work. I could hurry into the mall food court and get something, but I would be at least fifteen minutes late, even if I ate as I walked. No need to give anybody a hint that I did anything besides eat during my lunch break.

Then my second thought was: *What does it matter if I'm late?* How many lunch hours had I worked through, to get big projects done on time? The ones dumped on me at the last minute when someone else hit panic mode. How many evenings did I stay late? Despite all that dedication, I was getting sacked because I expected to be paid a decent wage for my time and talents. What happened to "the worker is worthy of his hire"?

"Miss Clydesdale?" Zach lightly rested his hand on mine.

"Sorry. My mind kind of ..." My face felt hot enough to melt all the snow piled up in the mall parking lot.

Sorry, God. I'm feeling sorry for myself, when I should be grateful how everything is working together. The thing is, how come I seem to be surrounded by the selfish jerks who wear a Christian button, but never pay attention to the owner's manual that tells them how to act to match the label? How come it's the nice ones who get no press, and who get run over by the jerks who do get the press? And how come I'm whining and sounding like Mrs. Rizetti all of a sudden?

That last thought snapped me out of my pity party. I looked into Zach's big, gray, sympathetic eyes, took the pen he offered me, and started in on the questionnaire. After all, I had to get back to work on time. No matter what, my service was for God, not for the egotistical, money-grubbing, self-righteous -- *Sorry, God. Feel free to slap me out of this pity party.*

Bottom line: I still had responsibilities, no matter how long or short a time they remained mine.

Zach stayed with me, offering explanations of some of the questions when I was stumped, clarifying my answers depending on how I interpreted the question. He also offered suggestions, based on what Mr. Phillips had told him about me. I actually finished those fourteen pages in half an hour.

"The next step is to put all your answers into the computer and create a profile for you," Zach explained as I gathered up my coat, gloves and purse and we walked out of the conference room. "I know your next question -- how come I didn't have you do the questionnaire on the computer?"

"Yeah."

He had a nice laugh. It made me feel included in the joke, instead of being the subject of it. "I've found that despite our high-tech age, people still respond better to the personal touch -- talking to a real live human instead of facing a screen. And I got details you couldn't have told a computer."

"True." Still, I couldn't help thinking it would have been easier to answer some questions without Zach in the room. I wouldn't have hesitated to tell a computer screen I didn't have a boyfriend or husband to consider when facing the question of moving to another part of the state, or even out of the state. Zach had a curious look in his eyes when I hesitated to answer that question, but he didn't ask. I didn't have to explain I was on the verge of breaking up with Thad.

"Besides," Zach added with a shrug, "we only have two computers. We can't afford to have them tied up with filling out the questionnaire, if other tasks come up. When we're bigger, we'll have computers for our clients to use, and then online access for our clients. I don't suppose you know any computer programmers out there looking for side jobs?"

I almost opened my mouth to tell him that between the computer problems at church, learning necessary software as I went along, and hanging out so much with Thad, I almost had a degree in computer science.

"Are you in love, honey?" Aunt Gertie asked, as we stepped out into the main office.

"Gertie," Zach said on a sigh.

"No. Definitely not." I tried to laugh, to cover up answering just a shade too quickly, and too sharply.

"Broken heart?" Her wrinkled little face got even more wrinkly in sympathy.

"Just disappointed."

"Let me sign you up for my matchmaking service. It's free, since you're already signed up with Zach."

"Uh, no thanks. I want to sit back and stay out of the dating scene while I take care of my job hunt."

That sounded so worldly-wise and weary, didn't it? The honest truth was, I had never really been "in" the dating scene.

Guys always treated me like a pal, a sister, or acted like I was invisible. Maybe that was why I had latched onto Thad so eagerly when he showed some interest in me.

"But don't you know, when you fall off a horse, you need to get right back into the saddle again?" she said, all eagerness.

"Gertie, Dinah's first priority is finding a new job. When she's settled, then she can come back here and let you play faerie godmother with her love life, okay?" Zach met my gaze over Gertie's head, widening his eyes in a clear plea to play along.

"Absolutely." I had a hard time not laughing when he mouthed, "thank you."

Walking back to church, I wished Zach went to my church. He was good at handling awkward situations. We could have used his help defusing the tensions and backbiting and power ploys in Singles. Then again, he was smart, he was nice, and while he wasn't exactly handsome, he was nice to look at. Some lucky girl would have snapped him up and dragged him to the altar fast enough to make all our heads spin.

Zach was probably married, anyway.

<><><>

Mrs. Grant called me first thing Wednesday morning, before the volunteers sauntered through the door. Well, that wasn't quite fair. Some new ones who showed up that day were very nice ladies who genuinely wanted to help. They made little remarks such as, "I don't know how our church would ever function without you. You do so much."

The ones who were in on the plot vowed to find "more efficient" ways of handling the jobs I was teaching them. They always said such things when I left the room, their voices pitched loud enough I was sure to hear them.

However, for a touch of irony, some of them had stopped their snide remarks by afternoon. I didn't notice until later, because I was a little stunned and worried and waiting for a second and third shoe to drop after the call from Mrs. Grant.

"Dinah? My, you're early," she said, when I took the phone from Mrs. Babcock, who was on duty that morning. She came in with her husband, one of our custodians, at 6 a.m. and stayed until lunchtime, helping out wherever she was needed.

"No, actually, my day starts at 8. What can I do for you, Mrs.

Grant?"

"I do admire a hard worker. Dear, would you mind too much coming over for lunch on Friday? We have some important matters to discuss, about your future."

I nearly dropped the phone. Mrs. Grant's word alone often changed the course of church board meetings. She found out details of deacon and trustee meetings *before* some deacons and trustees figured out what had happened. If she didn't approve, she had the ability to change minds that were set in concrete.

Had Mrs. Grant found out about Mrs. Rizetti and her cronies invading, and the fact I would be jobless soon? Maybe she had seen me going in or out of Match Made For Heaven yesterday, deduced I was looking for work, started asking questions, and decided to save my future.

I would have let out a celebratory shriek, but I had to come up with a gracious answer for Mrs. Grant.

With all the behind-the-scenes nastiness, and starting to enjoy the idea of a new job ... maybe I didn't *want* to save my job? Zach's questionnaire had gotten me thinking in new directions. He said my skills and experience were valuable. Was it wrong to want a little more appreciation for all the hard work I did? Sometimes it wasn't enough to know I'd get my reward in heaven.

Mrs. Grant was waiting.

"I'd like that very much, but the travel time would take up more than half of my lunch hour. We wouldn't have much time to talk, and I wouldn't want to hurry you," I said after scrambling through all my racing thoughts.

"Don't you worry about that. I'll have a word with Pastor Marcus. I'm sure there are enough people who can fill in for you for an extra hour. You leave it to me, dear."

What was going on? Mrs. Grant called me "dear" several times.

My hand shook a little when I put the phone down. At least she liked me, and she was pleased when I asked if I could bring something. So? Mom trained me right. *In any social situation related to church, assume there will be food, and always offer to contribute something to the spread.* Mrs. Grant had said she wouldn't expect a guest to bring something. Then she added that in the future, when I was a more frequent visitor, she wouldn't mind if I brought some of my mother's special recipe braided cheese bread.

Frequent visitor?

"Oh, heckety heck heck," I muttered, and stumbled to my workroom.

"Something wrong, honey?" Mrs. Babcock called.

"No. Fine." My standard answer. I should have put it on a tape recorder to save me having to speak.

Then the first trickle of volunteers arrived, and I had no time to muse and brood. However, I did find quiet moments during the morning to stop and contemplate banging my head against the nearest cinderblock wall.

It wasn't my *job* Mrs. Grant was calling about -- she wanted to grill me about my relationship with Thad. Maybe she thought I was railroading him into marriage. Of course, if she told Thad she liked me, he might have said I was the one dragging my feet. Not that I would have blamed him for such a wimpy answer. Mrs. Grant frightened me, too. No one wanted to disappoint her.

I needed to call Reggie and have a long, frantic consultation with her, but there was no way I would do that within the walls of the church. Not with Mrs. Rizetti and her cronies snickering on one side, and on the other side the ladies giving me guilty, sympathetic looks.

My cell phone rang the moment I stepped outside at lunchtime, before I even had my coat buttoned. I fumbled it, getting it out of my purse, and it landed nose-down in the pile of cinder-filled snow next to the sidewalk. It kept ringing as I dug it out and wiped off the cinders and ice.

"Dinah Clydesdale, please," a vaguely familiar male voice said, while I tried to hold my phone to my ear without it touching my skin or dripping on my coat.

"This is Dinah."

"Hey, Dinah, good news." He laughed. "Sorry, let me start over. This is Zach Foster. We have a job match."

"You're kidding -- please, don't be kidding." All the pressure in my chest evaporated, leaving me feeling kind of breathless. I laughed. "That's fantastic. What do I do first?"

"Well, we have some follow-up paperwork and questions, and I have a profile on the church. When can you be available for an interview?"

"Right away. I don't suppose there's time for me to get over there during my lunch hour..."

"Are you at lunch right now?"

"Just stepped out the door."

"If you don't have plans, how about coming up here and we'll see what we can do?"

"Sounds great."

I did a little dance, something akin to *We're off to See the Wizard,* after I jammed my phone back into my purse. If anybody was watching me as I hurried down the sidewalk and off church property, they probably thought I had lost my mind.

What did it matter? I was out of there as soon as possible.

If the church Zach had matched me with was a good place. It wasn't like I was desperate for work. Even if the severance package Pastor Marcus talked about was embarrassingly small, I had money in the bank. The house was mine -- well, mine and Dad's -- and I had money to pay for food and utilities while I continued my search for a place where I could be happy. I hadn't done calculations, but a good guess would be six months, if I was careful. I wasn't going to let panic railroad me into taking a job that would have me miserable.

Gertie was waiting in the doorway when I got to the Match office. Today she wore neon red velour tunic and pants and gold jewelry. She chimed when she moved, and Gertie moved constantly. She hugged me when I walked through the door, jumping up and down a little bit like a third-grader.

"Consider that a hug from both of us," Zach said, when I froze. He stood in the doorway to the conference room, grinning. "Don't let it frighten you, but we're highly motivated to find someone for this church. Be sure, we wouldn't have matched you with them if you weren't right for each other."

"What the big goof doesn't want to tell you is that it's our home church." Gertie gave me a nudge in Zach's direction. "Oh, honey, I'm so happy you're going to be working at our church."

"But -- you hardly know me." I stumbled, then caught my balance and let her herd me to the conference room.

"When you left yesterday, I started asking questions." She giggled. "I thought your name sounded familiar. I worked with your mother a long, long time ago, when you were just a baby.

And what everybody has been saying about you -- oh, honey, you're just perfect."

"Gertie ..." Zach shook his head, but as I stepped past him into the conference room, the corners of his mouth twitched. Then he laughed when he had closed the door, and saw me staring at the table.

Lunch for two sat on the table, with a stack of forms.

"I hope you don't mind. It occurred to me after you hung up that I was taking up your lunch hour, and you're probably going to pick up something on the way back to work and ..." Zach shrugged. "I hope you like tuna."

"Love it."

"You're joking, right?"

"Nope." I set my coat on one end of the table. "I have a lot of good memories tied up with tuna sandwiches and long bike hikes with my folks when I was a kid and ..." I probably didn't stop soon enough. Zach was unusually kind and thoughtful, providing lunch for me, but that didn't mean he wanted all the mundane details of my childhood.

"I heard there were some good bike trails around here. Do you still ride?"

"I haven't been, but I plan on starting up again."

I mentally made a list of all the fun, ordinary things I had stopped doing when I became so involved in running Singles. When Thad and I were over, I would have more free time on my hands. The thought of lazy Sunday afternoons spent reading or watching movies instead of in planning sessions sounded like a slice of heaven. I could start bike riding again in the spring.

Zach made a good tuna sandwich. I assumed he made it, and not Aunt Gertie, but I thought it might be a little too personal to ask about his culinary skills. Plus he had more to drink in the little refrigerator besides Coke. I'm a ginger ale girl, myself, and Zack had plenty of that. We worked through the forms and ate, and I told him which were the best bike trail sections of the Metroparks.

The church Zach had matched me to was only fifteen minutes away, by bus: Holy Spirit Independent Alliance. He caught me muffling a grin and demanded an explanation.

"They've just been our rivals in inter-church league sports for forever, that's all. It's kind of funny that I might work there.

Ironic. Maybe a little ... cosmic justice?"

"You didn't really say why you were leaving this job. I'm guessing a change in the administration?"

"Something like that. They want to give people an opportunity to minister in the church more -- and if that means saving some money, all the better."

"Gravity."

"Gravity?"

"Pulls you down. Better than saying it sucks." He snorted. I had to laugh. "Will it be a problem, working at a rival church and attending your old church?"

"I've been considering leaving. All the ugliness, and people taking sides. Why do Christians have to be such children?" I couldn't believe that had slipped out of my mouth, but I didn't feel embarrassed. Zach was a Christian. He understood. It wasn't like I was trash-talking my own team in front of the enemy forces.

"I've found a lot of people think they're the pipeline from heaven. Therefore, their way is the only true Christian way, whether it's outreach, Sunday school lessons or even decorations. It never occurs to them that God uses everybody differently. God is a whole lot more flexible and understanding than most old church folks," he added, shrugging.

"I don't suppose it's a requirement that I join the church where I'm working? If I get the job, that is."

"Nope. Pastor Paulson is pretty flexible and understanding about such things. He'd like you to join, but he's also aware that sometimes people are more comfortable *not* being church family, when they're in a service function."

"Ain't that the truth?"

Zach had a nice laugh, and later I wondered if I was a little more witty than usual just because I liked hearing him laugh.

When I got up to leave, I had five minutes to walk back to church. More important, I had an interview set up for that afternoon, after work. Pastor Paulson was working late to make up for office days lost to the holidays. I liked him already.

"Running late?" Zach said as I checked my watch.

"The sidewalks are clear. If all the lights are with me, no problem." That was a blatant lie, but I couldn't say it didn't matter if I was late, because what could they do, fire me? That wasn't a good attitude, period, but especially bad in front of the guy who was trying to get me a job, fast.

At *his* church. Meaning I'd see him there regularly. Especially if I attended there, too.

That idea made me feel a little unbalanced, so when Zach offered me a ride, to get me back to work on time, I accepted without thinking.

"Do you offer this kind of service to all your clients?" I had to ask, as I climbed into his dark green pickup truck.

"I don't know." He winked at me before he turned the key in the ignition. "Never had this kind of situation before."

That was a pretty safe answer, nice and neutral. I was relieved, because it wasn't until the words were out of my mouth that I realized how flirty they sounded. I wasn't a flirty kind of girl -- proven by my pitiful track record in dating.

I asked Zach to tell me about his church. He barely got started before we were pulling into the long driveway that took us behind the sanctuary, to the office wing. The lights had been with us the whole way. I learned Holy Spirit Alliance was a big church, twice as many members as mine, and the Singles ministry had just won an award from their association.

"That's something I was wondering about," I said, as I slid out of the truck. Zach had pulled up next to the curb, so I didn't have a long way to go down to the ground. I didn't have much experience dismounting from trucks. Zach thought of everything, obviously. I could really get to love hanging around a guy who thought ahead and paid attention.

"Our Singles group?"

"No, the name -- Independent Alliance? Kind of contradictory, don't you think?"

"Oh. Yeah." He grinned, nodding, and glanced over my head. I turned just enough to see two carloads of trainees coming into the parking lot. "Alliance just means being one body. But you're right -- how can we be independent? It's a delicate balance. The association is there to provide help and resources, not hand down regulations and directives. I stay out of the politics."

"I knew you were smart."

He laughed, then glanced over my head again. I felt the stares burning holes in my coat. Zach must have caught some of the weird looks tainting the atmosphere. He mock-scolded me to get to my appointment on time, said he'd be praying for me, and reached to put his truck into gear. That was my cue. I thanked him, said goodbye, and closed the door.

"I don't recognize him," Miss Slandowski said in her kitty-cat voice as she paused beside me and watched Zach's truck drive away.

"He's a new friend, from one of the businesses up past the mall." I knew better than to try to ignore the question.

"What about you and Thad Grant?" Mrs. Rizetti said as she minced her way up the sidewalk with her cronies.

Chapter Four

"What about us?" I met her gaze, truly curious to know what the gossip -- excuse me, "sharing" -- around church said, concerning my relationship with Thad.

"We assume the two of you --" She looked around at her friends. "Well, the general expectation is that you and Thad are going to be walking down the aisle in the next year. You certainly won't need your job here in the office, now will you?" She smirked and scurried away, with her friends following her like prune-faced ducklings.

"That's news to me. Is that how you and Pastor Marcus are justifying firing me, without any warning? Oh, she's going to get married soon and she can live off her husband?" I unclenched my fists. "For your information, Thad hasn't said anything about marriage, and I hope he never does."

A few jaws dropped and a few sets of eyes got wide. I waited until everyone had gone inside, and the warmth in my face and the thudding of my heart both receded to normal. Then I walked up the sidewalk and into the building.

The trainees were unusually quiet, assembling the bulletins for the New Year's Eve service. Occasionally, I caught one sneaking out of the workroom, phone in hand. The busybody hotline was buzzing that afternoon, for certain.

Fine. Let them. If the powers-that-be became irritated or embarrassed by the reaction to the gossip, they might just let me go sooner. I honestly hoped Pastor Marcus would tell me to clear off my desk that afternoon, but he was conspicuously invisible the rest of the day.

The bus dropped me at the corner in front of Holy Spirit Independent Alliance with ten minutes until my appointment. A big, white-haired man stood in the doorway between the sanctuary and the gymnasium wing. He was one of those broad-shouldered, heavy-set older ethnic gentlemen who seemed to predominate in the neighborhoods of Cleveland populated by

Croatian, Slovak and Polish immigrants. He wore a green plaid flannel shirt and a gaudy red felt vest sporting reindeer and snowmen. I hazarded a guess that his grandchildren had bought it for him, and he only wore it because he loved them.

Just as I guessed, he introduced himself as Pastor Paulson and ushered me down the hall to the office complex. He explained we would be meeting in the outer office so the custodians could see us as they worked, to comply with a strict policy of accountability and behavior, to avoid compromising situations. The building was newer than ours, bigger, and the office had lots of glass walls and half-walls, creating an open feeling. Everything looked neat and clean, with pots of poinsettias, green garlands, and personal items on the desks I passed -- photos, a Nerf basketball hoop poised over a wastebasket, pictures drawn by children, candy dispensers. I thought I could feel comfortable working in this office, just getting good vibrations from the place itself.

Pastor Paulson made small talk as he led me to an empty table in the center of the room, bringing up mutual acquaintances. He knew Dad from several inter-church efforts at Faith-and-Family Day events at Progressive Field and the Browns' stadium.

"Here's our situation. Our resident miracle-worker is with her sister in Calgary, who is having a difficult pregnancy, with triplets. We've been making do with temps and volunteers from our church family for the last month. Veronica called last week to say she's going to be in Calgary for at least three months, and is considering moving there permanently. It seems there's a young man who caught her eye." He winked. "While you coming here feels like the Lord's timing, I have to wonder why you're looking for work at the holidays. What happened?"

I wasn't sure how much I should reveal. This interview was my only chance to make a good impression. Still, if I painted things too nicely, and the truth eventually came out, everything I said would be tainted in retrospect.

In for a penny ...

I took a deep breath, nodded, and said a quick prayer for God to guide my tongue.

"Up until Tuesday morning, I didn't know I was leaving. I'm afraid nobody would have told me I was out of a job until they let me go if I hadn't caught on to what's going on." In as few words as possible, I explained the volunteers in my workroom, and the budget and stewardship portion of Pastor Marcus's reasoning.

"Do they know you're looking for a new position before they let you go?" he asked, after several minutes of silence.

"I told them I was looking." I let out a wry little laugh. "They seem to expect me to be loyal and adjust my schedule to suit their needs. If the volunteers aren't ready to fly solo until March, I honestly think they expect me to stay until then."

"How much praying have you done about this situation, young lady?"

"Not as much as I should," I admitted. Something about being addressed as "young lady," accompanied by that sympathetic smile, made me feel like I had passed some test. "I'm still working past the feeling of being betrayed. It doesn't help that I'm going through something like this with the guy I'm dating -- or maybe I should say *was dating*, past tense."

"Uh huh. That answers one of the questions I was going to ask." He nodded. "Tell me a little about yourself. I got your resume from Zach. Let's look between the lines, shall we?"

When I headed for home, I wasn't sure what I felt. Interested in the job. Comfortable with Pastor Paulson. Uneasy at having revealed part of the situation at church. Despite how they were treating me, I felt like a traitor. Then there was the whole stupid inter-church sports rivalry. We Clevelanders are rabid when it comes to our sports teams. Maybe I was starting to cool down from the first burst of indignation.

We didn't talk salary, but we did talk responsibilities, hours and benefits, confidentiality, and what he called "above and beyond" expectations. I would be involved when women came into the church seeking help in one form or another -- shelter, food, clothes, money, counseling. If a woman on the pastoral staff wasn't available, I would sit in on any counseling sessions or discussions the women had with Pastor Paulson or his associates. My input would be more than just serving as a chaperone and a shield against charges of impropriety.

I was a little afraid and a little excited at the thought of having meatier responsibilities. Other than Rev. Gilbert, most of the old pastoral staff had this attitude that the most input I could offer was to make coffee and type up notes.

When I got home, my answering machine had a three on the display. Since when did three people leave messages in one day? Then I remembered I had turned off my cell phone when I went into the meeting with Zach and hadn't turned it back on yet. They probably tried my home phone when I didn't answer my cell. The only other option was church people calling after office hours.

I listened to the answering machine while I searched my refrigerator, hoping for some leftovers I had forgotten about, to hide under barbecue sauce and heat in the microwave. Reprieve. All three messages were from people handling chores for the Singles' New Year's party -- Joy was bringing a party tray from her father's deli; Gary was in charge of the beverages; and Reggie had the pastry tray. Joy and Reggie reported in, mission accomplished, including what time they were coming to set up on Sunday night. Gary, however, was very sorry to dump the beverage detail on me. He was on his way to the airport to fly to Canada for a ski trip his boss gave him as part of his Christmas bonus. I didn't blame Gary for taking the trip. At least he remembered to call, so I could take care of the hole in the menu.

I found leftover fried rice, some fake crab sautéed with onions and sweet peppers -- a cooking experiment last time Reggie was over for some last-minute shopping -- and the remainder of a jar of mushrooms. Barbecue sauce could cover a multitude of culinary sins. Once dinner was nuking in the microwave, I turned on my cell phone.

The phone rang just as I read the display saying I had four messages. It was Thad.

"What's going on at church, that you're talking to people about us getting *married*?" he demanded before I finished saying hello. "Dinah?" he barked, when I was silent for five heartbeats.

"Mrs. Rizetti --"

"Oh, great. What were you talking to her about your personal life for, anyway?"

"Let me finish, and you won't have to ask any questions." I waited, expecting him to argue, but he surprised me by staying silent. "I was coming back from lunch, a friend offered me a ride, and Mrs. Rizetti and her clones were coming back at the same time. Because my friend was a man she didn't know, she accused me of being unfaithful to you. Then she said everyone expects us to get married. And since those idiots on the board expect me to be married and living off you, I don't need a job. That's why they're training Mrs. Rizetti and her idiot friends to do all my work. For free."

"You're getting fired?"

Right then, Thad almost made up for his lame Christmas present. He listened, instead of focusing on the horrifying thought that people expected us to get married.

"And they weren't planning on telling me until the day they told me not to come back."

All right, that wasn't very mature, but it was rare when Thad showed any kind of white knight tendency. I was going to milk it for all it was worth. Why not get my money's worth, even this late in the game?

He actually got angry when I told him my much-edited version of the argument with Pastor Marcus.

"So you're looking for a new job, right?"

"That's the plan. It'd be nice if I had a place to jump to before they give me a push."

I didn't want to tell him about Match and Zach. So I didn't.

"I don't know -- maybe we can find something for you to do at the store?"

Panic choked me. Now was not the time for Thad to start taking a deeper interest in my life. Not when I had decided I was closer to "happy" than "okay" with him dumping me soon.

"I don't think so. What if we can't work together? Or we break up? Whatever happens, it'll affect the other relationship."

No way was I admitting that while I could work with Thad, and work around him when necessary, I couldn't and absolutely wouldn't work with his cousins. Thad and Reggie were the best of the Grant grandchildren. They had grown up at our church and stayed there, which made their grandmother very happy. Maybe a third of their cousins had moved out of state for college and work. The ones who remained in the area had bad track records, church-wise. Whenever they got their feelings hurt, they quit and moved to a new church. I wouldn't work with Thad's cousins, even if it meant the difference between keeping my house and living in a cardboard box.

"Yeah, there is that," Thad finally said after another one of those silences that meant he was thinking hard. Always dangerous. "Still ... do you ever think about us ... you know."

"No. I don't know what you're talking about," I lied, and tapped the controls of the microwave to send my dinner through for another minute.

"Come on, Dinah." He laughed. "Maybe Mrs. Rizetti was right --"

"Go see a doctor right now. You're delirious." I forced a laugh through blockage in my throat. "We've just started dating. We have a long way to go to even think about -- that. If ever."

Silently, I added, *Not never.*

"Okay, I was ticked when I heard you were talking about us getting married. But the thing is, that stupid old woman made me think ... it wouldn't be so bad, you know?"

That sort of crystallized things.

Marriage should be in the category of "can't live without you," rather than "wouldn't be so bad."

"Thad, do you really want to talk about something like this with Mrs. Rizetti and her stupid gossip in your head?"

"Oh. Yeah." He laughed, that creaking, awkward sound that meant he felt stupid. If I didn't change the subject, or offer him an out, he would get angry.

That was my default reaction to situations like this, through all the years we had been working together. Maybe that was why he asked me out. I was good for his ego.

"I have too much to think about right now," I finally said, offering him an out, as usual, "with finding a new job and taking care of New Year's. Let's leave this talk for the future, when things are ... nicer. Okay?"

"Okay. But promise me something, Dinah?"

"Like what?"

"Promise you'll think about us being together, okay?"

"Thad ..." I was too tired and hungry to be tactful any longer. "We're not together. I have no plans for us to be together."

"Yeah, but we could be."

It was on the tip of my tongue to tell him there was a long distance between a gift certificate to *his* favorite store and "could be together." But of course, I held it back. Then a ruckus in the background came through the phone. Perfect timing.

"Dinah? Sorry -- gotta go. See you in church."

I heard someone say something about pizza and paying, before the phone went dead.

"Okay, I thought about us being together," I whispered as I closed my phone. "It's a definite no."

<><><>

Thursday morning, my phone rang as I was walking from my car to the office door. I nearly let it take a message, when I didn't recognize the number on the display. Then I did, and flipped it open, pausing almost on top of a new icy patch on the sidewalk.

"Dinah, good." Pastor Paulson's voice was warm and had a richness that made me think he laughed a lot. "I know this is short notice, but I just got out of a meeting and a few members of the board would like to meet with you, get to know you a little better. Are you free at lunch today?"

I looked over my shoulder at my car. Usually I didn't drive to work, but took the bus to spare my car daily exposure to the salt and cinders that filled the roads from November to April. Today I had driven because I had to get the cases of soda Gary would have picked up if he wasn't swooshing down the slopes.

"About how long would the meeting be?"

"Half an hour at the most, just a few questions to clear up."

"Sure. What time?"

I had a new spring in my step as I finished my walk to the church door, despite the icy patches on the sidewalk.

This morning, my volunteers didn't even begin trickling in until nearly ten, which gave me a chance to get work done without having to answer questions or someone watching over my shoulder. Plus, I had the satisfaction of Pastor Marcus and Mr. Flannery of the ever-shrinking budget pausing in the doorway and looking around with wide-eyed, panicked expressions.

"Umm -- Dinah --" Mr. Flannery took a step closer to the table, where I was making notes on the church directory changes.

I was smiling, because this was another item on my mental list of "never have to deal with this headache again."

"Mr. Flannery?" I bit back the urge to tell him to address me as Miss Clydesdale, since we were *not* friends.

"Where -- where is everybody?"

"You mean the women training to learn my job so you can

fire me?" I batted my eyelashes. I didn't feel the least bit of guilt when he flinched. "That's the thing about volunteers -- if they don't feel like keeping regular hours, you can't make them."

Mr. Flannery and Pastor Marcus got red in the face and their mouths moved a few times without any words coming out. I liked them better that way.

"What are we going to do if nobody completes the training?" Mr. Flannery muttered.

"Dinah is here for as long as it takes to train the ladies to do her work." Pastor Marcus chuckled. "How long could that take?"

"If you're so sure my job is so simple, why do you need *me* to train anyone at all?" I raised my voice a little when I saw a Cleveland Browns jersey glide past in the office behind them. Mitch, my favorite among the custodians, had probably come to check with me about tables or which doors to leave unlocked tonight for a social event.

"Come now, Dinah, we went over this before." His voice lost its jolly notes. "This is an opportunity for the ladies to serve as unto the Lord, giving of a little of their time every week, providing necessary services to the church body as a whole."

"But if *my* job is so *simple*, why does anybody need any training at all?" I persisted. Which probably wasn't very nice, but I had a craving for him to stick his head into a noose made of his words, with witnesses. "In fact, why don't you just let me leave tomorrow? Finish out the year cleanly. Save the church another week of payroll. No fussing with all those nasty old tax documents and the payroll going into the new year."

I bit my lip to keep from smiling, as I added yet another item to my list of things I wouldn't have to do anymore. Usually I had to retype all the tax forms a minimum of four times, because the treasurer and other people involved with church finances kept disagreeing over figures and procedures.

From the sudden widening of his eyes, maybe Mr. Flannery was starting to realize I did more work than the penny pinchers and bean counters gave me credit for.

"Now see here, Dinah --" Pastor Marcus had a new sheen on his upper lip and his high forehead. Panic sweat, maybe? Or maybe he was embarrassed?

"That's *Miss Clydesdale*. It's been made very clear to me that I am not part of the church family, I am *just* an employee."

Mitch loomed up behind Pastor Marcus and Mr. Flannery, a good head taller than them both. He frowned, making gestures at them, asking if I was all right. I had a sudden image of him grabbing each of them by an arm and hauling them out of the building. He could and had done it. Just not to church leaders.

The problem with having a church directly across the street from a big, busy mall was that people sometimes wandered in. Some were looking for free phones or bathrooms, others stayed to wander around and explore where they had no right to be. Because we were a church, there was an expectation for more things to be free to use than just the bathrooms. We learned during the Christmas shopping season to have ushers and trustees posted at the doors during services, as security.

During the week, only the doors by the office were unlocked. It was all too common for strangers to try to help themselves to coats and Christmas presents left sitting on shelves and coat racks, or even cake savers and tins and bags of refreshments people brought for class social time. What was really sad was that when such thieves were caught, they were usually angry, as if their rights were being violated. One nasty creature I confronted a year or two ago argued that churches were public property, and that meant anything left unattended was up for grabs. He threatened to sue us for ejecting him from the property and taking back the bag of Christmas presents intended for Mr. Orcutt's fifth grade boys. He stank of alcohol, which explained, but didn't excuse, his belligerence. He never followed up on his threats. Any lawyer he contacted probably laughed in his face.

Mitch was our version of a bouncer during the work week, when people managed to sneak in despite security measures. I would miss seeing him every day, to share a joke or a friendly gripe. He also had a talent for tapping the pop machine in just the right place to get me a free ginger ale when I needed it most.

I nodded to him. He shrugged, rolled his eyes, and stepped out of sight again.

"Dinah." Pastor Marcus looked a little sad, a little tired. None of the guilt I needed so much to see, to soothe my own aching ego. "This isn't like you, holding a grudge for so long."

"A grudge? Is that what you call this? Mr. Flannery, I had to put the clues together. Nobody had the guts or the courtesy to tell me I'm losing my job. And as I understand it, the board expects me to stay until you're sure the volunteers can handle the job. But if I find a job before they're ready, you think it's unfair if I leave."

"That's not what I said. That part is a regrettable misunderstanding."

"The plan was to give Dinah her severance package next Tuesday, when the volunteers were *supposed* to start," Mr. Flannery said slowly. "She was supposed to sit down with representatives of the deacons, trustees and finance committee, to explain the situation, our reasoning, and to thank her for her years of dedication. And she was to be *asked* to *consider* staying until everyone was trained. No one was to assume that she owed us anything. We were to offer her help in finding a new position." He turned back to me. "Dinah, I assure you, no one involved in the decision wanted you to find out this way. I was shocked when my wife told me the volunteers had come in a week early."

I had the sneaking suspicion Mrs. Rizetti had jumped the gun, in her eagerness to have me out on my rear.

"Since I am on the way out, Mr. Flannery ... a lot of things happen around here where I end up being the last person anyone ever thinks of. This situation is just par for the course."

Let me point out that I kept my voice calm and reasonable, which made me very proud, looking back. Granted, the knowledge that I had a possible new job to flee to helped me keep my cool. I didn't break down in angry tears, with my voice rising to the point only dogs could hear me.

"If you want to keep your volunteers, pay a little more attention to things like communication. This work is a ministry, but you have to work with *people*. Slap them around enough, they start thinking about bruises instead of spiritual things."

"Of course," he said quietly. He and Pastor Marcus exchanged looks, then he muttered something that sounded like, "Excuse us, please," and they walked out.

The first volunteers did show up about fifteen minutes later.

Later that morning, after I took the ladies to the kitchen to teach them about the refrigerators, I had a few minutes alone in my workroom. It was ten minutes until lunchtime, and they were busy conferring over where they wanted to go to eat. When I went into the bottom drawer of the filing cabinet where I stored my purse, to freshen up for my meeting, I found an envelope sticking out of it. It was in Mr. Flannery's distinctive square handwriting.

Inside was a severance check. A good one? A well-deserved one? Well, considering what I was expecting, it was a decent-sized check. At least it wasn't a gift certificate to the grocery store, but it was only two weeks' pay. Along with the check was a handwritten note, apologizing again for the way the "revelation" had been handled. Under the note was a copy of the meeting minutes where my termination and the process had been discussed.

I considered analyzing it to identify who had sided for and against me, then I folded up the papers and put them back in the envelope, unread. I would only be hurting myself. Besides, I didn't have time for that nonsense.

I left a few minutes early for my meeting at Holy Spirit Alliance and deposited that check right away.

The office area was bustling when I walked into Holy Spirit's building. My first thought was that with so many people working there, what did they need me for? Then I realized most of them were retirement-age people, taking down Christmas decorations and doing an assembly line to put together what looked like a bulletin.

"You looking for somebody?" a man asked in a quiet voice, off to my right.

I turned and saw him leaning out of one of the offices that had been closed when I was there last night. He wore a dark green shirt and a sweater vest with Santa appliqués on it. My first thought was that his mother had probably given it to him for Christmas.

All right, I scolded myself immediately. *Snap out of it. Just because you started the day in a snark is no reason to continue it -- or to take it some place new.*

"I'm Dinah Clydesdale. Pastor --"

"Dinah! There you are." Pastor Paulson came striding down the long hallway from the conference room, holding out both hands for mine. "Right on -- no, you're a few minutes early." He grasped my gloved hands and turned, looking around the room at the people who had for the most part stopped what they were doing to look at us. "Everybody, this is Dinah Clydesdale, the young lady Zach Foster's office sent us."

The smiles and nods from the people as they went back to work made me feel like I had fallen into one of those dreams where you don't know anybody, but everybody knows you. Worse, they expect something from you, and if you don't figure it out, the world is going to blow up. Yeah, one of those dreams.

Chapter Five

"Oh, yes, you've met Russell, haven't you?" Pastor Paulson continued, turning and guiding me with him. He nodded to the man who had questioned me. "Russell Prince. You two will be working quite closely for a while. Russell is in charge of the computer network, the sound system, the display screens in some of our bigger classrooms. Anything technical, he's your man. I don't know how we'd survive without him."

"Nice to meet you." Russell nodded to me, blushing in a way that made his previous complexion seem doughy in contrast.

I echoed him, and we exchanged smiles before Pastor Paulson led me down the hall.

In the conference room, a nice mix of men and women of different ages waited to talk with me. With plastic domed trays of sandwiches and cookies for lunch. What was with the people of this church -- first Zach, now the board here -- that they thought of things like lunch? I wasn't used to such consideration. Maybe because I usually had to think of such things for everyone else. I sat down at the table next to Pastor Paulson, and smiled during the blessing, as I thought about the next staff meeting at Central Avenue. They would sit down at the table and look around, and realize there was no coffee prepared. No cans of pop and bottles of fruit juice and tea in a big metal bowl full of ice. No cookies and fruit. Would anyone realize that was something else I handled without any recognition?

Attitude? Yes, I confess it freely. I wasn't in any mood to repent quite yet.

I had a nice surprise. Aaron Randall, who had been working part-time at several local churches after graduating seminary, was on staff there. I hadn't heard where he went or why he left Central Avenue. A few rumors said he had been arguing with several members of different church boards. He just didn't show up for work one day. I was glad to see him, but didn't get a chance to talk to him that afternoon. He nodded to me and smiled from across the room, but we had no more contact than that.

The various representatives of the ministries, committees, and boards of the church all had a few questions to ask, relating to their areas of concern. Some had scenarios to present to me, to see how I would react to a problem or need. I came away from that meeting with a growing feeling of ... not quite dread, but the certainty that this church was involved in twice as many outreaches and missions and service projects as my home church. I would be involved in all of them, in one degree or another.

I kind of felt excited, too. Leaving my old situation and moving to a new vista of ministry would be a good thing for me. I would certainly get a chance to grow and learn.

When I got back to church, only fifteen minutes late, I had ten twenty-four-pack cubes of beverages for the Singles party. Mitch met me with one of the wheeled carts he used for hauling tables around the church, and followed me back out to my car to get my load.

"Don't look now, but we're being watched," he said, as he bent to reach into my trunk.

Of course I looked, but used his broad back to hide my action. Pastor Marcus stood at his office window.

"What are the chances I'll be asked to turn in my keys and not come back tomorrow?" I murmured, as we headed to the door with our load.

"Honey, you can only hope." He winked. "So, looking?"

"Not only looking, but I think I might have a new job lined up already."

"Great." He looked around as I pulled the door open and held it for him, then lowered his voice. "Don't tell anybody, though, okay?"

"I don't plan to until something is concrete." His grin warned me. "Why?"

"Me and the guys have a pool going."

"Pool?" I followed him into the building and lowered my voice too, in case anyone was in the front office and heard us. "Like, betting on the Super Bowl kind of pool?"

"Kind of."

"Betting in church." I shook my head, and *tsk*ed. "So, what's your bet?"

"We're betting on the day they finally turn you loose, or you tell them to take a hike and walk. And we're betting on how long it takes for you to find a better place."

"Uh huh."

"I took the first week of January, for both."

"I'll try to live up to your faith in me."

He barked laughter, then we could say nothing more as we hurried down the hallways to the kitchen, to lock up the haul in the closet assigned to the Singles.

<><><>

Nobody approached me for the rest of the day, other than my volunteers. A couple times as I went about my duties, I met up with the other custodians, and they all gave me winks and grins. It was nice to know I had their support. I would miss them. Most of them were friends of my father, and I had grown up seeing them around the house, or going to the bowling alley for league tournaments and seeing them play.

Just before quitting time, I had to run down the hall to meet the social director for the Young Marrieds and Pre-Marrieds class, to hand over a refrigerator padlock key. When I came back to the office, everyone had left, except for Mrs. Carr and Mrs. Whickle, who answered the phones two afternoons a week. Mrs. Whickle had a pink message slip in her hand and Mrs. Carr stood in the doorway of my workroom, glaring, with her hand out. Since she was a Rizetti clone, it was a good guess the message was for me, and she was trying to spy.

"Dinah." Mrs. Whickle's face lost about half her wrinkles as she handed me the paper. "Message for you, dear."

"Some people think they can get away with mixing personal matters with work," Mrs. Carr muttered.

"Some people don't know how to verify facts before they make false accusations," I snapped, and folded my pink message slip into sharp creases before sliding it into my skirt pocket.

Her nostrils flared so widely with her fury, if she tipped her head back any further I could have seen into her sinuses. I offered her one of my blandest troublemaker-handling smiles. She huffed three times, then stomped into the workroom. Mrs. Whickle blinked, fighting not to smile, and we waited. I silently counted to ten before Mrs. Carr appeared with her coat on and stalked out of the office.

"Some people." Mrs. Whickle sighed. "It beats me why people like her bother coming to church. They sure don't listen to the sermons."

I remembered something Dad used to say, when I complained about the bullies and Pharisees I ran into at church. I had begged him to let me quit going, or at least quit attending the youth events. He would always tell me that listening was one thing, and application of what I heard was another. If I knew better than everybody else how to live, then I had a duty to show them how Christians were supposed to act, instead of just complaining all the time.

Suddenly I felt very tired. I certainly hadn't been acting like a good, self-controlled, forgiving, patient Christian lately, had I? Just because nobody else was, that was no excuse for the things sliding out of my mouth and the thoughts in my heart and mind.

"What's Victoria Grant want with you?" Mrs. Whickle asked, stepping back to her desk. Time to turn on the answering machine for the evening. Everyone else was gone for the day.

"I have a meeting with her tomorrow. I think she heard about this whole mess." I gestured around the office. "And she probably wants to talk to me about it, maybe just let me know she was against it."

"You're dating her grandson," she offered. "That has to count for something."

"I *was* dating Thad. I'm pretty sure he's breaking up with me. Just as soon as the New Year's party is over."

"Yeah, typical." Her eyes sparkled with mischief as she took her purse out of the bottom drawer of her desk and walked over to the coat rack in the corner. "All those Grant men -- use 'em and lose 'em."

"Is that what they do, or what we should do to them?"

I had always loved Mrs. Whickle's bubbly laughter.

I read the message in the car. Mrs. Grant had called to say she had gotten permission for me to take Friday afternoon off. That meant whatever she wanted to talk about, it was important, and she planned on me staying for a couple hours. As I drove home, I thought about calling Reggie to get her take on the situation, and maybe find out if she knew what her grandmother was doing.

Reggie was busy with rehearsals for the children's theater

production she had been tricked into doing. Even if she hadn't been, I hesitated to call. Getting her input would mean explaining everything that had been happening to me all week. Other than my first wailing, can-you-believe-those-jerks-are-doing-this-to-me griping session on the phone Tuesday night, we hadn't talked.

I didn't want to tell her about A Match Made For Heaven and Zach Foster and Holy Spirit Alliance, until everything was settled. Reggie might urge me not to go "work for the enemy," even if she couldn't care less about the inter-church sports league rivalry.

Later, I wished I had told her about the invitation from her grandmother. It could have saved us all a lot of embarrassment, discomfort, and frustration.

<><><>

Mrs. Grant had one of those big houses that were called "estates," back in a more gracious time. The driveway curved around from the street about one hundred yards, past landscaping that hid the front of the house from the street traffic. The huge porch wrapped around the entire house, and the two sides I could see when I arrived on Friday had furniture sets in what Mom always called "conversation groups." I looked at the wrought iron tables and chairs and wondered if they were exchanged for wicker in the warmer months. At the rear of the house, the driveway curved around behind walls of hedges taller than my head. She might have had a tennis court, pool, and a six-car garage hidden back there.

Everything was neatly shoveled and salted and tastefully understated in the decorations. Electric candles sat on the sills, with ribbons and garlands above them in every window. No electric light display bright enough to be seen in the next county.

I did find it funny that the driveway was lined with those plastic luminaries made to look like paper bags, with star-shaped cutouts. The battery-operated candles inside were glowing. At noon? On a day only slightly overcast? I shook my head and filed that detail away to ask Reggie about at the New Year's party.

I went to the driveway side door and rang the doorbell. The glass of the storm door was just frosted enough on the inside that it caught my attention. That was condensation, because the inside door hung open. A few seconds of concentration let me figure out the shadowy outlines through the frost, to reveal a long hallway with pegs and benches down one side. Coats and boots enough for an army filled those pegs and sat on and under those benches.

Then I heard the low rumble of voices. Lots of voices.

Mrs. Grant had company.

I suddenly felt like I did in those horrid dreams where I walked into a classroom and found out that I was not only late, but I was supposed to teach. With no idea what the class was about. Forget the stupid dream of showing up naked. I took two steps back on the deep porch and tried to look around the hedges hiding the back yard. Sure enough, I glimpsed at least four cars.

Please, please, let this be the wrong day.

But I knew it wasn't.

Mrs. Grant had told me to come at lunchtime on Friday.

What I had forgotten until that moment was that Reggie told me the required, all-day, family holiday get-together was Friday. It was always between Christmas and New Year's.

A sensible person would have the party on a Saturday, to ensure more people could come without interfering with work. Mrs. Grant, as matriarch of her enormous clan, obviously saw no need to accommodate others' schedules.

My brain froze up on the question of why exactly Mrs. Grant invited me to come for lunch, and to talk about my future, in the middle of her annual family party. I mean, yes, if I pushed it, stripping some gears in my frozen brain, I could come up with an answer. I had the horrified feeling I didn't want to know.

Time to get out of there. What did it matter if I insulted the most powerful old woman in our church by not showing up? I was leaving anyway -- job and membership. I would just walk away. I would tell the committee that I was sick and wouldn't be coming to the New Year's overnighter. I would start attending Holy Spirit Alliance right away. This very Sunday.

First, I had to get off that porch.

Please, please, let there be a bus coming, as soon as I get to the corner. Please, Lord? I know I've been griping a lot, and thinking very un-Christian thoughts about people who haven't been acting very Christian themselves, but on the whole, I've been a good girl. I deserve a little bit of grace, a couple of miracles, don't You think so?

Too late. A human shape appeared against the frosted glass. I took two steps backward to flee, and wasted time praying the latch would stick on the storm door.

"What are you doing here?" Reggie said, laughing, as she pushed the door open and took one step out.

"I have no idea, but whatever it is, I'm dead meat." I grabbed her and pulled her outside. The storm door slammed closed. "Reg, your grandmother invited me to lunch today. She got permission from Pastor Marcus for me to take the entire afternoon off."

"But why --" Reggie's eyes got big and she looked like she was about to choke. "Oh, this is all my fault. I knew I should have just brushed off Grammy's questions. When will I learn not to try for damage control?"

"What kind of damage control?"

I knew. I just didn't want to admit it. Part of me wanted to scurry around the back of the house and assure myself Thad's BMW wasn't sitting among all the other cars.

"Grammy put me through the inquisition Sunday night about you and Thad. I thought I could fix things, prove to her that it was over. I told her how much work you put into finding that jerk the perfect Christmas present, and how lame his present was for you, and I had to push him to get you anything. Oh, I'm so sorry, Di!" Reggie wrapped her arms around me, and for a second I felt like I was holding her upright.

"Grammy just thinks you're the perfect girl for Thad. She said something about what an idiot he was, because he didn't invite you today. And I tried to tell her, I really did, that you and Thad just started dating, but obviously he isn't serious, because he would have got you a better present and he would have told Grammy about you. I mean, honestly, he's such a wimp, and he's her pet, and he knows how much the other guys hurt her feelings by getting involved with girls she didn't approve of and ..." Reggie sank down into the nearest wrought iron chair, only lightly dusted with snow.

"I think I convinced her you were in love with Thad, and he was so cautious, and he was protecting you by not bringing you around because of the Witches."

Honestly, for about three seconds, I couldn't remember who Reggie was referring to. Which just showed how much my brain had short-circuited. I had made up that label for her three cousins who had made our lives miserable in school and whenever they deigned to return to our church.

I felt a little sick when I realized that Susan, Lisa, and Charlene were inside right that moment. Even if I wasn't horrified at the thought of coming face-to-face with Thad in his grandmother's matchmaking schemes, I was nauseated at the prospect of having to face those three.

"I'm gone," I said, at the same moment Reggie blurted, "You can't come in."

As usual, we agreed completely. I said a short, silent prayer of thanks that God made Reggie come to the door instead of Thad, or their grandmother. There would have been no escaping, then. I took two steps, then Reggie shrieked and leaped out of her chair and grabbed hold of my arm.

"You can't leave!"

"But -- "

"Grammy knows you're here. She has to. She told me to see who was here." Reggie shot a panicked look at the door. "We've spent too much time out here already. She's going to come looking for us any second. Or worse, she'll send Thad."

"Tell her I was someone with a flat tire and you called Triple-A for me." I headed down the steps again, with Reggie still holding onto me. We skidded down two steps before I stopped and tried to pry her hands off my arm.

"Dinah --"

"Dinah. There you are," Mrs. Grant said. I had never heard someone actually purr when they spoke, until that moment. "Why haven't you brought her inside yet, Regina?"

"I'm sorry, Mrs. Grant, there must be some mistake. I didn't realize you were having your family party. I was just telling Reggie that I have to get back to the office because of an emergency that came up before I left. They need me."

"Don't be silly, dear." She stepped out and held out a hand, and I swear, Reggie and I got lifted up the steps by some unseen power. Mrs. Grant was that impossible to say no to.

Especially when she addressed me as "dear."

"I'd like to start considering you part of the family, and what better time to do that than at the holidays?" She looped her arm through mine and gestured for Reggie to open the door.

Reggie gave me a "don't kill me" look, and opened the door

and held it for us as we went inside.

"I think you should know that Thad and I are breaking up. In fact, the only reason he hasn't broken up with me already -- and I haven't dumped him -- is our obligation to the Singles New Year's overnighter. Once that's through --"

"I had a nice long talk with Thad, and we've straightened out his thinking." She patted my arm. "Take your coat off and come downstairs. We just started lunch. Your timing is perfect."

No, I argued silently, *my timing is rotten stinky lousy.*

"Mrs. Grant, I think you should know that I'm leaving our church in a week or so."

"Leaving?" She gave Reggie an interrogative look. The kind an insane alien telepath would use on a *SyFy*-made movie to yank information out of someone's brain. Reggie just shook her head and gave me a panicked look.

"I'm being fired -- they're having me train a whole crew of volunteers right now to take over all my duties -- and I've already lined up a new job at a new church. It's natural that I would be expected to join that church."

Okay, I lied a couple of teensy lies, but looked at from the right angle, they *could* be true. I hadn't been *officially* offered the job at Holy Spirit Alliance, but it looked like I would. And it just made sense for me to be a member of the church where I worked, so I could get to know the people, the ins and outs, the political factions, the routines.

"Those idiots," Mrs. Grant said quietly. I swear, the temperature in the big entryway, with the smells of Christmas feasting drifting up the stairway, dropped about twenty degrees in five seconds.

"So if I'm leaving the church, Thad and I won't be seeing each other anymore. And we weren't very serious. We only went out six times."

"Yes, but you work so well together," she murmured, her gaze shooting somewhere over my left shoulder. "I've always liked you, Dinah. You work hard, you keep your nose out of trouble, you're respectful, and you're Regina's friend. That says a lot for your character. You'd be very good for Thad."

"He doesn't love me, and I don't love him."

"Your feelings are hurt, which is reasonable. I had a good talk with him about that. He was mortified at the message he gave you about your relationship, when he gave you that -- what was it you called it, Regina? Lame? Very applicable term, yes. That lame Christmas present." Mrs. Grant chuckled softly, then tugged on my sleeve. "Off with that coat." She reached for my collar, and I had a horrified vision of her unbuttoning my coat for me if I didn't act quickly. So I did.

The next thing I knew, we were going down the stairs, Mrs. Grant leading the way, with me behind her, compelled by an invisible force, and Reggie bringing up the rear. I silently called her a wimp for not coming to my rescue. Of course, I couldn't come to my own rescue, so why expect it from my friend, who could never stand up to her grandmother?

"At one time, Thad was considering going into the ministry. Did you know that?" Mrs. Grant stopped halfway down the stairs to smile up at me, over her shoulder. I shook my head. "Computers were always his hobby. He only went in to help his cousins when they had trouble with their business. He could never seem to extricate himself and get back on track. I think you could help him."

Considering how many times I had gone to Thad for some computer tutoring, and how much he visibly enjoyed working with computers? I doubted I would have any influence, getting him to leave the computer business and head for seminary.

The plan was clear to me now. Mrs. Grant was going to guilt-trip Thad into believing he was in love with me. She would make him acknowledge me as his girlfriend in front of the entire Grant clan. They would expect me to show up at family functions and holidays from now on. Thad would become comfortable with the idea of the two of us together.

Eventually, he would have one of his great-great-grandmother's diamonds made into an engagement ring. We would have a respectable engagement period, a lavish wedding at our home church, and head off to seminary. I would work to put Thad through seminary, and then "retire" from working outside the home -- meaning I would be caught between the church and the house for the rest of my life. Doing what I was doing now, but with no paycheck of my own. Even worse, pastors' wives lived in goldfish bowls.

Nuh uh. Not this girl.

I came out of my visionary daze just in time to turn the corner at the bottom of the stairs and walk into an enormous greatroom. A long buffet table went down the center of the room with a dozen card tables set up around it. From the decimated looks of the bowls and platters filling the table -- long enough to need three different tablecloths -- everyone had been through the buffet line. People were jammed into the room, sitting at the tables or on the couches at the far end or on the floor, everyone with a plate and cup and talking at the top of their voices.

Of course, the first person to look up from his plate and see me standing there between his grandmother and Reggie was Thad. He stopped with a fork three inches from his mouth, his eyes big and stunned. Probably what a skunk looked like just before the oncoming car sent it flying. He went pale. Then he flushed a dusky pink, put his fork down with deliberation I had seen during tense Singles meetings, and got up.

"Is there a problem with the overnighter?" he said, as soon as he got close enough to us to be heard without shouting.

"Don't be silly." Mrs. Grant patted him on the shoulder. "I thought it only right that your girlfriend join the family for Christmas. Get the new year started off on the right foot."

"I'm not Thad's girlfriend, Mrs. Grant," I hurried to say, and avoided looking at him. "We're good friends, yes, and we work together a lot on the Singles --"

My voice snagged in my throat when Thad caught hold of my hand. He never held my hand in public. Certainly not in front of his grandmother or the Witches -- who I just found among the noisy, eating crowd. From their sneers, they had seen me.

"Dinah, I realize how I hurt your feelings," he said, "and I'm sorry. I'm going to make it up to you."

Then help me get out of here, and explain to your grandmother that I've decided to start an order of Protestant nuns.

"That's not necessary," I said instead.

"Where are your manners? Get Dinah a plate and find her a place to sit and eat. Let her get used to us." Mrs. Grant hooked her arm through Reggie's and led/dragged her away. Without Reggie as a lifeline, the only person to cling to, in this crowd of mostly strangers and a few enemies, was Thad.

To my relief, most of the family had finished eating. They started trickling out of the room while Thad escorted me down the buffet table, pointing out what dishes were made by what aunt or cousin. Either Grant *men* didn't lower themselves to cook for family get-togethers, or they weren't allowed to cook. We got back to Thad's table, but that was no relief. His three cousins in the computer business with him shared the table. They had finished eating and were slouched back in their chairs, talking. Thad gave me his chair and grabbed one from another table that had been emptied. Then I sat there and nibbled at my food, and listened to the four of them talk about their plans for the new year. I was grateful they ignored me.

Eventually, they got up and joined other conversations, or got drafted to help clear the table of emptied dishes. None of them were married, meaning some poor, brainless girls had yet to fall for the "I want an old-fashioned girl" line.

"So, what's going on with the job search?" Thad said, after we ate in silence for a few moments.

I had to give him points for remembering my most important crisis, in the middle of the crisis created by his grandmother. I told him about the possibility of more interviews next week, and signing up online for some job search sites. I didn't mention Zach and Match in particular, or the fact that I hoped to be employed at Holy Spirit Alliance very soon. I had heard Thad gripe too many times about how our rival church had allegedly employed questionable tactics during a football game five years ago.

"I told your grandmother that if I got a job at another church, I would be leaving our church," I offered.

"Makes sense."

Thad was too calm. He should have either argued with me or taken it as the easy out I was offering him.

"Look, it's Debbie Budweiser," Lisa chirped, sauntering up to our table with the other two Witches right behind her.

I always told myself it could have been worse -- they could have associated my last name with different breeds of horses, big horses, rather than the beer company with the Clydesdale horses as their emblem. It was almost funny, how Thad just frowned and gave them a confused look. Laughing wouldn't discourage their teasing and snide remarks, and getting angry wouldn't either. I knew, because I had tried those tactics when we were younger, to get them to leave me alone.

"That's a horrid shade," Charlene added, stepping up and reaching out like she would wipe the blush off my cheek. "You're painted up like a hooker on Prospect Avenue."

"Been spending a lot of time down there?" Reggie offered, nudging aside Lisa and Susan, to take the empty chair next to me. She fluttered her eyelashes at her cousins, who all sneered and walked away.

Susan smirked, glancing back at us once as the girls headed up the stairs together. They laughed at something she said, and I had the awful, stomach-twisting feeling we had just had a hint of nastiness yet to come.

"They don't know what they're talking about," Reggie said, and patted my hand, just before I picked up my paper cup of ginger ale.

"Considering you're the professional? And the right kind of professional," I added with an attempt at a grin.

I knew Lisa was just giving me grief because I was wearing the makeup Reggie had given me for Christmas, specifically chosen for me through the latest color analysis system. I had the entire line, including the designer scent, and an instruction manual to create the look I wanted.

"They're just peeved because I don't give them my employee discount. Susan had a snit when she realized I was giving you the top-of-the-line kit."

"Why would Susan know or care what you gave Dinah for Christmas?" Thad paused with his mouthful only half-chewed.

Another reason to be glad we would be breaking up soon.

"She stopped by the counter when I was checking out at the end of my shift, and saw me paying for it. She turned on the slime-charm, ooing and cooing, and then made a remark that it would be nice if I gave all the cousins the same gift, instead of playing favorites." Reggie sighed. "I shot off my big mouth and told her I would only give something that great to my best friend, which meant none of them. Sorry. As if they need more reasons to hate either of us."

"Spoiled brats," Thad muttered, and filled his mouth with the last of his strawberry-gelatin-pretzel-cream-cheese salad.

We had that in common too -- we despised his cousins. It wasn't enough for a long-term relationship, though. The sooner I convinced his grandmother of that and ended her dynastic and ministry plans for us, the happier we all would be.

It definitely was a good thing I was leaving our church.

For about five minutes, I let myself hope that after the encounter with the Witches, and sitting with Thad where Mrs. Grant could see us, the worst was over. Maybe Reggie could go in another room and call my phone. I could pretend to get an emergency call from church, and make my escape.

No such luck.

Before I could lean over and whisper my idea to Reggie, Susan came back with Mrs. Grant to herd us upstairs for the gift opening. There were enough children running around, I assumed we would be just watching them tear into their loot. That could be fun. At least I thought so, until I saw the malicious sparkle in Susan's eyes. Before I could open my mouth and try to make an excuse, she repeated her complaint about my shade of makeup and how much I used.

Mrs. Grant frowned at me. That frown had always struck fear into the most innocent child in our congregation.

"I'm not sure I approve of those darker colors on any young woman," she said after hmm'ing a few times. "But with your darker coloring, Dinah, it looks quite becoming."

That response would have been enough to make me kiss Mrs. Grant. Susan went white and her mouth dropped open. Reggie and Thad muffled snickers and grinned at each other.

"However, a minister's wife can never be too careful," Mrs. Grant added. "You do have a few years to make adjustments, so I wouldn't worry." She patted my hand, hooked her arm through Susan's, and led her away. The solo Witch's feet skidded a few times, like she was being dragged.

"Minister's wife?" Thad said, his voice low and tending toward dangerous.

"All Grammy's idea," Reggie hurried to say, waving her hand in front of his face, like distracting an angry bull. "Dinah was just as shocked when Grammy brought the whole thing up. In fact, Dinah expects you to dump her after the New Year's party," she added with a shrug.

"Why would I dump you? Just because you thought my Christmas gift was stupid?" Thad was becoming the master of confused expressions, tending toward hurt-little-boy.

"Not stupid." I sighed, and wished I was back at the church, dealing with Mrs. Rizetti and her clones. I didn't care what they thought of me. "If Reggie hadn't reminded you that Christmas presents are expected when you're dating, would you have bought me anything?"

"You bought me something."

"Because it's expected," I lied. "Thad, we're nowhere near as close as your grandmother wants us to be. Agreed?"

He looked around the room, which was nearly empty of people. The Grants took Christmas presents pretty seriously, it appeared. He sighed. Finally he nodded.

Reggie and I exchanged nods, and I suspected I saw as much relief in her eyes as she saw in mine. One step taken in dismantling and discouraging the expectations his grandmother had instilled in him. Once we were officially broken up, Thad could deal with Mrs. Grant. If he wanted to make me the bad guy, that was fine. I was leaving the church, so I wouldn't have to deal with her ever again.

That settled, the three of us headed upstairs.

Can there be anything more uncomfortable than going to a family party where only one person expected you? More uncomfortable than watching everyone unwrap presents, feeling like you should have been given warning so you could at least bring a token present for the hostess? And feeling a little abused because you knew there was no present for you under that enormous tree that scraped the cathedral ceiling?

Think again.

Susan and Charlene distributed the presents. Their smug looks cast my way every so often made me edgy. What were they waiting for? Soon, everyone had ripped off the wrapping paper, and the children vanished into another room to play with their toys. At least the Grants had the good sense to give the children toys and books for Christmas, instead of boring clothes.

Let me say right here, I didn't expect anything, even knowing what a stickler Mrs. Grant was for protocol and appearances. After watching the adults open little packages with cell phones and iPods and jewelry (Mrs. Grant and her three oldest sons owned a jewelry store with four branches), being empty-handed didn't bother me. Even when Susan, Lisa and Charlene settled down on the hearth, giggling and whispering to each other and watching me, I had no clue.

Then Mrs. Grant came over and stood there in front of me. "You don't like your gift?" She looked pointedly at my hands. I was making notes on my iPod for chores to take care of on my way home that afternoon. Which I hoped would be very soon.

"Uh, this is mine." My mind went blank, except for the fear that she thought I was ungrateful, not even thanking her like Thad's sisters and cousins had when they got their iPods.

"I know that's yours." She *tsk*ed and shook her head. "You don't like your gift?"

"What gift?" Just about that time, I got that drop and shift in my spirits that I hated, just like in those horrid fever dreams where the masks came off the monsters and the floor dropped out from underneath me and I fell forever.

I took a psychology class in college and developed the theory that a lot of my anxiety dreams came from my family. What little I had. My only relatives were on Dad's side. They had never wanted my parents to get married, and once Mom died, they switched to punishing me for every imagined crime she committed. It took me until I was in college to finally get up the courage to cut all ties with them.

Having grown up with that kind of nastiness, I had a tendency to curl up and protect my softer underbelly. So when Mrs. Grant stood there, her elegant hands neatly folded in front of her, giving me that disappointed look, as if I had wiped my nose on the heirloom lace tablecloth, I started to shrivel.

"What do you mean, what gift? Your Christmas present."

"Uh, Gran -- " Thad waved his hands. That got the attention of half the people in the room. The sudden quiet was like that frozen moment when a swarm of sharks scented blood and they hung still in the water, getting their bearings. "Gran, Dinah didn't get anything." He gave me the same apologetic smile when he handed me the envelope with my Christmas gift.

"Ridiculous. I chose her present and had Susan wrap it." Mrs. Grant looked around the room, and people flinched under the weight of her gaze.

"That explains everything," Reggie murmured, next to me.

It did indeed. Susan had either tossed the present, or hid it. For a few seconds, I let myself wonder what kind of present Mrs. Grant had given me. I had already figured out that the elegance and price tag indicated where the recipients stood in the Grant clan ranking.

"It's on the mantle, right where you told me to put it," Susan said, her expression and voice so sweet, no one would ever have guessed that her car was a broom.

Mrs. Grant snapped her fingers. A grandson jumped up to fetch the gift. She stood there, watching me unwrap it. With most of the family watching me.

Now, considering the watches, necklaces, and bracelets I had seen others open already, I was justified in expecting the two-inch-wide by seven-inch-long package to have at least a simple bracelet in it. Maybe a watch. Right?

A tube of lip gloss. Cinnamon gloss. The same shade as I had put on in the church bathroom to freshen my makeup before I took the bus to the Grant house. This one had slightly different packaging from what Reggie had given me for Christmas. This was a knock-off brand that tried to capitalize on the visual recognition of the name brand, sold in discount stores where the floors needed mopping and the shelves needed a good dusting. The sale tag on the back was a bright yellow that could be seen from across the room.

A few snickers off to the side flipped that switch I had finally learned to install, attached to the new stiffness in my spine. Mrs. Grant owned a jewelry store, for goodness' sake. What could have been so hard about yanking a sale watch off the discount table and slapping a bow on it?

Chapter Six

"Thank you, but I hope you still have the sales receipt." I stood up and held the package out to her. "So you can get your money back. I'm allergic to this particular brand. Sorry."

Where in the heck were all these good lines coming from lately? Usually I froze up and stumbled through arguments and verbal attacks with ridiculously lame lines that made me feel sick to my stomach when I thought about it later.

Everyone inhaled on cue, and a second later, I could have heard a pin drop, the silence was so complete.

Mrs. Grant didn't move, and she didn't take the package. I turned the blister pack over so the sale tag was visible, put it into her hand, and wrapped her fingers around it. Somehow, my hands didn't burst into flame for my disrespectful actions.

Then I picked up my purse. "Excuse me. Bathroom?"

Thad's cousin Dave's wife pointed down the hallway. I didn't know her name because she had been introduced as "Dave's wife" when we sat down. I never got a chance to talk with her beyond that. She probably got the same treatment when Dave brought her to the first family gathering. I glanced at her hands as I passed her. She had one red envelope on her lap, and what looked like a mall gift card. Well, she had graduated up from the discount bin, but she hadn't gotten jewelry or high-tech electronics. Maybe she had to produce a great-grandchild first?

The silence held until I walked down the hall to the bathroom. I thought I heard Mrs. Grant's voice after I closed the door. Then a wave of laughter rolled down the hall.

Thank You, God, that Thad showed me how he felt before I got too emotionally invested in him. Marrying him would mean spending holidays with these people. I could never love a man that much, to endure this treatment. It would be even worse than the emotional abuse and rejection Mom suffered from Dad's family. I loved my Dad, but there were times I just wanted to slap him until his eyeballs rattled, for how oblivious he was. How little he stood up for Mom. All the things he should have done for her, but never got around to.

Dang, I've been dating my own father! I nearly heaved.

Thad was like Dad. That was why he was so comfortable to be around, and why I put up with so much obliviousness from him. Because I was used to it. Because I saw Mom put up with it and work around it for so long.

"Not anymore," I told my reflection.

The long hallway where I had left my coat was between the bathroom and the door. I didn't have to go through the living room to get my coat or make my exit. I slipped down the dark hallway, weighing my options. Find a bus, or start walking home? How long before anyone realized I was gone? Take the high road and go back to the living room, and say good-bye? I had already told a couple dozen lies today, starting with how nice it was to be included in their family gathering. Tell them I had gotten an emergency phone call and had to leave?

"Where are you going?" Thad said.

I honestly didn't expect him to come looking for me. Which crystallized just how I felt about him.

"I think it's quite clear how un-welcome I am. The polite thing is to spare your family more discomfort, and leave."

He had the intelligence not to argue with me on that.

"Let me get my coat -- "

"I can take a bus. That's how I got here. Don't inconvenience yourself any more than you already are." I picked up my coat and slung it around my shoulders.

Okay, I was snarky. I'm not proud of it. But honestly, didn't I have some justification?

Thad's lips went flat. Did I dare hope he felt some guilt over how this very promising Christmas season had fallen short in the romance department?

"Good-bye, Thad. Merry Christmas." I turned my back on him and made the mistake of rubbing some of that hot wet from my eyes. Why did I have to let my feelings get hurt like that? Why did I cry in front of that unworthy bozo?

"Hold on. Let me -- "

I was out the door before he got any further. When I reached the end of the driveway, I had no trouble seeing down the street to the bus shelter two intersections away.

Someone honked behind me when I reached the first intersection. I didn't connect it with Thad until the car pulled into the driveway in front of me. I made the mistake of stopping, instead of going around the car. He leaned over and opened the door. I swear, if he hadn't opened the car door, I would have kept walking. Next mistake: getting into the car.

"Susan bought the lipstick," he said.

"I figured that out already." I refused to look at him. And I bit my lip to keep from correcting him, that it was lip gloss. He would have laughed at me for splitting hairs. "They all hate me, so what does it matter?"

"They don't all hate you." He sighed.

"They were waiting for me to open it. They knew what it was. I wonder which of them hid it in the first place." Not to deprive me of a discount tube of lip gloss. To make sure everyone saw the cheap present I had been given and maximize the face slap.

"You know, Dinah, you have to get over being so sensitive about such things."

"Is that what Dave's wife had to do?"

"Her name is -- "

"Nobody could be bothered to tell me her name. She doesn't have any identity in your family except as Dave's wife." I almost said, *And that's what'll happen to me when we get married.* I held off because I didn't want Thad to get the mistaken idea that I wanted to marry him. "Everybody else got real gifts, and she got a store gift card. Yeah, really nice belonging to this family."

"Dinah ..." He sighed and slammed his fist against the steering wheel. We had come to the end of the street on a red light and needed to turn left. "I'm really starting to think twice about giving you that ring."

"What ring?"

"Your engagement ring." He glared at me and rolled his eyes, like he thought I was nuts.

"What engagement ring?"

"We were talking about getting engaged."

"No, your grandmother was talking about us getting married, but I know better."

"Oh, yeah, that's right -- you think I'm going to break up with you just because I got you a wimpy Christmas gift. When are you going to drop it?"

The car behind us honked. The light had changed. When Thad opened his mouth to say more, I told him the light was green. He glared at me as he pulled out and made the left turn. Away from the bus stop I needed.

"Like I told your grandmother, I hope you can get your money back."

"That's what really bothers you, isn't it? Money. The price tags. You spent more money on me than I did on you -- "

"If you gave me a hundred-dollar gift certificate, I still wouldn't be able to buy anything at that stupid bookstore."

"Stupid?"

"It's the thought that matters. The fact that you spent time and thought on me, instead of money. Reggie told you what to get me, but you ran out of time, and the bookstore was convenient. Am I right?"

Thad sighed as we came up to another stoplight, at the street leading to the mall. "Look, Dinah, you can't be so hyper-sensitive anymore. Not if you're going to be part of our family. Big families make allowances for each other."

"First, you don't have any right to tell me how I can feel. Because second, I'm not going to be part of your family."

"When we get married -- "

"You haven't even asked me yet, so what makes you think I'm going to marry you?"

"But we talked about -- "

"No, we never did. What alternate reality are you looking at?" I saw another bus shelter with the right route numbers on it. Now was my chance. "Good-bye, Thad." I flipped the door lock and pushed the car door open and got out before he stopped gaping like a stranded fish.

Too late, he hit the door lock control -- I was already on my feet and shoving the door closed. Traffic was fairly sparse around me for the moment. I hit the crosswalk and dashed for the curb. The light turned green just as Thad got his door open. The cars behind him laid on their horns. He glared at me, slammed the door, and went through the intersection.

I acted like the mature church worker I was and stuck my

tongue out at him.

Then I went into the grocery store conveniently placed on the opposite corner and bought myself some comfort food before I went to the bus stop. By five that afternoon, I was in my pajamas with a stack of DVDs waiting to be played, gooey bakery, cheese and crackers, and shrimp arrayed on the coffee table in front of me. The phone ringer, answering machine, and my cell phone were turned off. I didn't expect Thad to call, except to try to get the last word in. Whether he did call or not, I didn't want evidence either way.

Yeah, happy holidays to you, too.

<><><>

Saturday morning, Reggie and I ran last-minute errands for the New Year's party. She said not only did Thad come back to the family get-together, but he spent some time in the kitchen alone with their grandmother. Then they called her in to find out what she thought of the whole mess.

"I swear, I told them a dozen ways from Sunday that you were embarrassed and wanted to run yesterday, long before the makeup blowup." Reggie spoke in undertones. We wandered the aisles of the wholesale club, looking for the coordinated paper plates we had been eying for the party for the last month. We had played a calculated risk that everything even remotely New Year's-ish would be on sale on December 30. We were right. The risk was that there might not be enough to coordinate -- dinner plates, dessert plates, bowls, cups, utensils, streamers, and those metallic-looking plastic sproingy things for centerpieces.

"Are you sure Thad knows I had no idea it was a family thing and I wasn't trying to trap him? That's the feeling I was getting. All a setup to force him to take some steps in our relationship."

"Oh, he knows it was definitely a setup, but all from Grammy's side. I put a lot of blame on the Witches." Reggie snorted and looked around, making sure nobody in the double-wide aisles on either side of us could hear. "Grammy is so furious with them, she even slipped and called them the Three Witches, and didn't scold me when I said it. She knows they tricked me into doing the kiddie theater, when they're supposed to. I mean, Grandpa endowed the theater, so a Grant always has to be involved, but ... They went too far this time."

She sighed and pressed the back of her hand against her forehead. The melodramatic suffering look was ruined by the sparkles of laughter in her eyes. "Grammy got them together for a good lecture. I could smell the scorch on their clothes when she set them free. She seems to think that it's the bad influence of the other churches they've been visiting that makes them so nasty. I still don't know why she thinks attending our church, with all the stupidity going on now, is going to reform them."

"Uh -- no. They were that way every time they attended our church. They were just held in check." I let out a low cheer when I saw the end-cap display of all the on-sale party supplies, and the colors we wanted were in the majority.

"Anyway, I did my darnedest to convince them that you were more than ready to break up with Thad *before* you came to the party, and the ambush had nothing to do with the way you said good-bye to him yesterday and made it sound like forever."

"Uh, hello? It had everything to do with it. Lard and sugar frosting on a rotten cake." I paused in counting the packs of paper plates.

"Yeah, but you don't know the way Grammy and Thad think. If they can just blame the Witches, and how nobody introduced themselves unless Thad dragged you over to them -- which is generally the way everybody who marries into the family is treated, so don't think they were singling you out, by the way."

"*Not* marrying into the family. Love you, hate the rest of them. Wish we could be sisters, but then the Witches would be ..." I shook my head. "Forget it. Don't even go there."

"Yeah, too gross to think about. While it would have given you pounding rights when we were kids, now it just means you have to be nice and you can't get away from them. They're allowed to show up at your house and barge in and borrow things. Do you know, they've all showed up at my apartment in the last year and convinced the super that they had keys but they lost them and they needed to get their stuff from my apartment? I finally had to tell the super and anybody doing maintenance that if anybody shows up claiming to be relatives, wanting into my apartment, they were to call the police."

"You're kidding." I tossed stacks of cold drink cups and hot drink cups into the cart. "Please tell me they did at least once."

"Oh, yeah. The brats went whining to Grammy that I was being mean to them and telling lies about them. It's even worse than when we were kids, because their parents won't even try to make them behave." Reggie smirked. "Grammy almost always sides with me, so it doesn't do them any good."

"So what does all this delicious revenge have to do with convincing them that I wouldn't take Thad if he was the last straight man without STDs on the face of the planet?"

"Grammy says Thad needs a good woman like you."

"The nastiest judgment I've ever heard," I muttered. She snickered and slapped my arm.

I had told her about Pastor Marcus's lame response to the whole issue of my finding a man who needed me to complete him. Excuse me? I certainly would like to find a man who spent some time thinking about completing *me* for a change. A man who would fulfill some of *my* needs, too. The way I read the Bible, it's a partnership, not a situation where the woman stands on the bottom rung and hands everything up to the man and he gets the view, the acclaim, and the credit.

"And I pressed the point that you would be leaving the church anyway with your new job, so the two of you would be breaking up anyway, so it didn't matter." She smiled, but a twitch in one side of her mouth hinted all was not settled.

"What?" I grabbed her arm when she tried to take the cart and turn it around to head back down the aisle.

"Well, I hope you find something incredible and put in your two weeks' notice soon. Because if I know Grammy, she's going to call an emergency meeting of the board -- all the boards -- and pound it into their thick, male heads what a mess they're making by getting rid of you. Grammy is very well aware of all the hard work you do, even if those men aren't. Even Thad admitted that nothing in Singles would have succeeded without you."

"Yeah, but I bet nobody will say so when I tell them I'm leaving."

"Once you're gone ..." She stopped and gripped my arm. "You're not ever coming back, are you? Not even if they beg?"

"I'm seriously considering putting in my two weeks' notice on Tuesday morning, whether I have a firm job offer or not. Zach has a couple more job leads, so it's looking good."

"But?"

"But some jobs are more than an hour away. I might need to move."

"Just make sure you move south and west. Then it's still a decent drive for me to visit."

"Yes, master. Everything must be done to convenience you." I bowed, she snorted, we exchanged slightly teary grins and continued down the aisle. There were still tablecloths to find.

I still worried. After all, Reggie hadn't done that good a job, convincing her grandmother Thad and I were through. That was what had brought about the invitation for lunch.

When we were loading our haul into Reggie's SUV, my phone rang. I turned it around to show her the display, which read Match. She gave me a thumbs up.

"Dinah, honey, it's Gertie," she crooned when I answered. "Sweetheart, I have a match for you. Isn't that great?"

"It sure is. Umm, how come Zach is having you call me?"

This was the first time Gertie had called me. For some reason, little prickles of warning raced up and down my spine.

"Oh, honey, this has nothing to do with the job matching. I'm talking about the matchmaking service. I found a nice young man who really wants to meet you."

"Gertie --"

"And the timing is just perfect, what with it being New Year's tomorrow."

"Gertie, I don't --"

"He wants to take you out for New Year's Eve. So can I give him your phone number?"

"Gertie!"

This time, I got through, stopping the flood of words. My volume made some icicles break off the awning of the store.

"Is that a yes?" she said, after a couple seconds of silence.

"Gertie, I did not sign up for matchmaking. Just the job matching."

Reggie's eyes got wide and she mouthed, "matchmaking?" She grinned and continued loading the back of the SUV.

"But honey, don't you want to go out with a nice young man for New Year's? Start the year off right. Falling in loooove!" she crooned, and ended on a giggle.

I had the feeling this nice little old lady with her eye-watering taste in clothes had already started in on the New Year's champagne. Then again, I suspected she could get a buzz from non-alcoholic sparkling grape juice.

"Thanks, but first of all, I'm busy running the Singles party at my church. And second, I didn't fill out a profile."

"Oh, well, I used the profile you filled out for Zach --"

"The questions for matchmaking have to be very different from the job search."

"Well, yes, a little bit -- but honey, I just couldn't let you start the new year without a boost from finding the right man, who'll stand by your side through all the upheavals and problems that come with switching jobs. You know?"

Gertie was definitely buying into her own advertising.

"I appreciate your thinking of me, but I swear, the last thing I need to think about is adding a man to my life. It's complicated enough as it is."

"You got that one right, sister," Reggie muttered, and slammed the hatch of the SUV for punctuation. I stuck my tongue out at her.

"Besides, I just can't justify spending that kind of money --"

"Oh, honey, didn't I tell you?" Gertie giggled. It didn't take much to raise her spirits again. "It's on the house!"

Somehow, that did not make me feel any better.

"Thanks, but I'm going to have to pass."

"He's going to be so disappointed. I promise you, he's the nicest young man. I've known him for years."

"Gertie, are you sure this was a genuine match made by your computer, and you're not playing matchmaker yourself?"

"Dinah, that's just uncalled for." She giggled before I could take a breath and apologize. "I promise you, I put your profile into the system, and it matched with his profile right away. Honey, won't you at least consider going out with him?"

"Gertie, I have to run a party for fifty people tomorrow."

"Well, how about tonight?" she asked, her voice softening. Maybe this time her hurt feelings weren't faked?

"Tonight?" I barely kept from banging my head against the side of the SUV. "I'll be busy putting the party together."

"Liar, liar, pants on fire," Reggie muttered as we got into the

SUV.

"Well, then how about --" That whine was a lot stronger in Gertie's voice.

"Gertie, I have an appointment to see Zach next Wednesday during lunch. We can talk about it then, okay?"

"Promise?"

"Cross my heart."

"Whew!" Reggie said, when I finally got Gertie off the phone. "What was that all about?"

She laughed, but had a thoughtful expression when I finished explaining all the background, even describing Gertie's outfits.

We spent the rest of the morning hauling our supplies to church, filling our assigned refrigerator, locking it, and putting the non-perishable supplies in the Singles' closet in the hall.

"I'll be passing all this over to you tomorrow night," I said, as I tucked the keys into my purse.

"That's the nastiest thing you've ever said to me." Reggie reached to flip off the light switch as we headed out of the kitchen. "What's the Singles group like at your new church?"

"I've heard it's pretty big and active. But it's not my new church yet. I don't know if I have the job."

"Oh, you'll get it. If they have any brains at all, they'll snap you up in a heartbeat. You know, you should really turn in your two weeks' notice tomorrow, get a jump start on the countdown. It's awkward if you give notice in the middle of the week."

"Are you trying to get rid of me?"

"Trying to help you escape as soon as you can. That's what best friends are for." She shrugged. "And maybe I'll just follow you to your new place."

"Aww, that's sweet, but you don't have to."

"Sweet, nothing." She paused as we hit the panic bars on the double doors at the end of the hall and stepped out into the parking lot. "Survival tactics. I bet half the social committee bails, without you to do most of the work."

"And the other half?"

"Those are the girls who will sink their claws into Thad in a last desperate attempt to avoid being old maids." She snorted. "Starting with Anita."

"She's welcome to him."

<><><>

I deliberately sat in the back row in class the next morning. Reggie sat with me, and Beth next to her. Thad came in late, and looked positively panicked when he didn't see me sitting in the front row, holding a seat for him. Not that I always did, but on days when there were announcements to make or we had important events coming up, like the New Year's overnighter, we usually made our announcements together.

I now understood why people just assumed we were a couple, even before we officially dated. We had fallen into a rut, a routine, like an old married couple who didn't need to talk to know what the other was thinking.

That was kind of comforting and cozy, from one angle -- and terrifying from another.

Thad settled in the front row, nodding silent apology to Pastor Steve, who had started into the lesson. Anita moved up from her place in the second row and settled into the seat next to him. Beside me, Reggie da-dummed the opening notes from the ***Jaws*** theme. Beth and I muffled giggles.

In between class and the service, I slipped into the office and left my two weeks' notice. What Reggie said made sense -- why wait until I heard Tuesday or Wednesday if Holy Spirit Alliance wanted me? At the very least, if they called me back for a third meeting, that had to mean I was almost to the finish line, right? I left copies on Mr. Flannery's desk, Mr. Phillips' desk, and on the desk of each of the pastoral staff. I wondered how surprised they would be when they got my official resignation. Did they honestly expect me to hang around, put my life on hold, until they were ready to get rid of me?

The problem, I realized on that short walk from the dungeons of the Singles classroom to the office, was that I had *let* them put me in my invisible-until-needed, please-ignore-my-rights position. I should have been a little more vocal when I was stepped on, when I was given more work than I could handle, and when I was expected to take up the slack for everyone else.

I had to set some ground rules with my new job. This time it would be my fault if they turned me into a doormat.

My brain was so full of this epiphany, I didn't see Mrs. Grant lying in wait for me at the T-intersection, on my way down to the sanctuary. I only appreciated the irony of the staging later. This was where Reggie had caught me last week, to interrogate me about Thad's Christmas present, and Mrs. Grant had overheard us, and realized Thad and I were dating.

Were. Past tense. If Friday didn't give him the message, my leaving him to handle the announcements by himself should have clarified it.

"Dinah, dear." Mrs. Grant caught hold of my arm before I realized she had stepped into the flow of traffic.

Years of conditioning made me stop and then step out of the current of people heading for the sanctuary, when she pulled on my arm. We stepped around the corner, and I had this panicky feeling she would pull me into the kitchen, where Thad was no doubt waiting to confront me.

"I'm sure Thad has told you how sorry, how embarrassed we both are, over the nasty trick Susan pulled on you Friday."

"No, he hasn't talked to me since Friday. I honestly don't expect him to talk to me about anything except our duties with the Singles." I silently sent up a prayer that the predicted snow would turn into a blizzard and the overnighter would be cancelled. Would it be so bad, bringing in the new year with a new book, a homemade pizza, and that *Lord of the Rings* marathon?

"That's odd. He assured me that you were going to have lunch with us today." She frowned, and her hand on my wrist tightened a little.

"He didn't speak to me in class, and I have plans all afternoon, to prepare for tonight." True, my plans included a long nap, but that was none of her business.

"Oh, dear, yes, how would Thad survive without you to look after him and remind him?"

"Mrs. Grant --" I hesitated a few seconds, trying to decide how to free my wrist without being rude, or giving her a hint of the panic that shot through me. No way was I going to sign on for a lifetime of picking up after Thad Grant, reminding him to do his homework and tie his tie and go on visitation. I had just made a resolution to stand up for myself and stop letting people walk all over me in the name of alleged "Christian humility and service." Maybe this was God's first test of my resolve?

So be it.

I managed to stick a finger between one of her fingers and my wrist and used it as a gentle lever to break her grip, then slid my hand free. Not quite used to not being a wimp yet, I changed the movement to fix my hair, as if that was the reason I needed my hand back.

"Mrs. Grant, I have no plans to be part of Thad's life."

Chapter Seven

"I was so afraid you would say that." Her eyes glistened. For a second, I thought that was the legendary icy, refined anger I had heard of from church board meetings where she and her husband and their inner circle had saved our church from making disastrous choices in the past.

Was that glistening … tears? Over me? Maybe Mrs. Grant valued me a whole lot more than Thad did?

"You have been unfairly treated by our family, and that is as much my fault as those …" She snorted. "Regina is quite accurate -- those three witches. Thad assures me that he does have far deeper feelings for you than he has demonstrated lately, and he intends to pursue ... well, to pursue you." She patted my hand. Then she reached into her knitting bag purse and brought out a slender box, just about the size of that lip gloss from Friday, but not wrapped. It was a deep, dull, textured red, and I suspected that wasn't faux leather. It was a hinged box, the kind to hold a diamond bracelet or a fancy wristwatch.

I took a half step back, as far as the press of people passing us would allow. She turned the box in her hand and opened it.

Please, God, don't let it be -- Thank You, Lord. It's just a wristwatch. No diamonds or emeralds or anything fancy.

But it did look very elegant, and expensive.

"This is what you were supposed to open on Friday," Mrs. Grant said, and held the box out to me.

I put my hands behind my back. Of course, the movement made my purse slide off my shoulder, and then someone passing me ran into me as I turned to shift it back into place. Not one of my more graceful moments, but Mrs. Grant got the message that I wasn't going to take the watch. She drew it back and gave me a sorrowful look I was sure had cowed her children and grandchildren when dignified anger couldn't move them. I almost reached out and took the watch, just from the pressure of guilt.

"I expect never to see Thad again after tonight's party is over.

It wouldn't be right for me to take that watch, as ... as lovely as it is." Never mind that I really needed a new watch. I only had one, with a blue leather band I had replaced three times. The glass was scratched and the face steamed up when I went out in the rain.

"I don't understand." Funny. Despite the soft tone, I could hear her quite clearly. How could she not hear me?

Looking around, I realized the hall traffic had declined. The noise level had dropped to civilized decibels. Thad was coming down the hall with the social committee. Anita was giving him that adoring look I had seen her practicing in the mirror at skating parties. Just before the Sadie Hawkins waltzes, when girls had the right to drag guys out onto the floor to skate with them.

"Gran!" Thad's face split in that big smile that always made a happy little double-throb in my chest. Now I remembered why I put up with his neglect, and I was so happy when he asked me out on the first date in such a backhanded, *Hey, since we're working together on this, why not go out and talk over dinner?* way.

"Well, what do you think?" Thad hurried to cross the T-intersection and join us.

I saw Anita stop while the rest of the committee kept moving. Several rolled their eyes and shook their heads. Maybe they felt sorry for me? From the way Anita's eyes and mouth sort of puckered up, Thad had obviously let the entire group know he was trying to find me, and probably why. Now that I thought of it, the social committee knew before I did that Thad and I had been on our first date.

Yeah, that was how he ran our relationship. Why didn't I see things a lot clearer and get out of there sooner?

"Isn't it great?" Thad took the wristwatch, case and all, from his grandmother's hands and shoved it at me.

I took another step back.

"Thad, I really think you should clear things with your young lady before you make promises to me. It's rather embarrassing to mention to her our plans, and find she knows nothing about them," Mrs. Grant said.

On the positive side, Thad was the bad guy here, not me.

Obviously he didn't realize that, because he took a step closer, still holding out the watch.

"Dinah -- okay, so I didn't catch up with you in class. Why

didn't you save me a seat? I mean, we're together."

"No, we aren't. Mrs. Grant, I appreciate so much the fact that you're trying to fix things. The watch is gorgeous, and I wish I could take it, but it wouldn't be right. If you'll excuse me? I don't want to be late for the service." A lie, but I figured God would forgive me a lot faster and easier than the Grants.

Anita gave me a wide-eyed look as I passed her, heading down the hall. I tipped my head back toward Thad with a smile. I hope she understood I was saying, "He's all yours, honey."

I didn't look back, but I was pretty sure she glommed onto him as soon as he stepped away from his grandmother. She didn't grab onto his arm, but walked as close to him as she could without interfering with his stride.

I caught up with Reggie heading into the sanctuary. We ducked under the rope that was supposed to keep people out of the balcony, reserving it for overflow attendance. As usual, there was a scattering of middle and high school students settled in with their pocket video games or homework. In the balcony, they could do what they wanted during the service without parents seeing them, or ushers nudging them to sit up and put things away and pay attention to the sermon. Reggie and I took seats in the back right corner, and I whispered what had happened. She muffled giggles behind both hands pressed over her mouth.

"If I were you, I wouldn't even bother going to the party tonight," she whispered, just as Mrs. Dukes shifted from the prelude music to the opening bars of the first hymn.

I wanted to do just that, but I didn't dare. I had to be there to coordinate everything and cover for the ones who had a better offer at the last minute and dropped out. I had let Singles get used to "let Dinah do it." Tonight would be the last time. With the new year, I was turning over a new leaf.

<><><>

Anita was waiting when Reggie and I showed up to start putting everything together for the overnighter that afternoon. That surprised me because she rarely volunteered. Her talent was delegating. I admit, she had a gift for figuring out people's talents, but she couldn't actually *do* anything. In Singles, leaders had to be ready to do a majority of the work. Which she couldn't.

At least she wasn't the super-spiritual type, like Marianne

Pastorini, who had to be in the front row of every service, Bible study, and prayer meeting. She was in church every time the door was open. The only service she performed was to offer quotes from the latest best-selling theological book. Oh, yeah, and accuse people of depending on works rather than faith to get into heaven.

Someone said she was church-hopping, trying to track down Aaron Randall, the only single ordained minister within driving distance. Someone so super-spiritual would only be satisfied as a pastor's wife, don't you know?

"Hey, nice of you to help out," Reggie said, as the rest of the work crew pulled into the parking lot. We didn't linger outside. Another storm was blowing up, but not the blizzard I prayed for.

We all hurried into the church and headed for the big kitchen. The fellowship hall was ours tonight, leaving the gym for the senior high and college-age group. The main kitchen was between the two rooms. We had four big, heavy-duty plastic coolers, safely locked away in the Singles' closet. Jack and Kyle took some serving carts out to their cars and brought in the bags of ice they had bought at the grocery store around the corner. They got our evening's supply of bottles and cans on ice and hauled them down to the fellowship hall.

"I'm not here to help -- I mean -- well, yes, to help," Anita began, after Reggie went through the checklist of chores to set up the party. She gulped hard and turned to look at me. "Thad told me to come get the keys and tell you he doesn't need your help tonight." Her eyes glistened for about two seconds. Embarrassed? Then she took a deep breath and held out her hand for my notebook.

"Say what?" Beth stepped up behind me. "Who does Thad think he is, throwing Dinah out?"

"He's having a snit fit," Reggie said. "He's punishing you for not taking that watch, with witnesses. The one he should be angry with is Grammy, for doing it in public."

"What's going on?" Beth demanded. The rest of the team gathered around. Minus Thad, who had sent Anita ahead to do his dirty work.

"I'm breaking up with Thad. He doesn't want me here, so he sent Anita to take over my chores," I told them. Amazing how relatively painless it was to say.

A chorus of disagreement and disbelief burst out. Anita flushed, and a couple muscles twitched in her jaw. I had seen her survival mode trick before. She hadn't considered what she was getting into when she latched onto Thad. Now, she mentally switched to make me the bad guy, with them the victims.

Later, I vowed I would never be so desperate for a man in my life that I would play such mental games. Of course, for all I knew, Anita wasn't even aware of what was visible on her face.

"You all are witnesses, right?" I looked around the group. They gave me "huh?" looks that almost made me laugh. "Thad is using his authority as president. Anita is taking over, at Thad's instructions. Agreed?"

They made grudging agreement, the guys giving Anita disgusted looks, the other girls giving her sympathetic ones. Reggie shook her head and walked away. She hunched her shoulders, and I had a good idea she was hunting Thad to give him what-for.

Honestly, I felt relief more than vindictive delight at the impending mess. Anita had no idea of the schedule, the coordination, where everything was stored. If she thought Thad knew, she needed to think again. I always ended up doing most of the work while Thad played master of ceremonies.

"Okay, let's sit down and I'll go over the schedule and lists with you." I waved my notebook and gestured to the table and chairs at the far end of the kitchen.

"It's all written down." Anita held out her hand again. "Don't bother. I can figure it out from your lists. I mean, how hard could it be?" She offered a breathy, embarrassed giggle.

Why did people insist on saying that about the jobs I did?

"You'd be surprised what can go wrong. I just wanted to give you some warning."

"I'm sure everything is so organized, nothing can go wrong." She held out her hand again. "It's kind of a no-brainer at this point, right?"

"Right." I had a lot of notes and reminders in my notebook, but it was *my* notebook, and barely used. If I handed it over tonight, I probably would never get it back. I tore out the pages with the charts and schedules and handed them over.

"You're kidding me, right?" Jake stopped in the kitchen

doorway with a cart full of foil trays full of appetizers to be put in the oven. "You're not going to let her explain anything? Big mistake."

"How hard can it be?" Anita's jaw tightened up again.

"You're a witness that she didn't want anything explained, right?" I wavered between leaving and staying. Leave, and spend the evening imagining the mess she would make of all my hard work? Stay and watch her succeed, reinforcing her assertion that the job was a "no-brainer"? Stay and have people angry with me if it was a mess? Stay and hope people would feel sorry for me?

Hard choice.

"Dinah?" Pastor Steve strolled into the kitchen, with his wife, Marybeth, and Reggie right behind them. "What's this I hear about Thad --"

"Thad and I have broken up, and he feels uncomfortable with me around. He asked Anita to fill in for me, so nothing goes wrong tonight," I offered.

"What are you going to do?" Marybeth stepped up to hook her arm through mine. Pastor Steve and Marybeth had the onerous duty of taking care of the Singles, the entire Sunday school program, supervising the youth groups and their leaders, and visitation. I had no idea where they got the energy.

"We're blowing this Popsicle stand and having a girls-only night." Reggie smiled, but the brightness in her eyes was sharp and she bared her teeth just a little. "Anybody want to come with us?" She addressed the other committee members, and a handful of single girls who had trailed into the kitchen with the food they had signed up to bring.

"Reggie, maybe I should stay, just in case --" I began.

"We don't need you," Anita snapped, and stomped out of the kitchen.

"Can we come too?" Jake said, pitching his voice to be heard out in the hall. "Can we be girls tonight?" He gestured at Bob and Hector, who had come into the kitchen behind him.

"Ahh, guys, I don't know what's going on, but I don't think this is smart," Pastor Steve said. "Does this have anything to do with you quitting in the office, Dinah?"

"She didn't quit," Reggie blurted, stomping up to the stainless steel counter where I stood. "They're tossing her and bringing in a bunch of volunteers and they weren't going to tell her that she was gone until everybody was trained. Then Pastor and his yes-men had hissy fits when Dinah found out and started looking for a job."

"Really." From the closed, thoughtful expression, I was pretty sure Pastor Steve had been given a very different story.

Only later did I wonder why he hadn't known about the plan to save the money for my salary from the beginning. Was it possible the pastoral staff didn't communicate? Maybe the trustees and deacons didn't communicate with all the pastoral staff? What was going on in our church? Who was in charge?

Great. Now I had to contend with gossip and conflicting stories. Two minutes ago, I had leaned toward getting out of there. Now I had to stay, if only to ward off nasty gossip.

"I'm staying," I said. "I paid to attend this party and I don't waste money. Like Anita said, how hard can it be to do my job? As I've been told repeatedly, my job isn't that vital, and my contribution isn't that important."

Okay, so I couldn't resist twisting the knife.

"I'm still thinking of walking," Jake said, looking a little mulish. Some of the others in the room nodded and muttered.

"Don't guys. Don't punish the rest of the group. I'll be available if Anita needs any help, but for the sake of peace, I'm going to just sit this one out." I picked up my purse and my notebook, and headed for the church library, to sit and read until it was time for the service.

Yes, I said what I did mostly because Pastor Steve and Marybeth were there, watching. I had the stomach-twisting certainty I should sit and pray for the evening to be a big success. If it bombed, I would be blamed. Not Thad. Not Anita.

Maybe this last week affected my viewpoint, but I had flashes of the fallout when the story went around the church and everyone added their spin to it. The people who disliked my parents would support the stories that made me the villain. I knew how church gossip worked. Those who stayed in the church were given the benefit of the doubt. Those who left because they were hurt, worn down, and ignored were considered overly sensitive, arrogant, even rebellious. The judgment being that the church "family" was well rid of them.

It only took twenty minutes for Anita to come running to find me. She looked flustered, her hair was getting frizzy from humidity, she had dark spots under her armpits, and she was flushed. Her mouth twisted somewhere between embarrassed and nauseated and angry. She didn't want to be there asking for help any more than I wanted to be there giving it. I had worked myself into a self-righteous "serves them right" attitude by then. Obviously, I hadn't picked the right book off the library shelves.

She needed to know where the paper supplies had been stored, so the tables could be set up. Thad couldn't remember which door off the fellowship hall was the Singles' storage closet? He had the only other key. I told Anita that, because I wasn't about to hand over my key. Good thing I had unlocked the refrigerator already.

"Have they put the hot appetizers in the oven yet?" I asked, after Anita mumbled thanks and turned to leave.

"What hot appetizers?" She looked at the list she clutched.

"Other side. You have the second half of the preparation schedule," I offered. "Set a guard on the refreshments tables until the senior high leaves for bowling. Last year, they tried to confiscate the shrimp and the ice cream cake."

"Okay, thanks," she called over her shoulder.

I almost hoped she forgot the warning by the time she got back to the kitchen. Then again, we didn't have shrimp or ice cream cake this year. Anita was flustered enough already to think I was telling her we *did* have that on the menu. She didn't have screaming fits, but she might just get in a little trouble accusing the senior high kids of stealing from us.

Yes, I was vindictive. Sue me.

Reggie and Beth joined me just about the time I thought about going to the sanctuary for the service.

"How bad is it?" I asked.

"Thad finally dared show his ugly mug, and he's shot off his mouth a dozen times already, declaring we don't need you -- with lots of witnesses. On the bright side, nobody will blame this disaster on you." Reggie dropped hard into the couch on the other side of the reading corner.

"Meaning?"

"Jake got in his face and told him you were smart to dump

him." Beth settled down a little more demurely next to Reggie. "Thad claimed he dumped you, because you had embarrassed him at the family Christmas party."

"Uh huh." I shrugged, and tried to smile, despite that hot, wet pressure at the back of my eyes and a headache beginning at the base of my neck. "Didn't I tell you last week he was going to dump me?"

"Can't we just get out of here and order a pizza?" Reggie whined. "Go back to your place and watch a bunch of romantic movies and have a sleepover in your living room?"

"Sounds like heaven ..." I sighed. "But I don't dare."

"Yeah, she has to worry about what the creeps will say. If she doesn't have a good time," Beth said, "everybody will claim she went home to cry with a broken heart."

"Relieved heart," I hurried to assure them both. "We need to feel sorry for Anita."

"She knew what she was getting into."

"I do not want her as a cousin-in-law." Reggie shook her head sharply enough it made my neck ache.

<><><>

We headed down to the sanctuary for the service. I felt sorry for Anita, who was probably getting no help from Thad. So I gave her some important advice: first, lock the fellowship hall. Then make sure nobody used the age-old remedy of a coat hanger in the outside door, which was supposed to be locked, to hold it open for stragglers.

I wasn't there at the time, but I had heard horror stories of the time someone had left a door open on New Year's Eve. The fellowship hall had been invaded by some people who had been drinking heavily at a mall restaurant, until they were thrown out. They saw the lights left on in the fellowship hall and didn't realize it was a church. Or so they claimed. They came over to see if they could join the party. No one was there, because everyone was in the service. By the time the service ended, the drunks had knocked over one table of refreshments, looking for beverages more to their liking. They tore up a lot of the decorations in their anger at not finding any booze, and had helped themselves to the prizes for the games.

Fortunately, they were drunk enough they remained at the

scene of the crime and were easily caught. Unfortunately, they were also sick drunk. Having to deal with the police and clean up after a bunch of sick drunks was no way to bring in the New Year. With everything else that had been going wrong, the drunks or their stupid younger brothers would show up again.

Anita wasn't too happy to get my advice, but she did stomp over to Thad and demand he lock up before they headed down the hall to the sanctuary.

I didn't have long to recuperate from Thad's glare. Maybe he felt I was interfering instead of helping. When I got to the hall leading to the sanctuary, I saw the last face I ever expected to see at our church. I didn't recognize him until he stumbled through the current of the crowd and called my name. He had one of those goofy, slightly bashful grins that just made his face look more doughy than the first time I saw him.

"Russell?" he said again, when I just blinked and let him lead me out of the main flow of traffic. "Russell Prince? From Holy Spirit Independent?"

"Oh. Yeah. Hi." I looked at Reggie and Beth, who had stopped in the doorway to the sanctuary and looked back for me. "What are you doing here?"

"I heard you had a New Year's party, and I thought maybe I'd spend New Year's with you." He shrugged.

Today he had exchanged his sweater vest for a matte black suit with a thin crimson pinstripe, and a matching crimson vest. Very spiffy. If only he didn't look like a slightly squashed teddy bear. A little less pudge, nicer hair, a firmer chin, he could have been good-looking.

"That's nice, but don't you have a really active Singles group at your church?" I assumed he was single -- because any reason why he would ditch his wife to come spend New Year's Eve with me just boggled the mind. My brain was too sore already from exploring other unpleasant possibilities.

"Yeah, we do, but ..." Another shrug. "I wanted to get to know you without the rest of the church office watching."

"Oh. Okay. That's ... nice." Out of his field of vision, I gestured for Reggie and Beth to come join us and rescue me.

We took our perch in the balcony during the service, even though there was plenty of room down in the main sanctuary. By the end of the service, I hoped to come up with a story that wouldn't make it sound like I was trying to punish Thad. I was more concerned about people finding out Russell came from Holy Spirit Alliance, and how we knew each other, than I was worried they would think he was my new boyfriend. I mean, honestly, he was nice, but I hadn't done anything to encourage him, so why would he come looking for me in the first place?

How had he found me? Well, duh -- after a couple minutes of gnawing on that question instead of listening to the sermon, I had the answer. Russell ran the church's computer system. He could get into anything he wanted, and he had just snooped in the files for my application.

Still, I couldn't figure out how he had known I would be here, tonight, now. Finally, I asked him, as we were descending the balcony stairs.

"Oh, I asked Miss Foster." He grinned, looking like a delighted, slightly mischievous, geeky little boy.

"Miss -- Gertie Foster? Over at the job agency?" The pieces fell into place in my head. "You're the one she was telling me about. From her matchmaking service."

Russell blushed, and nodded harder.

Should I feel like I was being stalked?

Reggie gave me that wide-eyed look and tilt of her head toward Russell, and a raised eyebrow -- our signal for *Do you need rescuing?* I nodded without thinking.

"You know, Russ -- can I call you Russ?" She rested her hand on his shoulder.

"Everybody calls me Russell." He shrugged. I couldn't decide if he was trying to get rid of her hand or he was nervous.

"Okay, Russell." She looked around as we stepped out of the sanctuary and into the hall. "We just have this little problem. Everybody pays ahead of time, to take care of the refreshments. I don't see any problem with you staying for our party. Dinah always buys way more than the hogs in our group can eat, but she isn't in charge anymore -- "

"She's not?" His head snapped around like a homing missile to stare at me. "You're not? But Gertie said you ran things -- "

"Dinah got dumped by her boyfriend," Beth offered, "and the bozo told his new girlfriend to take over her job. And he won't stay away and let Dinah enjoy the party she put together."

I groaned when Russell got that indignant look on his face, even as something inside me thrilled to see it. Okay, I was needy enough to like some angry sympathy.

"That's not fair. Who is this guy?" he demanded, his voice raising just a little bit as we turned down the hallway to the fellowship hall. We were near the end of the crowd, and we had lost most of the traffic as people exited the church, so his voice carried better than normal. There was always something about the sounds inside a church at night. They carried.

"So even though we would welcome you to join us, you really need to clear things with Thad and his team. You understand, don't you?" Reggie finished up.

"Who is this Thad? What right does he have treating Dinah that way?" Russell stopped short. "Your cousin? You said your name was Grant? Thad Grant?"

"Yeah, you know the big bozo?"

Being a computer geek, Russell probably did know Thad. I felt the pressure of impending disaster gathering around me.

We should have herded Russell out the door right there, but Reggie was on a roll. Yes, Thad was her cousin, only she didn't like admitting it. If Russell knew the big arrogant jerk, he understood, right? We came around the corner. Thad stood in the hallway in front of the kitchen, looking at a much-mangled schedule. Anita stood with him, wringing her hands and bouncing a little on the balls of her feet -- she wasn't wearing her high heels any longer.

I swear, Russell got fire in his eyes, straightened his slumped shoulders and clenched his fists. He left the three of us behind in just a few steps as he stomped up to Thad. Russell knew Thad, but from the blank look and the frown Thad gave him, he didn't know Russell. What did that say about the two of them?

Then Thad looked beyond Russell and scowled at me. He jammed his fists into his hips. "I hope you're happy."

"About what?" I didn't do anything to hide my irritation.

Or maybe it was irritation with myself, because I had witnessed many times when Thad had used that "I'm so disappointed in you, I expected better of you" aggrieved tone on other people. I had never really questioned Thad's rightness in giving someone else a tongue-lashing for letting down the Singles. Now he was using it on me, when *he* had brought about the current messed-up situation. Maybe I owed all those other people an apology?

"You put the rest of them up to this. You told them all to stand back and let Anita fall on her face. Just to get at me."

"Hold it right there, Grant," Russell growled, and poked a long index finger in Thad's face.

Reggie muffled a giggle when her cousin blinked and took a step backwards.

"I heard that you took Dinah's job away from her. I heard that you sent your new girlfriend to take over." He paused when a delighted little squeak escaped Anita. "I heard you weren't man enough to work with her. So you just threw her out, didn't you?"

He kept poking that finger, getting closer and closer, making Thad go cross-eyed, until Russell lowered that finger and poked him in the chest.

Chapter Eight

"So what if I did?"

Oh, very intelligent rebuttal, Thad. Yes, I was pleased by how his voice broke. All the stragglers from the service had caught up with us, so we had more witnesses.

"So how can you blame Dinah for the problems you brought on yourself?" Russell pressed.

"Who the heck are you?" Thad demanded.

"I'm someone who hopes tonight means Dinah is free of you, so I can step in."

"Him?" Thad barked laughter and looked around Russell to meet my eyes. "You want to date this nerd?"

"Takes one to know one," I snapped.

Okay, I wasn't very intelligent or witty, either. With the pressure of all the whispering behind me, I had some excuse for suffering brain-freeze.

"Do something," Reggie whispered. "We're going to have a church split right here if you say the wrong thing."

"Thanks a lot. I couldn't figure that out for myself." I sighed. Typical -- cleaning up someone else's mess yet again. "Look, everybody, don't go punishing Anita for Thad's -- for Thad's and my bad timing, okay?" I looked around at the others standing behind us in the hall. "Just dig in and help out like you always do, okay? Go on in there and have a fun New Year's party. We've never been able to pull it off without a lot of people helping out and -- well, doing the Christian thing."

A few people snickered. Some looked a little ashamed. Far too many gave me and Thad speculative looks.

Running was probably the wrong choice, but that was just par for the course. As soon as everyone stepped around us to head into the fellowship hall, including Russell, I got out of there. My coat was in the nook next to the kitchen. I had my purse with me and my notebook. I grabbed my coat and headed for the door and my car. Maybe I should have waited for Reggie to come looking for me, but I had to get out of there.

I seriously considered not coming in to work Tuesday morning, just calling in sick. It occurred to me, as I headed down the long driveway out of our church parking lot, that I had developed a habit of running away to deal with unpleasant situations. Sometimes running away was the smartest choice, but was it the right choice right now, for me?

<><><>

Joe Cooper called at 10 a.m., New Year's Day, to ask me on a date. I was still in bed when he called, recovering from a sugar hangover. I had stayed up to watch the last half of the *Lord of the Rings* marathon and nibbled at a new carton of peanut butter chocolate ice cream until it was nothing but three tablespoons of brown syrup.

My brain was so foggy, I latched onto the first detail that stumbled through my brain: Joe sounded far too alert and energetic. He had been at the overnighter, which was supposed to end at 6 a.m., with breakfast at the Green Rooster.

"What?" I finally said, when my brain caught onto the fact that he had asked me something.

"I said, do you want to do something today?" Joe laughed. "There's a bunch of new movies. We'll get something to eat after."

"Why?" I finally got myself sitting upright, and made a mental note to keep my phone out of my bedroom. There was no phone call so important that I had to take it while I was supposed to be sleeping. Or semi-comatose.

"What do you mean, why?" Again, he laughed. Joe was one of those guys who laughed when he was nervous or uptight about something, and then he moved on to punching. Thank goodness we were on the phone.

"Why are you asking me out?"

"Well, you're not with Thad anymore."

"Oh. Okay."

"Great. Let's meet at --"

"No, I meant okay, I get it now." Memories were synching, and I had flashes of that ugly scene in the hall outside the kitchen, between Reggie, Thad, Anita, me, and ... Russell Prince. How was I going to explain that, if anybody asked?

I couldn't confess that Gertie Foster had tried to set us up.

"Get what?"

"You've never liked Thad. You can score on him by taking me out after that big public break-up last night."

"Aww, come on, Dinah, I'm not really ... well, maybe a little of that." He sighed, which was better than his creaky laugh. "The thing is, some of us started wondering what kind of a girl you are, and wondering what we didn't see. I mean, you and Thad have been together like forever --"

"Only on the social committee. We didn't start dating until a month ago. You could have asked me out a lot sooner."

But you never did. Meaning you weren't interested until you realized someone else wanted me. Yeah, real good for my ego. Not!

The question was whether it would do me any good to confront him with his hypocrisy and typical guy sexist double standard scheming mentality.

"Yeah, but everybody just assumed you and Thad were together, know what I mean?"

No, I didn't know what he meant, because if "everyone" assumed we were together for so long, his grandmother would have heard about it, and pressed Thad to make a commitment. I was hung over from the late night/morning and all that ice cream. And peeved that once again, the network played the theatrical version of the *Lord of the Rings* movies, instead of the extended versions. That made me cranky.

As much as I wanted to put Joe in his place for thinking I would believe such a stupid story, my doormat mentality kicked in. I couldn't burn all my bridges. Yes, I was definitely done with Thad, so why discourage some guys finally expressing interest in me? I might get a few date offers. Always good for my ego.

But should I accept them? Especially if they were all thinking along the same lines as Joe?

"Dinah?" Joe coughed. "Are you still there?"

"Look, Joe, I had a really rough night last night, and I don't think very well when I'm horizontal."

That got a nervous laugh from him. So okay, that meant Joe was a normal guy and he had some sort of sudden mental image of me lying in bed. Or a flash forward to trying to get me into the back seat of the car. I decided right then, we would *never* have a date. Just because Joe attended our church, that didn't mean he was a good Christian man who had promised to stay pure until his wedding day. Not in the least. Even if his body was pure, I had just had evidence that his thoughts (if we're confessing, mine too) weren't anywhere near pure.

All this was too much to handle on New Year's morning, when I had only been awake for about ten minutes. My mouth tasted like something had died in it and my eyes felt gluey.

"I'm going to pass, okay? Thanks. Some other time."

Yeah, like when they rent ice skates next to the Lake of Fire ...

He stumbled through assuring me it was all right. I had the distinct impression he was relieved and disappointed both. What had the guys talked about last night, after that scene in the hall? What kind of crazy plan had they hatched -- and what kind of stories had they made up about me and Thad? In a group as big as ours, with all the dynamics of people who had grown up together and knew each other's ugly childhood and teenage exploits, there were always cliques and rivalries. Guys who disliked Thad to any degree probably saw dating me as a way of settling scores.

So chances were good Joe wasn't interested in *me* at all. He just wanted to say he had taken Thad Grant's girlfriend out the day after we broke up.

I groaned and lay back down and buried my head under the pillow, as similar ideas surged through my aching, stuffy head. Some girls disliked me because I ran things, or they were just echoing the rivalries between my parents and theirs, or they wanted Thad. I had always pretty much been the good girl. Translation: too inhibited to step off the straight and narrow. That didn't mean I didn't play stupid, nasty tricks and gossip and earn long-lasting enmity, even in a church group. What had those girls said about me, after that scene in the hallway?

For a few seconds, I felt some pity for Anita. She finally had Thad, if only because he needed her to do my jobs. She might have already dumped him, or he dumped her because she messed up last night. How many girls were already moving in on Thad? How many really wanted Thad for himself?

Probably just as many guys would be truly interested in me.

"Lord, is it too late to start an order of Protestant nuns?" I grumbled into my pillow.

The answer came immediately -- but not from God. My phone rang again. My brain also woke up enough to wonder who gave Joe my number, because it wasn't in the church directory. Everyone on the social committee had it, though.

Reggie proved she was a true friend by holding off on calling me until that afternoon. In between Joe's call and hers, I had more than a dozen calls, all relating to the break-up scene or the downhill race of the New Year's party.

General consensus: Thad was to blame, because he was being insensitive -- a heartless jerk, according to the guys -- to what I was going through after being fired. Well, that was a relief. There were a few mutters from the malcontents, who never volunteered to help, were never happy with anything the Singles did, and always pointed out afterwards what we should have done differently. They had known all along Thad and I were never meant for each other. I supposedly had only been using him to rise in the social ranks at church. The Grants were such powerful, influential people, after all. The seeds of rumors had been sown. Time would tell what kind of fruit they would bear.

Reggie assured me, when she called, that the girls from our Christmas day get-together had done their loyal duty as friends. They let everyone know about Thad's totally lame Christmas present. She also did her duty as a best friend by letting people know how long she and I had shopped to put together Thad's Christmas present -- which she promised yet again she would return to me, so I could get my money back.

"I can never show my face in church or Singles class again," I told Reggie, when she ran down in her excited spill of information. It was a little hard to speak. I was choking on something that tightened my throat, but I couldn't figure out what it was. Amusement? Fear? Exhaustion? Relief? Embarrassment?

Shame was strongest, once I thought about it later. There must have been some way all these problems could have been handled in a more mature, spiritual fashion. I had gone into so much of last week without any preparation. Without praying about it. Without thinking ahead to how I would respond, even when I knew people would be cruel.

Some of this -- maybe a lot of this -- was my fault just through lack of preparation. What could I do about it? Could anything be done to salvage any of this?

I honestly tried to pray. A couple dozen times during that

day. Between interruptions. I suspected my prayers were bouncing off the ceiling, like in the Ragamuffins' song.

Three more guys called after Joe -- Jake, Truman, and Seth. They weren't exactly pals, but I could imagine them sitting in a back corner at the party, making disparaging comments about Thad, and speculating about me. When each one called, I had to bite my tongue to keep from asking if they had a competition to see who actually got me to go on a date.

I told them all it was too soon to think about dating, and I had more important things on my mind -- namely, finding a new job, figuring out what I was going to do with my life. My mind kept flashing to Gertie Foster, wanting to fix me up with my true love. Trust my heart to her or to guys who only wanted to score on Thad? Not much of a choice.

"You ate an entire carton of ice cream last night, didn't you?" Reggie said, after I reported on my four date invitations and the resulting speculations.

She knew me too well. I drowned my sorrows or flustered feelings or frustrations in ice cream, and then paid the next day. It was worse than the most depressed hangover ever portrayed in the movies.

"Yeah. So? It's not like I care right now about looking good for anyone. You know, that's what I need to do. Sit down and make a list of all the benefits of not having Thad or the Singles in my life. Think of all the free time I have now, to do things I haven't done in years. I can make a dent in my to-be-read pile of books. And go bike riding in the park again."

"In January?" She laughed.

Funny, but I was thinking of Zach Foster, rather than all the snow blocking the biking paths in the Metroparks. Maybe I should take up cross-country skiing? Did Zach ski?

We conferred over the online movie listings and found one at a discount theater neither of us had seen yet. I hurried to jump into the shower and get ready. My head still hurt a little. Blame the ice cream or the fact I hadn't had anything but tea since Joe woke me up at that unforgivable hour? Or maybe the growing certainty that I had burned a lot more bridges than I realized, and the fallout was only beginning.

<><><>

Reggie and I made it an early night, because she had a meeting for all department heads for Rockaway at the cruel hour of eight in the morning. She confided in me that the stores were consolidating, but I wasn't supposed to tell anyone until the official news was released to the media. Who would I tell?

I was in bed by ten, my brain filled with pep talks to face the new year. The countdown toward my freedom started ticking when I walked into work next morning.

Funny, but all our speculations and silly brainstorming and dreaming up crazy scenarios didn't even approach what did wait for me when I walked to the door of the church office.

The first clue should have been the number of cars in the parking lot. All the pastoral staff parking spots were full. Usually only Pastor Steve was at work when I arrived in the morning. Pastor Marcus rolled in about the time I had finished filling the coffee pot and turned on the computer. Today was unusual. Maybe they were all in early to make up for taking short days during the holiday slump week.

Mrs. Rizetti met me at the office door. Not the door to my workroom, but the church office. Mrs. Humphries sat at her desk, filing her nails and staring at the phone like she thought it would bite her at any moment. I glanced at it as I sidled around Mrs. Rizetti, who didn't say anything. She watched me and smiled like a shark. Maybe she had tried to take a bite out of Mrs. Humphries already? All ten extension lines on the phone were lit up. That had never happened in my memory since coming to work for the church.

My second clue was how Mrs. Humphries gave me a startled look and turned back to watching the phone. Usually she bubbled over with chatter about her weekend, her grandchildren, and a recipe she was adamant I had to try.

The paper ream box sitting on the end of the long table in my workroom should have been a clue. I didn't pick it up, because usually in such situations the box is sitting on the victim's desk.

"I'm to make sure you take everything that belongs to you, and nothing that doesn't." Mrs. Rizetti was practically purring. Another bad sign.

My last clue. I put it all together. What was with her, that she was unable to come out and say what was going on? Why did she have to insinuate and act like I had already been given the bad news by someone else? Did she expect me to read her mind? Believe me, if I could read minds, I would not read hers. No matter how much anyone paid me.

Just to spite her, I put my purse down on the worktable next to the box and took off my coat. Before she could open her mouth -- probably to tell me I wouldn't be there long enough to need to take off my coat -- I dug in my pants pocket and brought out my church key ring.

I kept my set of church keys separate from my personal keys. Dad had warned me to do that when I got the job. He told me horror stories about people with responsibilities in our church, who had blithely loaned their church keys to someone to open a closet or an office. Hours later, the borrower returned without the keys. Usually the excuse was they forgot where they left them. In the meantime, someone else had time to make copies of every key for their own use, whether they had official permission to get into those rooms and use the equipment or not. That was bad enough, but what if that ring had home and car keys, and other keys that gave access into the owner's private life and property?

Granted, most of the time, the keys were honestly lost. Just like people in our church tended to stand in the center of any hallway for personal meetings, they also tended to misplace anything that didn't belong to them. Dad warned me to think twice and sometimes three times about *why* someone wanted to borrow my keys. Had they lost their own set of keys, or had an authority taken them away?

So I kept my keys separate from the church's. The key ring, however, was mine. Yes, it was a big ceramic dove and a blue glass fish, which anybody could pick up for less than five dollars at any Christian bookstore, but they were mine. I put my thumb through the big loop to get a firm grasp on the key ring after I unlocked my filing cabinet drawer. Sure enough, Mrs. Rizetti was suddenly standing over me, reaching for the keys.

"You don't need those anymore." She glared, her eyes big enough to be stop signs, when I closed my fist over the keys and jerked my hand out of her reach.

"I'm not letting these keys out of my possession until I hand them over to Will Franks and he signs for them. That's policy," I added, when she opened her mouth, probably to shriek at me for defying her orders.

Her taking charge of the office when I was told to clean out my desk (metaphorically), proved my theory that all along, she was behind the push to (allegedly) save money.

"You cut your own throat, you know." She smirked as I began emptying my drawer. "Just like your mother, cutting off your nose to spite your face. Did you really think that you would be punishing us by handing in your two weeks' notice?"

Oh, so *that* was what this was all about. I turned my back on her to hide my sudden grin. I envisioned the panic and self-righteous fury that swept through the offices as different officials sat down at their desks and got the news. I wouldn't be their doormat and put my life on hold until they decided to toss me out. So they were punishing me by telling me to pack and walk now, instead of waiting the two weeks.

Who was cutting off their noses now? They were stuck relying on half-trained volunteers who only showed up to work when it was convenient for them.

Footsteps outside the workroom caught my attention. Mrs. Rizetti was on a roll and didn't notice. Mr. Phillips came to the doorway. He met my gaze and shook his head, a crooked smile taking one side of his mouth.

"This just goes to show you that your job isn't as all-consuming and vital as you think. Just like your mother, always blowing up your importance and making mountains out of molehills. We'll be fine without you. It was only sympathy that prompted Pastor to offer to let you stay and train us."

She snorted, probably infuriated as I kept on loading my belongings into the paper box and didn't react to anything she said. Not even the false accusations against my mother.

"Don't even presume to think you'll get that severance check now, after the way you slapped us in the face with your snotty little two weeks' notice," she finished, her voice rising about half an octave in triumph.

And then broke, as a snort of laughter escaped me. I couldn't hold it back any longer.

"Dinah," Mr. Phillips said, stepping into the room.

Mrs. Rizetti turned her head so fast, I fully expected it to snap off her neck. At the very least, she should have had whiplash. Her face went stark white with shock, except for two bright red spots high on her sharp-boned cheeks. Interesting. Was she afraid of Mr. Phillips? Or was she very aware that other people wouldn't approve of what she had been saying to me? Or was it something else I hadn't caught on to yet?

None of that mattered. The politics of this church were way behind me now, and I was relieved.

"You did cash your severance check as soon as you got it, didn't you?" Mr. Phillips continued, looking Mrs. Rizetti in the eyes and giving her that soft, clean conscience smile that amazed me. I knew he disliked her and was probably feeling pretty good about shoving some of her words down her throat.

"Oh, definitely." I put the box down on the table and set the lid on it. Now I had some choices to make. There were people I wanted to say good-bye to. Did I dare leave the box there and risk someone going through it while I was gone? Should I take the box out to my car?

Thank You, Lord, I thought to drive my car this morning, instead of taking the bus. There was no need to drive, no bad weather to consider or shopping to do on the way home. I just felt like taking my car for a change, rather than the bus. It made my imminent getaway just a little more dignified. Get in and drive away, as opposed to trudging down the long driveway to the bus stop, my paper box a visible signal to the world that I had been sacked.

"You shouldn't have gotten -- you have no right to that money. That severance check was only if you left on good terms!" Mrs. Rizetti was nearly spitting in her fury. Curiously, her face was so red that it hid the previous red spots.

"Good terms, Joyce?" Mr. Phillips sounded amused. "Dinah leaves on good terms if she leaves when she's tossed aside on the administration's schedule? But it's not on good terms if she leaves after giving two weeks' notice?"

She sputtered for a few seconds. Still spitting. "She wasn't supposed to get that money until her last day of work."

"Which is today," I offered, trying for an innocent tone, and failing miserably. At the back of my mind, I could hear Mom chuckling at seeing her old rival so flustered.

"You have no right to that money. If you were a *real*

Christian, you'd give it back. You should never have cashed it in the first place!"

"It's all about money with you, isn't it? Money and power. And punishing the children of the people who wouldn't give you what you wanted," I couldn't help adding.

She got in her digs about Mom, it was only fair to get something back. I didn't care right then about "right."

I put on my coat and picked up my box and took it out to my car. Then I came back in and stopped at Mrs. Humphries' desk. She wasn't staring at the phone anymore -- which wasn't all lit up, either. She had two pink spots in her cheeks and her lips looked kind of bitten, but she smiled at me and turned her chair a little bit to put her back to the workroom door. Mr. Phillips still stood there, visibly keeping Mrs. Rizetti in the room.

I took the time to go over with her the check-in lists for all the equipment and other items people had signed out for the events last week. I could trust Mrs. Humphries to take care of them, and to verify I hadn't walked out the door with no clues left for those who had to clean up after me. Reggie had the refrigerator lock and key, and she had promised to turn it in. I would turn in the key for the Singles storage closet when I turned in all the other keys.

Then I walked down to the other end of the church and worked my way back, saying goodbye to the custodians. I turned in my keys and got a copy of the paper verifying I had returned every key entrusted to me. The smell of damp mops and the bite of floor wax granules and Pine-Sol would always remind me of that morning. I had always been on good terms with the custodian staff. Most of them were Dad's friends and I had grown up hearing their side of the way the church was run. So I knew how and when to ask them for things, and when not to ask.

When I came back to the office, Mr. Phillips was nowhere in sight, and neither was Mrs. Rizetti. I considered walking out to my car and not saying goodbye to the pastoral staff. My feet were unwilling to go down that hallway, but I did it anyway, my mouth dry and my heart thudding a little faster than usual.

Yes, I had had time to think and realize that maybe, just maybe, Mrs. Rizetti was right. I had cut off my nose to spite my face. I was still hurting over how I had been sideways notified that my services were no longer required. Only a few had apologized, when they were shamed into it. I wanted to hurt someone.

Besides, my job at Holy Spirit Alliance hadn't been assured yet.

Mental note: Stop by Match and ask about any new job leads, on my way home.

I started with Pastor Dave and Pastor Steve. They were in Pastor Steve's office, conferring over checklists. I leaned into the half-open door and waved to get their attention. It was somewhat consoling to see they both looked a little sad to see me. So they knew what was up.

"I just wanted to say good-bye. It was nice working with both of you."

"Dinah ..." Pastor Steve sighed. "I wish things hadn't worked out the way they did."

"You'll be missed. Thanks, Dinah," Pastor Dave said, and turned back to his paperwork.

Okay, maybe he wouldn't miss me. I had never been too sure of him, always rather standoffish. Maybe he was one of those who supported taking my job off the payroll?

I was tempted to ask if they were going to take voluntary pay cuts, to save even more of the church's money. About that time, my doormat-for-the-sake-of-peace tendencies took over, so I kept my mouth shut. Burning bridges, and all that.

Most staff doors were closed, and muffled voices made me think they were on the phone. I didn't want to talk to Pastor Greg, the music and worship minister. He always struck me as having Broadway tendencies. He was performing, not worshipping.

Next stop was Mr. Flannery's office. The door was open but the lights were off, and his coat rack was empty. So he hadn't come in yet. Interesting. More interesting, my envelope with my two weeks' notice letter *wasn't* on his desk. Had he come in and read it and left, or had someone taken it off his desk?

"Not your concern anymore," I whispered, and continued back up the other side of the hall, heading toward the door.

Mr. Phillips was last. He hugged me. He opened his mouth like he would say something, then looked past me. Someone cleared his throat behind me, and I turned to see Pastor Marcus standing there. Rats -- his office was empty when I had stuck my head in, and I honestly hoped I could leave without speaking to him. Childish, yes, but there it was. I never claimed to be fully mature or a super-Christian.

Over the weekend, and especially yesterday, I had envisioned my last day at the church, making a grand speech. I was a little peeved that my rapid exit had taken that out of my hands.

"Well, Dinah -- err, Miss Clydesdale." Pastor Marcus glanced at Mr. Phillips before focusing on me again. "I have to say - well, I'm sorry that things worked out the way they did. I realize that you were hurt by our ... well, our thoughtless actions and bad timing. And it has been pointed out to me that people who are unjustifiably ... antagonistic to you were given an unfair opportunity to hurt you."

I wondered how long he had been working on this speech, and that made me smile. Just a little bit.

"This isn't the way that a dedicated servant of the Lord should leave a time of service and ministry. And I dare anyone to say you did not have a ministry here, as true and solid as any missionary or teacher or pastor." He backed up a few steps, probably just to give me room to make my exit if I so chose. "I hope you'll accept my sincere apology. My intent, at least, was never to hurt you."

I believed him. Despite all the friction over the last week, Pastor Marcus really had been good for our church just in the short time he had been with us. I wondered how quickly the ruckus over this would die down and things would go back to normal. How long would the bruise from this last week be a detriment to the growth and testimony of our church? I got that queasy feeling again, and the growing certainty that I had contributed to the mess a little more than I should have.

Heck, let's be honest -- I shouldn't have contributed at all. I was thinking about *my* feelings, *my* situation, putting them first, just as much as Mrs. Rizetti and the bean counters. Some of them enjoyed hurting me, but maybe, just maybe, some people had started with good intentions.

Please, God, could I wake up tomorrow and find out the last ten days have just been a bad dream?

"I should probably apologize for any flack you're going to get, or stories you're going to hear about in the next few days," I said. "Some of my friends in Singles aren't too happy about me being fired. Combined with my breaking up with my boyfriend in front of the whole group ... well, they're on the offensive for me right now. I'm sorry about that."

"Yes, well, in some sense, maybe no one is innocent in this, are we?" He held out his hand to shake mine. "I sincerely wish you the best. And I pray that you find a job quickly. One that fulfills you and feeds your soul."

That was somewhat poetic. I ruined the moment by wondering what book he had borrowed it from.

Then Pastor Marcus had to ruin the moment, as he and Mr. Phillips walked with me to the door outside.

Chapter Nine

"I hope we can call on you to help us out from time to time, when our volunteer staff runs into any trouble," he said, returning to that we're-all-just-a-loving-family smile. As if he thought his little speech had fixed everything.

I did take a moment for a deep breath and to weigh my words. Maybe not long enough?

"That's going to be a little hard to do. Considering that I'll be working full-time for someone else."

"Oh. Yes." His smile faded. "Sorry. Didn't think that through all the way, did I?"

He and Mr. Phillips stood in the door, watching me get in my car and drive away. I took my time, going the long way around the church, to get one last view of the building where I had grown up. The church had grown with me, nearly doubling in size thanks to three additions. All the trees in the back field that we had climbed during Sunday school picnics and Vacation Bible School were gone now, chopped down to extend the parking lot and the building. For a few seconds, I didn't recognize the place anymore. I got a thick, heavy feeling in my chest as I turned out of the driveway onto the road that ran along the mall, and told myself not to look back.

I decided not to stop to see Zach at Match about new job leads. I could do that tomorrow. Gut instinct said to get home. After a side trip to the grocery store for a replacement carton of triple chocolate ice cream. I got home, changed my clothes, and settled down to indulge in a *Young Riders* marathon.

A couple times, I noticed a trace of salt in my ice cream, but I ignored it the best I could.

Around one, I called Zach to let him know what happened: I had handed in my two weeks' notice, anticipating getting a job offer, and I had been let go. I had to leave a message on his answering machine. Either he was at lunch, or he was busy with a client. I hoped that was a good sign for his business.

I had an appointment with him at lunch the next day, so I told him I was flexible and could come in any time Wednesday, whatever was better for him. I had no life, now.

Then I called Reggie. If she couldn't talk yet, it would go to her voicemail. As if we hadn't had enough talking yesterday? As a good friend, I needed to return the favor of a listening ear, now that she was facing two crises: working the children's theater production with that guy who was still relatively new at church, and now the store consolidation. I wouldn't ask if she had news for me about Thad. I had had time to work up some righteous indignation, along with digging up more reasons to be glad he wasn't in my life anymore.

Although, along with the other revelations I had had lately, I decided it was more like I had been in *his* life, an accessory or assistant. I vowed once again not to become a doormat for anyone. There was a point where Christian humility and peaceable living ended and turning off my brain began. Never again would I go into a relationship where I was expected to put someone else before me 100 percent of the time. Especially not someone who never thought about putting me before him.

All right, maybe that wasn't the most humble or spiritually mature way of approaching relationships, but if nobody was going to look out for me, I had to, right?

Reggie picked up on the second ring. The meeting was over and she was running errands, because today was supposed to be her day off. I could never keep her work schedule straight, since she worked all sorts of different shifts at the cosmetic counter. Being manager of the department had its perks and its downsides. She practically lived at the store until Christmas.

It was good she was in the car and I was home, because she dropped a bombshell and I shrieked.

"Guess who's the outside consultant the company brought in to oversee consolidating twenty stores?" Reggie didn't wait for me to respond. "Nolan."

"Nolan? You mean the new guy at church?"

"The one who doesn't participate in anything. Whatsoever. Except the kids' play!"

I could hear Reggie's voice echoing off her car windows. She hurried on with the ugly details. Nolan Peters, I already knew, was the new director and manager for the children's theater the

Grant Family Trust had endowed. He had been making Reggie's life uncomfortable, but she refused to bail on the production of *The Bremen Town Musicians* and disappoint her grandmother. Besides, the Three Witches had done an about-face. After tricking her into working makeup for the children's theater production, now they wanted her job. Meaning access to Nolan. She wouldn't inflict them on anyone, no matter how uneasy he made her.

I almost felt sorry for the guy.

"This could really be a mess, working with him on the consolidation *and* the play. I can't believe he didn't say anything. He knows I work for Rockaway, because they're donating props and makeup." She sighed loudly. "I don't want to talk about it. Give me time to adjust. Just spill. What was the fallout from your two weeks' notice?"

"Fallout. Nuclear. I'm home right now. They fired me the moment I walked in the door."

"Did they tell you why?" Reggie demanded.

"Nope. I don't even know who made the decision. I should have done it Friday."

"You don't know what kind of snits they could have worked themselves into over the weekend, if you had done that." She sighed. "You know, for all the stupidity of your bosses -- I mean, yeah, they're mostly men, it's genetic brain damage."

Our mutual joke didn't seem so funny now, and kind of hung in the air with an almost silent sour note.

"The thing is, I really wouldn't have expected it of them, to toss you because you handed in your notice. I mean, come on, you let them know you were looking for a new job. They let you know they were letting you go. It's not like you were bailing ship -- so why punish you like this?"

"Did I tell you about the severance check?"

"I bet they held it back, didn't they?"

"No, got it and deposited it right away. Mrs. Rizetti held that over my head while I cleaned out my drawer. She said I wouldn't be getting it. Oooh, was she furious when she found out I got it, then she demanded that I give it back."

"That's just like her. Thank God your dad didn't marry her."

"Dad was too oblivious to realize she was chasing him, until she made such a big mess he had to run for his life."

I sighed. Why did she have to remind me? The last thing I wanted to do was call Dad about my being sacked. He was only moderately angry on my behalf last week, when I told him.

Dad was a peacemaker. Close on being a wimp with a "kick me now" sign, when it came to church politics. The longer we talked, the bigger the odds that he would turn things around, try to placate the administration to get my job back, and somehow make it my fault. He was always trying to make both parties responsible without punishing anyone. I was hurt, I was wronged, and if crying on Dad's shoulder wasn't going to do any good, why cry there at all?

I was sick of being surrounded by unreliable, oblivious men. I wanted --

"Dinah?" Reggie sounded a little uneasy. "You've been kind of silent, and you made a funny noise like you're choking. What are you thinking?"

"I'm still in shock, I guess. I was thinking I really needed someone who would get in fights for me, or over me, or something. And I got an image of Russell trying to take on Thad Sunday night. Ugh! What kind of a loser am I, that the only knight in shining armor I can scare up is a computer geek?"

"Maybe it's a sign from God that you're worth something, despite how everybody's been treating you lately?"

"Hmm. Maybe." But I really wished, if I had to have a knight in shining armor, he would look more like Zach Foster.

We talked for half an hour. Reggie had an uncanny talent for being able to shop, deal with clerks, haul her purchases out to her car, and a dozen other details while talking to me. After her errands, she drove through KFC to get dinner and joined my *Young Riders* marathon. We missed a lot of it as we grumbled about our situations. All she said about Thad (I didn't ask) was that she hadn't been called either by Thad's mother or their grandmother about Sunday night's showdown.

"Which means the big bozo is too embarrassed to complain to either one of them," Reggie said, eyes sparkling. She hit the pause, right where Hickok stepped out into the street to face down the gunslinger trying to make a name by calling him out.

"What makes you think he would?" I contemplated getting up and throwing away our trash in the break.

"Well, I figure Grammy is going to demand reports on what he's doing to win you back. By now, Uncle Theo has been dragged into the situation, and he'll pass it off to Aunt Miranda, like he always does." She shrugged and helped me dump the gnawed bones of our chicken back into the bucket.

In the space of two hours, we had finished off a ten-piece bucket with biscuits and double coleslaw. Emotional disasters and personal upheavals gave us an appetite. So, sue us.

"Silence means Thad at least feels some shame over what happened. Good sign, or bad?"

"It means he's ignoring Grammy's demands for a progress report. Once she sets her mind on something, she doesn't let go. I know she wants you and Thad together, and she's determined to get it, because she's been ignoring me every time I say you two are done, finished, separated, totally split. Right?"

"Right." I sighed and set the bucket down on the floor instead of hauling it to the kitchen. "Maybe I should just move to Arizona with Dad. Start totally fresh."

The landline rang the same moment Reggie opened her mouth to answer. She giggled. I grabbed the bucket and ran into the kitchen to answer it. Which was stupid, I realized as I picked up the phone. I was usually never home at this time of the day, so why would anyone expect me to answer the phone? It was probably a telemarketer or politician or a recorded message.

"Who was it?" Reggie said, when I finally returned to the TV room ten minutes later.

"Mrs. Winslow wants to reserve the parlor for a mothers of school athletes Bible study she's starting in February."

"Why would she call you? Wait -- school athletes?"

Mrs. Winslow was one of those women who loudly and frequently proclaimed that *real* Christians didn't read fiction. *At all.* They also didn't watch television or plays or movies. Since she believed the only "proper" reading material for Christian women was Bible studies, devotionals, how-to books, and cookbooks, she spent her time researching and writing them. She had instigated five Bible study groups so far, to research a new devotional she was working on.

At least she had a way to make a living, and she didn't depend on anyone to give her a chance to do it, either.

"She called the office, but nobody was able to help her," I said, settling down on the couch again.

"But why did she call you *here*?"

"A lot of people call me at home when they can't get what they want from the office, or it's after office hours."

"But you don't work there anymore." She got a wicked grin. "They aren't telling anyone you're gone, are they?"

I wasn't going to touch that particular speculation with a ten-foot pole. I snatched up the remote control and got on with Hickok's gunfight. Either the people who picked up the phone in the office didn't realize I was gone, or those who knew weren't talking. The ladies who answered the phone were used to me running around the church. Just because they couldn't see me didn't mean I wasn't there. A pile of pink message slips was growing even as I sat there watching TV. Maybe nobody would put the pieces together until a real disaster struck. Then the news would get around. Meanwhile, I would have to deal with calls from people who wanted me to fix the problems at church.

Part of me looked forward to telling every caller, "Sorry, I can't help you, I don't work for your church anymore."

Part of me felt ashamed of my bitter glee at the thought of putting emphasis on *your church.* Until people caught on.

By the time Reggie went home that evening, I had taken four more calls from people who wanted something for the next day or later in the week. I simply told them they would have to talk to someone else in the church in the morning, because I wouldn't be in and couldn't help them.

Reggie called me a wimp the first time she heard me use that line. Then she got thoughtful. By the last call, she looked a little concerned.

"You need to just flat out tell them the truth. You were let go. I know you're trying to be gracious and not cause trouble, but think about it. The longer you hold off telling the whole story, the more that Rizetti witch can tell her lies."

That was frightening. I wished she had thought of that a lot sooner. I wished *I* had thought of that a lot sooner. I agreed with her, and resolved to start telling the flat, unvarnished truth from then on. So of course, no more phone calls came from people who thought office hours didn't apply to them.

<><><>

Zach Foster didn't change my appointment, so I went to A Match Made For Heaven at noon, as scheduled. Gertie met me at the door, dressed in a purple and gold jogging suit.

"Well? How did it go?" she demanded, rosy-cheeked and bouncing up and down on her toes.

"How did what --" I nearly choked when I realized what she meant. A little of my anger at her matchmaking came back. "Gertie, I appreciate you wanting to help. But I told you, I need to focus on finding a new job and getting that part of my life settled. The last thing I need is another relationship."

"A nice girl like you needs a boyfriend to look out for her." She pouted as she flopped into her chair.

"I've lived most of my life without a boyfriend, so I doubt I'll wither up and die just because I lost one I only had for a month. My first boyfriend in six years, I might add."

"I find that hard to believe," Zach said, coming out of the conference room behind me.

I turned around to face him, my heart going triple its usual speed. I had to remember how small this office was, and there really was no privacy. The last thing I needed was for a guy like Zach to realize what a loser I was. It might impact how he saw me when he was trying to find me a new job.

"Believe it," I managed to say. I think I got a creditable smile in place. "I've been just too busy for dating, and guys never thought I was worth the effort of pursuing."

Oh, smart, giving that kind of information. My loser-ness was going to damage my job prospects. What was wrong with me? Too much ice cream, clogging the synapses in my brain?

"Take my advice. Give the dating scene a rest. You're smart to concentrate on the important things -- work, health, a life plan." His smile seemed sincere enough, as if he really did think I was smart, avoiding dating and the complications that came with it.

"Don't listen to that stupid advice." Gertie waved a scolding finger at Zach. "You need to keep on the move, get back up on the horse, let nice boys know you're available."

"I'm *not* available. I just want to find a job. So no more matching me up with other guys like Russell."

"Russell?" Zach frowned. "Aunt Gertie, you didn't send

Russell Prince after her, did you?" He groaned when she nodded, grinning so wide I thought her face might split in half. "Dinah, I apologize. Mrs. Prince has been in here five times since Aunt Gertie started matchmaking. She's desperate for a success."

"I wouldn't match Dinah up with a loser, and you know it. I have high ethical standards! Russell adores her already. He told me she was a damsel in distress, and he wanted to get on his trusty steed and defend her." Gertie's cheeks got rosier and she wrapped her arms around herself. "It's so romantic!"

I shivered at how her words matched some of the thoughts I had had the last few days. I really would have liked to be someone's damsel in distress for a change. But ... okay, Russell was probably a very nice guy. Maybe it was the computer connection -- he reminded me a little too much of Thad.

"He thought she was amazing, how she stood up to those idiots in her church on New Year's Eve," she continued.

"You sent him to her *church*?" Zach groaned. He braced himself on the counter, towering over Gertie. I felt like a spectator in the front row seat of a live soap opera. "Dinah ... I'm so sorry."

"Don't apologize." She slapped his arm. "Dinah, I understand you want to slow things down, but Russell thinks you're wonderful. Doesn't that make you feel so much better?"

"Yeah, everybody needs a white knight," I murmured. My gaze drifted to Zach and locked with his. I envisioned him in a suit of gleaming silver armor. The image held for about five seconds, until Russell peered at me through the helmet. It slammed closed on him. I muffled a little gasp of laughter. "Ahh, could we get to --"

"Back to work. Right. Sorry. Wasting your time." Zach flushed and pushed off from the counter. He gestured me into the conference room. As I stepped through the door and started to take my coat off, behind me, I heard him say, "Gertie, I love you. I know you're trying to help. But I'm warning you, stay out of Dinah's love life. She didn't sign up, and I don't care how much Kayla Prince pressures you to find a wife for Russell, you've got no business pressuring Dinah. Understand?"

Whatever Gertie said, it was muffled and I couldn't hear it.

"I don't care how great you think he is, those two aren't right for each other. Hands off. Dinah's in too much upheaval right now, and I am not letting you make things worse, no matter how good your intentions are. Got me?"

My heart skipped a couple beats. I wished someone would stand up for me, go all white knight on my behalf. Gertie responded again with more unintelligible mutters. Zach seemed satisfied. At least, he looked calm and professional and upbeat again when he came into the conference room, closed the door and sat down across the table from me.

<><><>

I was feeling pretty good about my prospects when I got home that afternoon. Zach had five more job possibilities for me, either at Christian schools or local mission organizations. Then I looked at my answering machine and saw five messages waiting. Symmetry?

Every call was from someone who couldn't get anyone at church to help them. I was left with the unpleasant task of telling people I couldn't help them, either now or in the future. I contemplated changing the message on my answering machine: *I no longer work for Central Avenue, so don't bother asking for help.* I only had the landline to protect my cell number from church people, and telemarketers. Then I thought about Dad forgetting my cell number again, calling me on the landline, and getting that message. I still hadn't called him about my situation.

It took me an hour to get back to the people who left me messages. All of them were home, so I couldn't leave a simple (cowardly) message. How come when we want to take the wimp's way out of a situation, God never lets us? I had to explain that I no longer worked for the church, I had no authority to promise them anything or do anything for them. I couldn't answer their questions because I had no idea who was handling my duties.

Of course, that answer wasn't good enough for anyone. I had to answer reams of questions. Most callers were family friends and were horrified and sympathetic. The peacemaker and wimp in me tried to clarify things. I envisioned the anger I heard on the phone turning into ugly rumors going around the church. What if people thought I had said those things, rather than the people who were angry on my behalf? Protecting my back, more than Christian charity, kept me on the phone too long.

I was exhausted when I finished, and I seriously considered

sending a bill to Pastor Marcus for time spent dealing with problems he or the church board had made.

But I didn't, of course. Wimp that I was.

<><><>

Sunday morning, Reggie showed up at 7:30. I was still in my robe, with wet hair, debating whether I should read all day or go check out Holy Spirit Alliance. I was panicky enough about the long silence regarding the decision to hire me, I hoped showing up to worship there would earn me some brownie points. Maybe nudge the dawdlers into making their decision.

"You are going to church, aren't you?" she demanded, as she stomped her boots off on the back step and came in through the kitchen door.

She had her own key, of course. She had lived with me for three months when she was between apartments, and I never thought it worthwhile to take back the key. I mean, she was my best friend.

Reggie had started taking night classes at Disciples Bible College about the same time she got promoted to manager for the cosmetic department. That meant she could finally move out of her parents' home. She let her Uncle Charles, who worked in administration at the newly started college, match her up with two girls from out of state who needed roommates. Disciples was so new it didn't have dormitories yet. After about two months, one roommate went off the deep end, insisting that Reggie's science fiction books were allowing demons to invade their apartment. She conveniently forgot that her previous lifestyle, dancing at a Vegas casino that offered fortune telling, Tarot, and Ouija boards, might have had something to do with it. Or that she was an unstable nutcase who insisted everyone else adhere to her latest extremist lifestyle changes.

Reggie came running to me, because she certainly couldn't move back in with her parents. We agreed it was only a temporary thing. We both needed our own spaces. Reggie was dating a pre-seminary student who was making noises about being serious, so she anticipated being a newlywed soon.

Here we were three years later, neither dating nor engaged, living in our own places, and she still had the key to my house. Which was fine by me. I had a key to her apartment, too.

I just wished she had thought to call ahead. At least she didn't show up while I was in the shower. That would have been a little creepy, stepping out of the shower, turning off the water, and hearing the radio in the kitchen -- meaning someone was in my house without my knowledge.

"Yeah. Just not sure which church to go to," I said, and tugged my robe a little tighter around myself. Would anyone really blame me if I took this Sunday off?

I remembered considering taking last Sunday morning off. I could have avoided a lot of unpleasantness if I had done that. I wouldn't have turned in my two weeks' notice, or encountered Thad and Mrs. Grant over the watch. Anita wouldn't have been drafted to take over my duties. Russell still would have shown up for the New Year's party, though. That might have been amusing, in a weird way.

Oh, ugh, did I really want to go to that church and risk seeing Russell in the hallway? What had he told Pastor Paulson? Had he told him anything? Maybe Russell was embarrassed over what he had done, chasing me down, he hadn't told anyone?

"Dinah? Dinah!" Reggie stood in front of me, both hands on my shoulders, shaking me, her nose nearly touching mine. "Snap out of it. You're thinking too hard. I swear there's smoke coming out of your ears."

"Where can I go to church?" I almost whimpered. Almost.

"I wouldn't go to our church. Not if they got down on their knees and apologized. And hung Mrs. Rizetti from the balcony by her ankles," she added with a snort.

That broke the dizzy, falling, funky feeling that had clogged up my brain. We shared grins.

"Honestly, I was thinking about staying home today. Just to make a clean break." I pointed at a notepad sitting on the table. "I've been listing things to do with my free time, and I was thinking I'd just spend today reading a book cover-to-cover."

"Sounds heavenly. But not smart. You find excuses to skip church one Sunday, and pretty soon you'll have excuses every Sunday." Reggie hooked her thumb over her shoulder in the general direction of my bedroom. "Get dressed. We're going to Holy Spirit Alliance."

"I'd rather you went to our church and did some spying."

"Listen to the gossip?" She glared at me until I actually took a few steps toward the hall.

"Gossip is such an ugly, un-Christian word. Sharing." I paused and leaned against the corner. "I've had another twelve calls from people wanting help with church stuff. Someone isn't getting the word out that I'm not there."

"The volunteers aren't working out, and if they don't tell anyone you're gone, maybe they can shame you into crawling back without anyone the wiser." She shook her head. "Ain't gonna happen. Are you going to get dressed, or do I have to do it for you?"

<><><>

I think God sent me a sign that I had done the right thing by going to the second service at Holy Spirit Alliance. Zach Foster came across the parking lot from the opposite direction and looked around when he reached the side door of the church. He saw us coming and stopped to wait for us. I introduced him to Reggie and he gave us a few pointers of where to go, the best door to take into the sanctuary, and how to get to the welcome center to get coffee or tea or hot chocolate before the service.

"No wonder you dumped Thad," Reggie murmured, when Zach excused himself to sign in at the usher station. Her eyes sparkled, and I had a funny feeling in my chest for a moment.

That was stupid. Zach was just a working friend. He thought it was smart for me to avoid all relationship entanglements until I got my job situation settled.

"Zach is helping me find a new job. It wouldn't be ethical to get personal until things are settled."

"Until?" She batted her eyelashes at me as we rounded the corner into the welcome center. Not only did it have stadium-sized urns of coffee, hot water for tea and hot chocolate, but they had mini cheese danish and donut bites. "Is that hope I see in your big, teary eyes?"

I glared at Reggie. I wanted to punch her in the shoulder. I would have at our home church, but we weren't in our home church. People weren't used to us being silly and a little rowdy. Nobody knew us here, and if I hoped to work here, I certainly couldn't cause a ruckus and make a bad impression, could I?

Pastor Paulson had the message that morning, and I

thoroughly enjoyed listening to him speak. He knew how to tell stories that didn't depend on someone -- usually a man -- being the butt of the joke, like Pastor Marcus did. His funny story made me think. He basically followed through on my first impression that he was a thoughtful, warm, caring leader.

I knew I would enjoy working for him, and my work would feel like a ministry, instead of a cross between kindergarten teacher and zookeeper at my home church.

It wasn't my home church anymore, was it?

When the service ended, I decided I would have to see about transferring my membership. Could I feel comfortable attending here if I didn't get the job? After thinking about it, as we made our slow way down the aisle to the back of the sanctuary and out into the hall, I decided I *could*. I liked this place -- even though I cringed at the prospect of having to settle in and make a place for myself somewhere new.

"Dinah? It is Dinah, right?" A tall, slightly familiar-looking girl with long, cinnamon-colored hair approached me. Reggie and I had paused to remember what path we had taken to the sanctuary. "Hi, I'm Stacy Tiernan. We didn't really meet, when you were in for your second interview, but ..." She shrugged, then gestured a few steps down the crowded hall.

I remembered her when I saw the husky, gray-haired man who waved to us. He was sitting in a wheelchair, with a toddler sitting on the cast-bound leg propped up before him, and three more hanging on the wheelchair sides, all chattering away at him. Stacy had pushed him out of the room after the meeting last week. He had been introduced to me as Pastor Bert, and I assumed she was his assistant. I found out I was wrong, when she went on to say her Uncle Bert wanted to greet me. Reggie and I went over to talk, while the traffic in the hall diminished a little. Pastor Bert was minister to the Seniors. He certainly seemed to be a favorite with the children, judging by the little ones who scrambled through the incoming and outgoing traffic to come say hello. Pastor Bert recognized Reggie. He coached the men's basketball teams for the inter-church sports league, and her Uncle Theo did the same for Central Avenue.

Before we got any further, a couple ladies who could have been swapped out for the silver-haired iron ladies of our church came up and asked for Stacy's help. There was a planning meeting for the Widows Fellowship right after the Sunday school hour, and they had run into a problem while setting up. Pastor Bert and Stacy apologized, said goodbye, it was nice to meet us, and trundled down the hall.

"Widows?" Reggie murmured.

"You didn't see the rings on the chain Stacy was wearing? Dad did the same thing when Mom died, took off his ring and put it with hers."

"Wow, she looks kind of young to be a widow."

I just nodded. No way was I going to admit the stray thought I had had, what felt like months ago, about marrying Thad and hoping to be a widow, so I could legally continue working at the church. What had I been thinking?

"Dinah! Sweetheart, it's so good to see you!" Gertie scooted out of the crowd in the hall to grab onto my arm. She started pulling me along behind her, but she saw Reggie with me and her eyes got wide and she stopped short.

Russell caught up with us while I was introducing Reggie to Gertie. He smiled at me and nodded politely. I didn't see any discomfort. Maybe he didn't recognize Reggie from New Year's Eve? If only ...

"So this is Dinah." A little, crooked woman stood next to Russell. She was dressed all in black, had a crumpled black hat decorated with cherries all around the hatband, and leaned on a cane with a brass eagle for a handle. She tugged her hand out of the crook of Russell's elbow and thrust it out to me to shake. She wore black mesh gloves without any fingers. "I'm Kayla Prince, Russell's mother." Her gaze swept over me with such force, it was like her eyeballs had been replaced by laser beams. "You're exactly as Russell and Gertie described you."

"Ahh ... that's nice." I swallowed hard. "Nice to meet you."

"Oh, let's get out of traffic." Gertie made shooing motions, moving us down the first hallway we came to.

"Tell me, Dinah, do you follow football?" Mrs. Prince said.

"Football? Like the local teams, or the Browns or -- "

"Dinah and I don't care about any sports except baseball." Reggie hooked her arm through mine, cutting off Mrs. Prince, who was reaching for my arm. "We're practically sisters. As far as we're concerned, there are no professional sports in Cleveland until spring training starts."

"How ... nice." Mrs. Prince blinked at her a few times, as if trying to figure out what she was doing there. "I hear you're at the top of the list for the secretary job. That's lovely. Gertie's nephew is such a reliable young man, I know he's properly vetted you. We can trust Match Made in Heaven for God-ordained matches."

I bit my tongue to keep from correcting her that it was Match Made *For* Heaven, not *In* Heaven. If Gertie didn't correct her, why should I?

"Where did you go to school?"

This time Reggie let me answer for myself. As soon as I told her about college and high school, Mrs. Prince wanted to know about my parents. She clucked sympathetically when I said Mom had died of breast cancer when I was in high school, and Dad was now in Arizona. She wanted to know where I went to summer camp, how long I had been a committed Christian, and what I thought of the governor's latest decisions. The questions went on and on, snapped out almost before I finished answering the last one. They had no pattern I could follow. What was she trying to learn? I didn't even have a chance to ask her why she needed to know all these things. She just kept pressing.

Russell came to my rescue. At the fifteen-minute mark, he patted his mother's hand, resting again in the crook of his elbow, and reminded her she had a class to teach.

"Oh, my. How silly of me. I lost all track of time. Well, you're such a lovely young lady, Dinah. So well-rounded. I like that." She nodded. "My boy is a treasure, isn't he? So good to his mummy." She yanked on his arm, bringing him down to her level, and smacked a kiss on his cheek, leaving a magenta smear of lipstick. Russell colored slightly and nodded to us as she made her farewells and toddled down the hall. I couldn't decide if she dragged him, or he supported her. As they turned, I saw him reach up with his free hand and wipe away the lipstick.

"Wow," Reggie murmured. "They don't make them like that anymore."

I could almost hear her thinking: *Thank God for small favors!*

"I have to apologize for Kayla," Gertie said with a chuckle. "She's my oldest friend. Russell is her treasure, and she's ... well, very protective of him. He's been hurt. Romantically." She waggled her eyebrows at me. "Kayla wants only the best for her boy. But she really, really likes you."

"That's nice." I didn't dare say that I really, really didn't like his mother. She made me nervous. Once Gertie said goodbye and wandered down the hall, I muttered, "I was waiting for her to demand to see my teeth, and the results of my last physical,"

"Weeeee-ird." Reggie chuckled. "Nobody expects the Spanish Inquisition," she said with a really bad British accent. We both laughed, because nice girls like us weren't supposed to know about Monty Python routines.

Holy Spirit Alliance was such a big building, with so many hallways, we got turned around and couldn't find the parking lot where Reggie had parked, even with the help of the maps posted at every intersection. I thought if I could find the church office, I could triangulate our position and get us back to the right place. So we ended up at the office wing door, planning to go outside and take the sidewalk around the building. Pastor Paulson was just going into the church office as we came by. His big smile when he saw me made me glad I had made the effort to come to church. He held onto my hand the whole time I introduced Reggie to him.

Chapter Ten

"Pastor, I think you ought to know..."

I swallowed hard, suddenly feeling guilty. Maybe a little queasy. I wasn't so stupid as to think that none of what had happened to me lately was my fault. I had made bad choices, reacted badly, and aggravated people who were looking for excuses to treat me the way they did.

"I handed in my two weeks' notice last Sunday, and when I got to work Tuesday morning, I was let go. You should know, in case any stories get back to you. In case it has any effect on your decision whether or not to hire me."

"Uh huh." He patted my hand, regarded Reggie a moment. "I was afraid something like that might happen." He looked around at the thinning crowds, frowning a little.

That gave me a sinking feeling. Had I just destroyed my chances of being hired? Then that frown brightened when Aaron Randall passed us, heading for the office.

"Aaron, just the person I need. You mentioned you know Dinah?"

"Yes." Aaron smiled as he turned to look at us. Then he gave us a doubletake. "And Reggie, too. How are you both?"

"Well, this works out better than I hoped," Pastor Paulson said once we exchanged greetings. He gestured at the office door. "Dinah has come to me about that matter we discussed the other day. With her home church. Since you know Miss Grant as well, that works out even better. First, we need to take this somewhere a little more private."

He led us into the office area. The thick glass blocked out the sounds of the people in the hallway. Comforting.

"I'm glad you thought it necessary to tell me, Dinah. Zach did let us know what happened," Pastor Paulson said, after Reggie and I had taken two chairs in the main office, Aaron sat on the edge of a desk, and he leaned back against the counter. "Aaron and the senior staff and I discussed it, and we're of the opinion your giving two weeks' notice wasn't the whole reason." He chuckled when Reggie and I both made confused sounds. "I called your Pastor Marcus last Friday. We've progressed enough in the hiring process, we need to get your references, talk to the people who worked with you. Some of the people I talked to were surprised I was calling. I'm still trying to figure out some of the reasons why."

"Inter-church sports league," Reggie said. "Don't you know you can lose your salvation, fraternizing with the enemy?"

He chuckled and shared a glance with Aaron. I was glad he took her remark as a joke. "Some were surprised you found a new position so quickly. Others, I think, still hadn't heard that you were being let go."

"Par for the course," I muttered, and braced for the other shoe to drop. With my luck, he hadn't talked to just those who were out of the loop. He had talked to at least one person who wanted me out. Eagerly. Anxiously.

"Some woman who claimed she was your supervisor felt she had to warn me that you were a flighty, vindictive girl who didn't know your place in the world."

"Mrs. Rizetti," Reggie said. "Gotta be."

"You were right," he said, glancing at Aaron again.

"I apologized for not warning him," Aaron said, holding up his hands as if surrendering -- or accepting blame.

"I didn't get her name. She wasn't willing to give it. That says something about her, as well as the things she said." Pastor Paulson shook his head, smiling. "Don't worry, Dinah. My conversations with the people at your church only emphasized the good points I've already seen in you. I hope you won't forget that there are a lot of good, well-intentioned Christians back at your home church. It's just that the opinionated, self-righteous ones are louder."

He stood up, pushing off the counter, and gestured at the door. We got up and let him escort us out.

"On the whole, I think you should be encouraged that most of them had only good to say about your work ethic, your reliability and confidentiality, and your spiritual maturity. You'll be missed. Several did express regret over the economic decisions that required them to let you go."

"Not enough regret to make some adjustments so she could

stay." Reggie offered him a fake smile, and batted her eyelashes. He laughed.

Pastor Paulson was my idea of the perfect minister. He wasn't so caught up in being pious that he was a pain to live with. *So heavenly minded he's no earthly good,* Mom used to say. And he had a sense of humor. I wanted to work with him.

"The bottom line," he said, as we paused at the door to the parking lot, "is that I can't promise you the job just yet. If it was up to me ... Well, this is a decision that impacts our whole church family. You will have contact with every member of our congregation. Everyone who will work with you has to weigh in. I can promise you'll have an answer by the end of the week." He winked. "If we offer you the job on Friday, could you start on Monday?"

I had no idea what got into me. Maybe the relief I felt at knowing he still liked me, despite Mrs. Rizetti's poison.

"Well, I was thinking about visiting the beach house for a week or two, take some time off, unwind. But I think I can accommodate you."

Reggie snickered. Pastor Paulson grinned and patted my shoulder as we said our goodbyes and went out the door.

Zach was driving away as we came down the sidewalk. I made a mental note to get a map of all the parking lots that surrounded the church, and all the exits. He saw us, pulled over and rolled down his passenger side window.

"So, how did it go? How did you like it?" He nodded and smiled when we said a few things about the service, the size of the church, some of the people who had talked to us before the service. "I have a couple more possibilities to show you, if you want to come into the office tomorrow. But I have to tell you, I really want you to get the job here."

"Why?" Reggie said.

"Well, it's my home church. I want the best for us." He grinned wider and rolled his eyes. "That didn't come out right."

"I don't know. It was kind of good for my ego," I quipped, which got a few snorts of laughter from him.

"The thing is, I have full confidence in my matching program, and this is my home church. You just fit the bill perfectly. And ... well, I admit, I'd like to get to know you better once you're settled in a new job."

Reggie nudged me so hard with her elbow, I almost stumbled off the sidewalk. Zach looked away, flushing, so I didn't think he saw that. A relief for me.

"Heck," Zach continued, "maybe I'm just making sure you're conveniently close, so I know where to find you."

We agreed on a time for Monday.

"He really blew it with that last part," Reggie said, as Zach drove away. "Conveniently close. Sheeeesh! It's like you're a -- a -- a spare roll of toilet paper."

I slapped her arm. "That's for being vulgar. You don't talk about toilet paper in public at church."

"Who says?" She wrinkled up her nose at me, then we linked arms and crossed the parking lot to find her car.

<><><>

Tuesday afternoon, I got home from running errands to find ten more messages on my answering machine. I couldn't delete without listening to the messages. I didn't want to. Despite constantly telling people I no longer worked at their church, they still expected me to help them, to tell them who to talk to, what they needed to do, and even talk to the staff for them. Time to unplug the answering machine? Leave a message that anyone calling from Central Avenue should go away? Or send an invoice to the church for time spent doing someone else's job?

That wouldn't be a Christian thing to do, and my attitude was definitely not nice, but I was tired of being nice. When would people be nice to Dinah for a change?

The flashing red ten on my answering machine kept nagging at me as I put away my few groceries, then brought empty boxes in from the car and went into the basement.

With so much free time, I had been doing some ridding. I started with junk in our tiny basement. I took a lot of things to the Salvation Army. I trashed lawn furniture that had been used when my parents bought it. This summer, I would have time to sit in the backyard and read in the sun, but it would be on furniture I had picked out, not faded, rusty, outdated junk.

Getting rid of books I would never read, dishes I would never use, and tools Dad didn't take to Arizona, I discovered a whole new room downstairs. I could refinish the basement. Maybe get one of those electric fireplaces. A place to curl up and read away the winter storms. There were lots of possibilities.

To do that, I would need money, and that meant a job.

Please, God, have Holy Spirit call me soon and offer me that job? Maybe I'm going a little stir crazy having all this free time?

I filled those empty boxes with more things to take to the Salvation Army and the recycling center. Then I settled in the kitchen and reached for one of my dozens of cookbooks, with a vague idea of making a recipe I had never tried before. The problem with filling my free time with cooking was that I would end up needing a new, larger wardrobe. Maybe I needed to rid out cookbooks, too. Mom had loved to cook, and Dad had often squeaked by at gift-giving time by buying her big, expensive cookbooks she had drooled over, but never could justify buying for herself. At least he didn't get her appliances.

The shelf of cookbooks sat next to the phone. That flashing red ten glared at me as I rifled through the shelves, trying to decide if I should check out each book, or just empty the shelves wholesale.

"All right, already," I grumbled, and pressed the button to play the messages. I snatched up the notepad tucked in between two cookbooks and prepared to write down any messages I needed to deal with.

Funny, but out of those ten messages, seven were frantic, half-whispered pleas for advice and explanations from the women in the church office. I imagined Mrs. Rizetti somewhere in the background, glaring at anyone who suggested, "Why not call Dinah and find out how she did this?" I could easily see those women distracting her, while someone made the next call.

One call was from Thad, sounding tired, asking if we could meet somewhere and talk and "fix things." I wanted to call him and say there was nothing to fix. Problem: that wouldn't be smart, it wouldn't be gracious, it wouldn't be mature or Christian. I wanted to be bigger than all this.

Dream on ...

Besides, Thad knew my cell number. If he really wanted to talk with me, he would have called my cell. He was taking the immature, cowardly way out by calling the landline and leaving a message. He knew my practice of using it to screen calls, so he knew we wouldn't talk. At all.

The other two calls were Russell Prince. No messages, other than to say he would call back.

There was no use wasting time, wondering what Russell could want. I went over my scribbled notes of what the ladies in the office wanted, then I picked up the phone to call back. I wished I hadn't already taken our fax machine to the Salvation Army. I could have written down the answers and faxed them over, and then I wouldn't have needed to talk to anyone.

Not very mature. But doggone it, why did I always have to be the mature one?

Mrs. Babcock answered the phone. I asked where Mrs. Humphries was, too surprised to remember my resolve not to ask for any news from the church.

"Oh, honey, she couldn't take it anymore. She had to keep getting up every ten minutes and go in there and explain everything they couldn't figure out. That's not good for her with her bad knees. Then you-know-who snapped at her every time she told them how *you* did things. She kept saying you got fired because you couldn't do anything right. How come they kept asking how you did it, if you didn't do it right?" She sniffed. "Nobody has to put up with that kind of treatment, especially when they're not getting paid."

"Why are you still there?" Yes, I confess, a little laughter caught in my throat. Ah, the sweet taste of vindication.

"Honey, I just tell them I don't know anything, and if they're so lost, maybe they shouldn't have shoved you out the door before you finished training them." She sighed, with a touch of weary laughter. "How are you doing? Please tell me you got a fantastic job that pays you three times as much for half the work."

"Not quite, but close enough to suit me. If everything comes together, I'll be starting my new job on Monday."

Well, that wasn't exactly a lie, was it? I did say "if."

Mrs. Babcock agreed to take my instructions as a message. A couple times, I thought I heard women's voices in the background, arguing. Maybe sounds of distress. Maybe they had broken some of that very old office equipment that I had nursed along for years. Gee, maybe someone else on the church staff would have to be let go, to have the money to replace equipment.

Not very nice of me, but I had years of being a doormat to work out, and lots of free time to think about it.

I hung up, stood up, and the phone rang. Expecting it to be Mrs. Babcock, asking for some clarification, I answered. Bad choice.

"Hi, Dinah," an unfamiliar, slightly thick male voice said.

"Uh -- yes?" Too late to say there was no one there named Dinah, he had the wrong number. Just proof my brain wasn't firing on all cylinders. I really needed to get back to work. All this free time was slowing my mental reflexes.

"Hi." He chuckled. "It's Russell." Pause. "Um, Russell Prince. From Holy Spirit Alliance?"

"Hi, Russell." What in the world did he want? I muffled a giggle, thinking maybe his mother had thought of another dozen questions. What was with that woman?

"Umm, are you busy tonight?"

"I have tentative plans with my friend. You met Reggie on Sunday, remember?"

"Oh, yeah." His voice got a little thicker, and I envisioned him slumping in little boy disappointment. "I was kind of hoping you would want to take the stargazing hike tonight."

"Stargazing hike?"

"Yeah, in the Metroparks. On clear nights, they take us out to the glacier meadow, and we set up telescopes and do some stargazing. There's a ranger on staff who has some pretty cool stories, mythology and science."

That did sound kind of interesting, if cold. I was tired already. Tromping through the woods to huge expanses of rippling granite, worn down by glaciers centuries ago, to stand there on a January evening and look at the stars, did not appeal to me. I wanted a warm, indoors evening, preferably with the option of crawling into bed whenever I wanted.

"That sounds cool, but I do have tentative plans." I paused, hoping he'd say goodbye, but there was just silence. I thought I could hear him breathing. "Maybe some other time?"

"Okay." What was it about Russell's voice, a little brightness that made me think of a puppy that had just been tossed a chewy treat? I quashed the mental image of him frisking around his desk, panting, with his tongue hanging out. "See you at church. Uh --

bye." Then he hung up.

<><><>

Reggie proved herself my best friend once again, bringing over a deluxe dinner for two from our favorite Chinese restaurant, and her Stuart Granger DVD collection. Give me *The Prisoner of Zenda* any time. Right up there with Zorro, the Scarlet Pimpernel, the Green Hornet, John Stranger, and Stingray. I liked my heroes tall, dark, dangerous, and mysterious.

We had invited our Christmas day gang to join us, but they were either busy with jobs, finding jobs, or they had dates. The traitors. Reggie didn't have a rehearsal for the children's theater because Nolan was busy with a meeting at the Rockaway headquarters. She was just closed-mouth enough about the whole consolidation, theater and church connection with the guy, I felt a tiny bit suspicious. But I didn't ask. We had learned when we could nudge, when we could ignore, and when we absolutely had to badger the truth out of each other.

"Oooh, she's got two guys lusting after her," she said, with a smirk and a growl in her voice, when I told her about the phone calls that evening.

"I don't think so. Not when Thad and Russell are both probably being egged on by your grandmother and his mother."

"Who said anything about Thad? I'm talking Mr. Match Made in Heaven."

"That's ***For*** Heaven." My heart gave a funny little leap at the thought of Zach. Now, he wasn't exactly dangerous, but he did fit a lot of my ideals for a hero.

"Same difference." She gestured with her chin at the cardboard tub of hot and sour soup. "Are you going to open that, or just stand there gloating over your possible love life?"

"Besides, Thad called me today." I pried the lid off the soup tub. Despite being frazzled, I knew my priorities. One did not let hot and sour soup wait to be eaten. Not when Reggie could slurp it all down without stopping to breathe, if I wasn't careful.

Yes, she had done it once. We were much younger then, and I had foolishly ordered a pint. We needed a quart between us.

"Thad? Oh, puh-lease. What did he want?" She stepped over to the cupboard and got bowls and plates out, while I told her about the phone message. "Straighten things out? What's to straighten out? He made Anita tell you, instead of facing you like a man."

"How are Thad and Anita doing, by the way?" I managed to say that without my voice catching or breaking, and I didn't spill the soup when I got the tub open.

"Not together. If they ever were. Anita's gotten over her snit and is grateful to escape. When she stopped by for her Clinique order today, she told me about running for her life. I have the feeling she told me because she knew I'd tell you, and to fix things without her really apologizing."

"Poor Anita."

"We warned her, didn't we? Guy isn't worth the powder it would take to blow him up. And I speak from intimate knowledge, having grown up with the big bozo." She brought over our dishes and utensils and we perched on our usual stools at the counter.

That night, we indulged in two Stuart Granger movies and made plans for the weekend. Reggie promised yet again she would retrieve my Christmas present to Thad. She refused to take the gift certificate he had given me, to leave in its place.

"Let the big idiot face you down to get it back."

"Reg, that isn't exactly fair."

"Nothing about your relationship with Thad was fair. He needs to do some groveling."

I let it drop, and made a mental note to mail the gift certificate back to Thad -- *after* Reggie got the present back.

<><><>

"Di, please tell me you're sitting at your desk," Dad said, when I answered my cell Wednesday morning.

Point of fact, I was sitting on the floor in the basement, with a pad of paper and some pencils, brainstorming the changes I wanted to make down there. It was going to be my retreat. I wanted a fireplace and an oversized easy chair, for reading.

"Ah, no, Dad. I'm in the basement."

"The church doesn't have a basement." He sighed. "So it's true what Rod and Calvin told me?"

"What did they tell you?" I tried not to groan.

Dad's golfing buddies, Rod Higgens and Calvin Smith, were the worst gossips. I should have known they'd tattle.

"You got escorted off church property after you told off the entire pastoral staff."

"Seriously? You believed them? Dad, you know me better than that."

"You're right." He sighed. "So, what really happened?"

"It's not as bad as it sounds. The fact is, I turned in my two weeks' notice and they let me go the next day. No one escorted me anywhere. I didn't tell off the pastoral team, but --"

"Why did you turn in your notice?"

"Because I'm close to getting a better job."

"Honey, you shouldn't need to get another job. You had a great job."

"Dad! Remember? They brought Mrs. Rizetti and her buddies to learn everything I did and take over my job."

"Uh huh. That scheming twit doesn't have me to punish, so she's taking it out on you." He sighed. I imagined him getting that hound dog sorrowful look in his eyes. "Now what's this about you missing church?"

"I have a new church, Dad. I'm not turning into a heathen."

"Very funny, little girl."

"When did Rod and Calvin give you the latest gossip?"

"They just got here for a week of golfing. I could have about strangled them, not telling me earlier. And I'm pretty riled at you for not telling me sooner."

"What could you do about it? The guys have exaggerated things. There's nothing to worry about."

"Nothing to worry about, she says. You *are* looking for a new job?"

That was another thing about Dad -- I had to tell him at least a dozen times before some details would stick. Like, duh, why would I turn in my two weeks' notice if I wasn't looking for a job? It was financial suicide, at the very least.

"Looking, signed up with online search sites and a local Christian agency. And I almost have a job nailed."

"Uh huh. Where?"

"Holy Spirit Independent Alliance." I held my breath. Dad was as rabid about sports as any resident of Cleveland and its suburbs.

He laughed.

When he finally got off the phone half an hour later, he was assured I was going to be fine. I got him caught up on the church news I had gleaned from Reggie and my few friends who cared to keep in contact. At least Dad was ready to discount any other stories his friends passed on to him. I should have been feeling pretty good. Impending lectures averted.

I felt deflated enough to give up my redecorating plans and go upstairs. Besides, all our talking had worn down my battery, and I needed to plug my phone in to recharge. For all his faults, Dad had taught me to pay attention to little things like power charges, turning off lights, blowing out candles, and making sure the refrigerator door closed all the way.

What had me down was the realization that came with my new insight into myself. Dad taught me to let people walk over me for the sake of peace. It affected every part of his life, with his disapproving and estranged family. His way of handling their criticism had been to avoid them, rather than face them down. Of course, Mom got blamed when Dad didn't keep in contact with anyone after they moved to Florida.

Asking if I was looking for work was the extent of getting involved in my problem. Dad had made an art form of ignoring situations where he couldn't do anything.

I remember when I was a kid, coming home from miserable visits with grandparents, aunts and uncles. They ignored me and constantly made snide remarks about Mom, in front of her, as if she wasn't there. She would be in tears on the drive home, and Dad would look over at her at a stoplight and say, "What? Why are you crying?" He honestly had no idea.

He was doing the same to me now. I had been primed from birth to think a relationship where a guy put me low on his list of priorities was healthy, normal, and acceptable.

The only difference between my relationship with Thad and my parents' marriage was that under his ineffectiveness, Dad really did love Mom. She knew it, and he did try. When he remembered. Thad had a long way to go to approach the outskirts of loving me. I didn't have that kind of patience. I didn't love him. Sure, we had some important things in common: loving the Indians, despising politicians, enjoying the Lake Erie islands. Still, beyond leading the Singles, what did we have?

Time for a high-fat comfort food lunch: raisin bread, peanut butter, three kinds of cheese, and mayonnaise, in my George Foreman grill until everything just started to melt together. And a bag of barbecue chips to wash it down.

I finished assembling the sandwich when the doorbell rang. Mrs. Grant, dressed all in black with a deep purple blouse and scarf, stood on my front step. I did what any intimidated, well-mannered girl would do: I invited her inside and offered her a cup of tea. Although I didn't have any tea made.

She declined the tea, though I did earn a tight little flat smile for my good manners.

"Dinah, I think you need to be aware of the falsehoods circulating the church regarding how you ended your employment there," she began.

So much for small talk.

Chapter Eleven

"I've already heard some of them," I said.

"Including that you were fired because you aren't married?"

"Something like that." I sat down on the couch facing her, feeling a little warmth blooming in my chest at the thought that she was angry on my behalf.

"Sometimes I wonder why we bring people into our congregation, why we welcome them so warmly and let them get involved so quickly, without at least a period of testing." She slowly pulled off her gloves with that elegant precision I had always envied. And feared.

"Excuse me?"

"I'm sorry, dear." She reached across the gap between our seats to pat my hand. "Old grumbles. Problems that have plagued our church, and the Body of Christ, for centuries. The short version of the story is that a fringe element that, I have recently learned, was essentially driven from their original church, is trying to change our church to suit them. Thad referred to it as terra-forming, though I'm not sure what that means."

"Science fiction, mostly. People go to an alien world and change the environment to suit them. Basically killing off the native life." I swallowed hard, having an awful idea of what she was about to tell me. "Go on."

"This group has volunteered at every level of our congregation. Everyone just loves volunteers, passing responsibilities off to others. Quite a few people are simply worn out with carrying the duties that ten times as many people should be handling. Everyone is so grateful to have helpers, they don't pay attention to what those helpers say, how they are changing basic principles, basic practices ..." For a few seconds, Mrs. Grant drifted off, looking a little sad, a little weary, and about twenty years older than she usually did.

Then she sat up straight and wrapped around herself that field of energy and crispness that so many women her age, and thirty years younger, couldn't hold onto.

"All this is still in the investigative stage. I would appreciate you not discussing this with anyone." She tried to smile. "I hope you are still in contact with your friends at church, that all this ugliness hasn't cut you off from them. The possibility of a church rift, which could destroy all the good we've done in the community, has required the investigators move slowly. Quietly. I was upset to learn that so many in the church leadership, the leading families, have been kept in the dark about both the infiltration and the investigation. Until now. The reverberations from your unjust treatment are having some good impact. Making people sit up and look around, and realize something is wrong."

What could I say? It didn't sound like I was the hero in this weird kind of politically charged scheme. Just a pawn.

"In simple terms, these newcomers are trying to turn us into a supposedly, *allegedly* family-oriented congregation."

"That sounds fine, but I'm guessing it's something totally different from what we think?"

"Exactly." She nodded for punctuation. "Their idea of family-oriented is that everyone *must* be married. They believe single men and women have no hope of getting into heaven. Not only must you be married to earn the Lord's approval, but you must produce children."

"What about the people who are sterile, or miscarry? Or the people too old to have children?"

"That's what got them driven out of their previous congregation. They insist such people are under God's judgment. Well, they insisted their minister and his wife had turned themselves over to Satan. When she miscarried for the third time, it was God's punishment. The congregation nearly shattered before most of the people came to their senses."

"And the gossip never reached us, to warn us," I said. As church secretary, I would have opened an email or a bulletin from the denomination, if people in authority knew about this ugliness. "How come stupid stuff spreads like wildfire, but the important information, to protect us, never gets past the church doors?"

"If we could solve that, dear, we would be that much closer to our Lord's return." She smiled at me, a little bit of grim humor, and for a few seconds there, I felt like we had reached some sort of unity of mind and understanding.

Then I got that shiver of warning up my back. The worst of the news was yet to come. I sat back and wrapped my arms around myself for a moment, but that was weak body language. I settled for clasping my hands in my lap, really tight.

"So what else are they doing and saying?" I asked.

"They're insinuating themselves into every ministry and committee. They haven't managed to get their hands on the checkbooks yet, but our investigators are sure that's the next step. After duping enough people into accepting their rhetoric without thinking what it means, they could oust everyone who disagrees with them. Under the guise of trimming excess from the budget and conserving resources and energy, they're deleting programs that don't conform to their idea of family-oriented."

"Uh huh." I nearly grinned at the flash of insight. "They attacked the Singles program, didn't they?" Now some of it made a twisted kind of sense.

First step, get rid of the most visible single in the budget: me and my salary. Now to trim out the Singles ministry. I nearly snorted at the idea of them bringing in a matchmaking service, like Gertie and A Match Made In Heaven, to force singles to pair off and get married.

These people would have trouble trimming the Singles program. It was mostly self-supporting, taking care of expenses through pay-to-participate. The church provided about $50 every month for refreshments, sending postcards for follow-up to visitors, and materials for the bulletin board. Participants paid for the gas when they used the church vans. Taking that money away from the Singles wouldn't close down the program. However, taking the Singles off Pastor Steve's list of duties would free him up for other work. The neglect alone would reduce membership.

"They're trying to trim the pastoral staff, aren't they? Get rid of the ministers and their wives who don't have children? Maybe fire the two custodians who aren't married? Maybe insist we only employ married men with families to support?"

"Exactly. Their mistake was arguing with people who have stepped up as your champions. They said too much to some married men who are friends of Thad. The silent type who don't let you know what they're thinking until it matters. Their silence led these people to believe they shared their alleged values." Mrs.

Grant sniffed with a delicacy that shouted her disdain. "Thad went on the Internet and tracked some of them down by articles they published on an obscure, lunatic fringe website and, well, it's all starting to unwind on them. Not fast enough to suit me, but eventually we will have the evidence and moral support to cleanse our congregation and put things back as they should be. As the first real casualty in this disgusting campaign, I thought you should know."

"I don't suppose our denomination practices excommunication?"

Mrs. Grant laughed at my lame joke. Just a sharp little chuckle, an even sharper gleam in her eyes.

"The element in our church that is always pushing to save money, to trim expenditures, and yes, to get more work handed over to volunteers, became their dupes. Their tools. Working by remote control, in Thad's words. All these extremists had to do was concentrate on the money aspect, put the right words in the money people's mouths, aim them at a target, and set them loose. Getting them to admit they were wrong, that they were used, will take some careful maneuvering. We must prevent a split that could put our building and resources in the wrong hands." She shook her head. "Listen to me. I sound as bad as them. It isn't the building that matters, it's the threat of a split. Damage to our congregation must be prevented at all costs."

"I didn't really believe what Pastor was saying, about not encouraging single girls to stay single. I thought he just didn't want to admit it was all about money."

"Oh, Pastor Marcus is infuriated, now that he can see he has been used. Believe you me, he is on the warpath now."

I muffled a snort, because quite frankly, I could envision it. Pastor Marcus was passionate about making our church a vibrant tool for Heaven. He had stepped on a lot of toes. Too bad he hadn't stepped on the toes of those involved in this plot.

I wanted to find out if Mrs. Rizetti was part of the "everybody must be married to get into heaven" clique. Call them a cult? I imagined she had gladly joined them when she realized what they taught. It certainly explained why she loathed me so much and blamed me for Dad escaping her planned trip to the altar. She thought I was denying her a ticket to heaven.

My head hurt, trying to figure my way through the tangle.

"So what do --" I refused to ask what she needed me to do. Central Avenue's problems weren't mine, because it wasn't my church anymore. Still, my conscience spoke up and reminded me with a good hard pinch that I should sit down and pray for them until they got through the whole mess.

"So what are you going to do about all this? I mean, I appreciate you explaining it all to me. I don't know if it makes me feel any better, knowing it wasn't personal, I was just collateral damage, but ..." I shrugged.

"My dear." She briefly squeezed my hands. "You have been hurt so badly, in so many ways, in the last few weeks. And at Christmas. You're essentially alone in all this, thanks to the silly political games even you young folks play." She sighed and sat back. "You don't have to be alone, you know."

"I'm not. I have lots of friends."

Well, to be honest, Reggie was the only one who kept up contact. I had talked to our Christmas Day group several times, but we were all busy with work or trying to find work, and personal issues. I knew the other girls were there for me, but I had my doubts about them dropping everything and running to my rescue at a moment's notice. Maybe because I doubted my ability to do the same for them. Hardly anyone else in Singles had made any effort to stay in contact with me. To be fair, I hadn't reached out to any of them, either.

"That may be, but I wish you would give Thad another chance."

"Mrs. Grant, I'm flattered that you want me to -- to be with Thad." No way was I going to say *marry*. "But I don't love him. I think he's proven he doesn't love me. If I wasn't useful, would he have anything to do with me?"

"Don't be silly. There's more to you than being useful. You're clever and pretty and wholesome and --"

I had heard that before, in too many forms. It was not encouraging.

"The bottom line," I broke in, "is that I've spent my whole life, it seems, accommodating other people and putting others first, without anyone ever putting me first. I'm tired of feeling useful instead of feeling appreciated."

Mrs. Grant's face lost its softness and she sat up a little straighter. "Well," she said, with a hint of frost in her voice, "your new job might make you feel admired and adored, but honestly, how long will the honeymoon last? There is a great deal more to marriage than love, and more to serving God than feeling appreciated. The sooner you learn that, the sooner you'll stop feeling sorry for yourself and expecting the impossible."

"Oh, I know that. I'm a realist. Maybe too much." I stood up, and to my surprise, she stood up too, and we headed for the door. "But reality is no excuse for expecting women to lie down and be doormats in the church and in marriage, and for people to be ignored and kicked around, and used like pawns in a big chess game of church politics."

She stiffened a little more, then that tired look washed over her and her shoulders softened and she sighed.

"Maybe you're right. Maybe you've been hurt too much, and ignored for too long, to forgive as easily as we could wish. But you have to forgive. I've learned that the hard way. Several times, I learned it too late." She patted my shoulder. No more hand squeezing. "I've done what I came to do. You have some explanation for recent events. If you could just think about what I said ... well, I'm still holding out hope for you and Thad."

The most I could manage was to thank her for coming. The mature, Christian thing to do would be to ask her to tell Pastor Marcus and the others who had been dupes that I forgave them, I understood they were being used, and I didn't hold any grudges.

Would it be the truly Christian thing to *lie* and say I forgave them? Truthfully, I *did* hold a grudge. I was tired of being the one who got hurt in the power struggles and had to forgive with only half-hearted and partial apologies, mostly done to look good. First with Dad's relatives, then the church youth group, Singles, and now my job. Former job.

When is it going to get better, Lord? When do I get happily ever after?

<><><>

Russell called that evening for stargazing Thursday night. The weather was supposed to be a little warmer, clear, no wind, and the location was next to a lodge in the Metroparks, with fireplaces and hot chocolate close at hand. Nicer surroundings. I was just rankled enough over Dad's phone call and Mrs. Grant's visit, still seething over the sense of being abandoned, I agreed. I got the sense he was nervous, and my going meant a lot to him. That soothed my wounded vanity. It was a win-win situation for both of us, I figured.

I had a nice time. Honestly.

Russell wasn't nearly so geeky in the dark. His voice sounded much nicer, warmer, when I wasn't looking at his face. He was running late when he picked me up, so we avoided the awkwardness of asking him inside while I got my coat and hat and gloves. He did most of the talking on the drive over to the lodge, filling me in on the stargazing group, telling me about some of the amazing things he managed to see. He had started with a telescope his father gave him when he was ten. The kind that could be found on a toy store shelf in the science and education section, with a few simple lenses. He worked his way up to more complicated equipment that let him change focus and filter out different kinds of light. The telescope he had in his trunk wasn't his best or biggest. That one was too big to remove from its permanent mounting on the deck at home, inside a special shelter he had built that let him study the stars in all weather and protected the delicate instruments. The one he had brought tonight had a digital camera.

Russell was smart, and he grew more assured with every sentence. He didn't strike me as doughy and uneasy. He certainly wasn't quiet. I kind of liked this side of him, and what he told me was interesting. At least, until he started using so many technical terms, I couldn't follow him. I let him keep talking without asking for clarification and prayed there wouldn't be a test later. I preferred him doing all the talking, focused on his interests and not asking me any questions. At the back of my mind, I was worried I was going to end up with another Inquisition like his mother put me through last Sunday.

There was something nice and quiet and safe, at the same time feeling very small in the grand scheme of things, standing there in the cold and darkness under the stars. There were perhaps thirty in the group, with twelve telescopes among them. We went into the trees beyond the lodge, which reduced the interference from city lights, according to the leader of the group,

Scott. The snow had been swept off the relatively flat meadow, and the grass crunched a little under our feet. Occasionally a soft touch of chilly breeze washed over us, but for the most part the trees on three sides sheltered us. Our breaths clung to us in softly drifting clouds that slowly dissipated as the warmth and humidity chilled and crystallized and fell. Everyone spoke just above a whisper. Like maybe they thought the stars would hear and hide?

There was a long pause as the owners of the telescopes set them up and compared notes and offered advice, and the rest of us stood to one side, waiting. I had no trouble picking out the first-timers from the regulars who couldn't wait to get an eye-full of the night sky up close. I kind of envied the regulars, and wondered what it was like to be in love with the stars, but unable to afford a telescope of my own. It had to be frustrating, maybe even humiliating, to rely on the generosity of others.

Russell offered me the first look through his telescope, once he got it set up. It really was quite an impressive arrangement, with multiple legs and several tubes sticking out of the side and electronic gizmos with all sorts of blinking lights and LED displays and buttons. It even had a little box that sent warm air around and through the telescope so the cold air didn't settle condensation on the lens.

When he proudly stepped back and gestured for me to come up and look, two guys stepped up with me. One opened his mouth, and the sour tilt of it hinted he was going to tell me to go away. Then Russell said my name, and grinned. Both of these strangers stopped short and their mouths dropped open. Likely, Russell had never brought a date with him before.

They stood a couple feet away, muttering to each other under their breaths, while I leaned in and put my eye to the viewing cup and tried not to touch anything. Russell sounded like a kid explaining his favorite video game. He walked me through the process of adjusting the tracking so I could scan the night sky and see the entire sweep of what looked like a long spill of sugar across the blackness. When I tipped my head back and eyeballed the approximate area in the sky where those stars lay, I couldn't see them. Not even a distant gleam. The pressure of those two guys glaring at me grew strong enough that I stepped back a little sooner than I wanted to, and gestured for someone else to take a turn.

"Don't you like it?" Russell asked, sounding a little disappointed. I could only imagine that kicked puppy look on his face. The darkness did wonders for my impression of him.

"It's incredible," I said, being totally honest, "but your friends have been waiting their turn long enough."

"Oh. Yeah." He chuckled nervously. "Sorry, guys."

He never introduced them to me, and they never introduced themselves. We just stood there, the four of us, taking turns in the dark looking through the telescope for the next three hours. They spoke in a lot of technical terms that went way over my head, and I seriously doubted they noticed when I stumbled to the lodge, surrendering to my frozen feet and fingers. I took time to defrost in front of the fire and enjoy a cup of hot chocolate before I went back out. I had a sudden fear I would find Russell had packed up and left without me. After all, Dad had done that to me several times growing up. Just in case Russell did miss me, and think maybe I had abandoned him, I brought hot chocolate in covered cups for all three of them. Plus another cup for me. Miss out on free hot chocolate with marshmallows? Nuh uh. My mama didn't raise no fool.

It was nearly midnight when Russell brought me home. That didn't really matter, since I didn't have to get up for work the next day. He did, though. He laughed when I asked him about it, and how many nights he stayed up late, stargazing.

"Whenever I can, as late as I can," he said, as we pulled into the driveway. Most of the drive home had been taken up with him spilling all his enthusiasm over the things we had looked at that evening. He finally named his friends, but only in passing, "Theo thought this," and "Roger was hoping for that," but of course, I didn't know what faces went with what names.

"What time do you start work? Don't you have a hard time getting going in the morning, if you stay up late every night?"

"Oh, my workday starts around ten."

"Nice," I muttered, and refrained from asking if he knew when my workday would start, *if* I got the job. Tomorrow was Friday, and I would hear one way or the other if I was hired. Suddenly, I was a lot more awake than I wanted to be at that late hour, jolted with a dose of pure adrenaline.

Please, Lord? I really need this job. It feels like such a nice place to work, and attend. Please?

It occurred to me that lately, most of my prayers had been self-pitying, and asking for the people who had hurt me to get a good slap from God, maybe a dose of their own medicine. That kind of stuff ran strong through the Psalms, which seemed like implied permission to grumble to God, but I didn't think the Psalm writers meant to say it was okay to always grumble and complain and dwell on our hurts and trials and injustices. Right?

"Yeah, well, I'm sort of on call, especially on Sundays. There's always something that needs to be tweaked around. So Pastor said it's only fair that my regular work hours be trimmed back a little, to compensate. He's come stargazing with me a couple of times."

I heard the grin in his voice, even though I wasn't looking at him right that moment, being busy digging for my keys in my jeans pocket. I got out of the car and thanked him for a fascinating evening. He asked if I would want to do it again.

"If you can guarantee another night like this. You know, quiet and clear and hardly any wind. And lots of hot chocolate," I added. Russell laughed. "Sure. That might be fun. If my schedule allows," I hurried to add.

One of the many dating rules Reggie and I had created over the years was to never, ever, on pain of death, give a guy the impression that we had nothing at all to do, or we were willing to drop everything to accommodate his plans.

"I've got a lot to teach you, Dinah. We're going to be so happy -- I mean -- um -- we'll have a great time together. You like me, don't you?"

"Well, I hardly know you. But I like the guy I've seen so far."

"Me, too. See you in church?"

"Sounds good. Good night, Russell. Thanks." Then while he was nodding, I quickly pushed the car door closed and hurried to my back door.

He didn't start backing out of the driveway right away. I waved, hoping he would take the hint, then put my key in the lock. I finally saw the brake lights turn to the white of reverse when I had the door open.

After I was safely indoors and Russell's car had vanished

down the street, it occurred to me that he was being a gentleman. He was making sure I could get inside the house, rather than waiting for a chance to leap out of the car and attack me. It did feel a little creepy to have him watching me.

Which just showed how little I had expected from Thad. Usually he had shifted the car into reverse as soon as I closed the car door. He was gone before I got the key in the lock.

If I had a diary, I would have written a couple paragraphs about my date with Russell Prince that night, and smiled. True, it would have been about the stargazing, rather than him, but I still would have smiled and written more than the bare bones.

<><><>

Friday morning, while I was making one of Mom's long-forgotten recipes, I got **The Call**. Pastor Paulson himself called me to say he was delighted to offer me the job. Could I start first thing Monday morning?

Of course I could. Not because I didn't have anything else to do. I had a huge list of things to do around the house, ridding and sorting and renovating. I needed to get to work, to be around people again. I needed to get on with making my new life.

"Would you mind letting us introduce you to the congregation on Sunday?" he asked, once we had the details settled, such as my starting time, a luxurious 9 a.m.

"Uh, I guess. What does that entail?"

"You would attend both services, and I'll call you up to the platform just before the sermon, to announce you're coming on board, let everybody get a good look at you, and then pray for God to bless your time of ministry with us."

"Well, I sure could use as much prayer and God's blessing as I can get," I quipped. Maybe not the most intelligent thing to say, but Pastor Paulson chuckled. "Sure. What time do you want me there, and where do you want me to sit?"

What else could I do but agree? It wasn't like they would rescind the job offer if I refused, but it was smart to get off on the right foot. Besides, I liked the idea of being open with the congregation. Tell them all at one time, everybody heard the same thing, and nobody could claim they were left out of the loop.

Reggie didn't come to church with me that Sunday. She had to attend our -- ***her*** -- home church, and assure her parents and grandmother she wasn't dropping out.

I sat in the second row from the front, primed to get up and come onto the platform, stand there and smile and try not to trip moving up and down the steps. I attended the first service, and planned to leave the sanctuary during the second service.

Zach surprised me by showing up and settling in the pew next to me, when I arrived for the first service. He grinned at me, and I realized I was staring at him, my mouth dropping open.

"Hey, don't look so surprised. Some of us do get up for the early service. These are the hard core folks, worship the Lord with the rising of the sun and all that."

"Hard core." I muffled a snort and looked around. There were only about fifty-some people in the sanctuary so far, so my first introduction wouldn't be overwhelming.

"Of course," he said, leaning closer and lowering his voice, "there's this theory that these folks show up so early so they can do some fishing or whatever the rest of the day."

"Fishing? In this weather?"

"Ice fishing. Don't you ever see those holes in the ice in the Metroparks in the winter?"

The organist shifted from the prelude music to the first hymn, and Pastor Angela, the choir director, stepped up to lead the congregation in singing. Zach kept giving me sideway looks, like he knew I was trying to come up with a smart-alec answer, and he was just daring me. I wisely kept my mouth shut.

It turned out he had to come up onto the platform with me, so Pastor Paulson could thank him for finding me. He looked about as comfortable being there as I felt. Zach and I were a lot alike in that aspect. We worked hard, we did the best we could, and most of the time we preferred to stay in the background, providing support and organization. It was nice to be recognized and valued for our contributions, but we didn't live for the spotlight and the applause. Facing all those unfamiliar faces, people who would expect me to be a miracle-worker, was a little daunting.

Zach was with me between first and second services. He was a witness when Mrs. Prince and Russell tracked me down. Of course, she did all the talking, dividing her attention equally between welcoming me to the church staff and casting adoring glances up at Russell.

"Of course, it's a pity that it won't last very long. We do need someone with your talents and servant's heart, so very badly."

"What do you mean, it won't last?" Zach asked.

Mrs. Prince looked startled, and I could have sworn she hadn't realized he was standing right there, listening.

"Well, when Dinah gets married, she certainly can't spend her days in the church office. She'll be needed at home." She wore that fake smile I always saw on Mrs. Rizetti at her sugary worst.

All the more reason to avoid her.

"I have no intention of looking for a husband," I hurried to say. "I'm busy putting my life back together."

"Yes, but when God puts the man He's chosen right in your path, don't you think it's sinful to ignore His leading?" She fluttered her eyelashes at me. I realized how stupid and affected that looked and made a mental note never to do that again, except to be silly or irritate someone. "How could a girl of any intelligence ignore the gift that God has sent to you?"

Then she looked up at Russell adoringly. My stomach took a nosedive, and I nearly clutched at Zach's hand for support.

Maybe it was arrogant. Maybe it was paranoid. I was suddenly painfully, nauseatingly sure Mrs. Prince planned on me marrying Russell. After one date!

That settled it. I might have had fun, but I was never going on another date with Russell Prince. Not even if he was the last straight, disease-free, church-going man in the entire Cleveland area. Heck, the entire state of Ohio!

<><><>

My first week in the office at Holy Spirit Alliance was exhausting, frustrating, exhilarating, humbling. They had equipment I had drooled over when looking through office supply catalogs. The worst part? I learned quickly that I did *not* learn quickly. The manuals were thicker than phonebooks for office equipment that seemed to do everything. Or they would do everything if I could figure out the instructions. With one touch, according to the manual (it lied), our printer the size of the Space Shuttle would scan, print, reduce to fit the paper, print both sides, collate, assemble, fold, staple, punch, and comb-bind.

If I could learn to speak its language, which wasn't any language known to human beings, or even in this galaxy. It wasn't just because the printer was made by a Japanese company, either. I was positive my counterpart in Japan was just as frustrated with the ridiculous, complicated thing.

Everyone was nice, willing and eager to help me straighten out the messes that I couldn't seem to avoid. More than one person shared his or her own harrowing experiences when the equipment first arrived. That was nice, but I was supposed to be there to help *them*, to take over jobs they had been handling since my predecessor went to help her sister.

Pastor Paulson sat me down after work on Thursday, when everyone else had left and I was staying late to finish up the bulletin. Oh yeah, and Russell, in the sanctuary, making an upgrade in the sound booth control panel.

"I can tell you're letting this get to you," he said, settling down on a chair by my worktable. "Don't let it. No job is worth tying your guts into knots."

"But I'm not this slow to learn, and I've just been making more work for everyone this week." I winced, hearing the whine in my voice.

"This week. Exactly. This is your first week." He shook his head, looking like a father who was amused despite the enormous mess the toddlers made with a bag of flour and a jar of grape jelly in the middle of the kitchen floor. "You're probably too irritated with yourself to hear this, but you're actually far ahead of a lot of people in the learning curve."

"Really?" I suspected he was just saying that to make me feel better, but I desperately wanted to believe him. Dad's side of the family had always made sure I knew I was slow, clumsy, and embarrassing to have around. Such treatment had a way of sticking with me and erasing all memory of praise and success.

"Really. You're picking things up faster than we had hoped, even given your record and recommendations." He sighed and cocked his head to one side. "We'll be sorry to see you abandon us when you get married."

"Married? Me? You've got to be -- you heard Mrs. Prince when she cornered me on Sunday, didn't you?" My face got hot enough I swore the ends of my hair started to curl.

"When Kayla gets something in her head, it's hard to persuade her otherwise."

"I swear, Pastor, I did not come here looking to snag a husband. I have no interest in marriage. I only went on one date with Russell, and I have no intention of going on any more."

His smile widened and he nodded. "That's what I thought, but I figured it was better to make sure."

"Just curious ... well, there's been a lot of ruckus over at my old church over the whole issue." Trying not to reveal the confidential information Mrs. Grant gave me, I outlined how the insistence on marriage and volunteering had been used to leverage me out of my job. "What is this church's stance on the whole issue of marriage and service?"

"Well, we consider ourselves family-oriented. But definitely not to that extent." He chuckled. "We firmly believe that family comes first. We urge our couples contemplating marriage to try their best to get by on one income, even if they're both working, and bank the rest. That way, when the children come, if they choose to have children, if the Lord chooses to bless them with children, they're used to one income so one parent can stay home with the children. We like to think we're open-minded enough to accept stay-at-home fathers and working mothers. We want at least one parent there to make the children their priority. Do you see what I'm getting at?"

I nodded.

"We want our people to stop worrying about money and the things money can buy, and focus on people. That's an ideal, of course. I dare anyone to say they fully live up to it." He smiled, but for a moment he looked sad, tired. "We urge people to devote their free time to service, yes, but not at the expense of their families. There has to be a balance, and we try not to condemn when parents put their children ahead of church service. I wonder sometimes how many young people leave the church at the first chance they get, because they saw themselves as abandoned by their parents for the sake of church service, rather than seeing the blessing of being in the Lord's service."

Something told me he spoke from experience. I didn't know him well enough to ask, but I hoped to be able to, someday.

"We have ideals about the family structure, and involvement in the church body, but there are always exceptions, depending on need. What good do we do the world if we stick so strictly to our doctrines, our policies, that we lose sight of mercy and common sense? We are very glad to have the help of the childless and the single, both as volunteers and as employees." He nodded to me as he said that last. Then he grinned. "Often the singles are the best, most dedicated workers in the church. Fewer distractions."

We both laughed at that.

I felt a lot better about my new job, and that someone besides Zach knew Mrs. Prince had made me a matrimonial target. I was actually able to smile, when I stopped in the grocery store on the way home.

Until I ran into Thad in the home cooking section, where the fully assembled, freshly prepared meals sat in long refrigerator cases. I didn't even realize it was him until we reached for the same package of sweet and sour chicken. We both paused with our hands nearly touching, looked, and grinned.

Chapter Twelve

I froze, recognizing him. His grin flattened, then turned to a scowl as he straightened up and stepped back.

"Hi, Thad." It was on the tip of my tongue to blurt that whatever he was riled about now, it wasn't my fault. Instead, I just nodded to him, snatched up the package that he had clearly abandoned, put it in my cart and turned to leave.

"That was a really low blow, Dinah." He yanked his cart around to walk beside me down the aisle.

I had the feeling he wasn't talking about my taking the last sweet and sour chicken.

"What are you talking about?" I didn't look at him but concentrated on the list I had made up. Gliding past the bakery, I snagged a package of sugar cookies. The soft ones with the icing almost as thick as the cookie, and candy sprinkles. I had the feeling I would need them before too long.

"Taking back my Christmas present -- your Christmas present to me."

"I didn't. Reggie did." I made a quick turn. He didn't take the hint and leave me alone. We headed through the deli section. If I stopped to fill up a deli tub from the olive bar, would he stay with me or leave me alone?

"What kind of a cold-hearted --"

"Fine. Follow me home and get your gift certificate back. Then we're even." Actually, we weren't, because I spent twice as much as he spent on me. While I would get the money back, I had spent time assembling the present, and I would have to spend more time returning all the pieces of the present.

He let me walk away after that. I didn't look back, so I had no idea of his reaction to my words. I felt a little odd, knowing Reggie had gone through with our plan. Sometimes we just mouthed off, making big plans for revenge and justice, but we hardly ever followed through. Mostly because we came to our senses. I would have to check with her and find out what had prompted her to make the raid. Something must have irritated her. I wondered why she hadn't called to say the deed had been done. I expected an earful when she did.

I didn't see Thad behind me when I pulled into my driveway, and he still hadn't shown up when I closed the garage and crossed my handkerchief-sized backyard to get to the house. Maybe he wasn't coming.

When I stepped into the house, the gift bucket was sitting on the kitchen counter. A queer ache shot through me when I saw it still wrapped in green cellophane, with the bow only half untied.

Thad hadn't even unwrapped it yet.

What did that say about his feelings for me?

I turned away, blinking hard against the totally unreasonable wet heat in my eyes. Habit had me check the answering machine next. Six messages. I was still listening to them, replaying each one and taking notes, when Thad came in the back door. I had left it hanging open, so he didn't bother knocking. He waited while I wrote everything down.

"It's nice to know you liked my present so much you didn't want to take it apart," I said, as I deleted the last message.

"Sorry." He closed his eyes, looking as tired as I felt. "I was just so -- well, on the way home, I woke up enough to think. You didn't even open the envelope. I figured you were mad. Which made sense. I started feeling guilty, and then everything blew up and ..." He shrugged and opened his eyes. "I'm sorry."

"Me, too." I had the gift certificate sitting on the counter, to remind me to give it back to him, so it was easy to hand over.

"Don't those people realize you're gone and you're not coming back?" he said, gesturing at my notepad.

"I don't know what they think anymore."

"Serves them right. Especially Mrs. Rizetti."

We both grinned. Mrs. Rizetti had lowered herself to leave me a message, scolding me for refusing to answer the phone when my church needed my help.

"I can't believe those calls all came in during the time you ran to the store," he added.

"The whole day."

"Why didn't you answer them?"

"Well, duh, because I'm at work. I have a new job. Believe it or not, someone *wanted* to hire me, despite what Mrs. Rizetti tells everyone." Just like that, my good feelings vanished, as quickly as they had come. "And I don't ignore any request for help. You think I write down all their messages just for the fun of it?"

"Maybe you should. Ignore them, I mean. Maybe if you don't bail them out all the time, they'll straighten out and apologize." He shrugged. "Even if it takes a while, like me."

"I wish ..."

His words did give me an idea. Before I could rethink it, I picked up the phone and dialed, and left a message on the church answering machine. Thank goodness the workday was over, because I did not want to have to deal with anyone.

I answered all the questions that had been left for me. No response for the griping or snotty editorial comments. Then I notified them I was working full-time, and would not be available during the day, so kindly stop calling me. Then requested they remove my name from the church membership, since I had found a new church to attend.

Thad headed for the door when I said that. He didn't say good-bye. I didn't follow him to the door. What was the use? We had essentially said everything that needed to be said.

I heated up my sweet and sour chicken and left a message for Reggie to call me. Then I burst into tears, all my thoughts in a tangle so I wasn't quite sure what I was crying about. Maybe everything.

I didn't want to cry for me and Thad, what might have been.

I didn't want to cry for all those years wasted, thinking that being the good girl meant letting people walk all over me.

I didn't want to admit that I wanted those self-righteous jerks to apologize. I knew I wouldn't forgive them. I knew I wouldn't believe any apology they made. It was too soon, and too many people had been shamed into apologizing, and then just kept being rude and demanding and abusive, which just proved they were never sorry in the first place.

I was too scorched to forgive.

Too bruised to forgive.

I just wanted to stop crying.

The sweet and sour chicken ended up down the disposal. I should have let Thad take it.

<><><>

Monday morning, bright and early, Zach called me at work. On my cell. I got as far as saying "hi" when the office phone rang. He heard it and laughed.

"That's okay. I should know better than to expect to have a real conversation during business hours," he said. "Call me back at lunch? I really want to talk to you. And not business." He laughed. "Hang up and answer that phone, okay?"

"Okay. Lunchtime." I laughed and clicked off. I caught the phone on the third ring. Not bad.

Even as I took care of the first emergency of the week, the back of my mind was churning over why Zach would call and say it wasn't business. What did he mean by "really" wanting to talk to me? I was hanging up the phone, and nearly dropped it, when I remembered his comment about me being conveniently close, where he could find me.

Was he -- ? Could he be -- ?

Interested in me, date-wise?

"Don't be an idiot, Dinah," I whispered, and got up to deal with the phone message I had just taken. Zach could have said something in church the day before. We had passed each other at least a dozen times. He could have sat with me in Singles class if he was interested that way.

When I got back to my desk, still gnawing on that little puzzle, Russell was waiting, leaning against the half-wall that separated my section of the office from the front area where the tag-team receptionists sat. He tried to look casual, but he wasn't a natural-born leaner. He kept fidgeting and changing which arm rested on top of the half-wall. It was somewhat endearing, and I felt a little uncomfortable for the poor guy.

"Hi, Russell. What can I do for you?"

"Saturday?"

"Excuse me?" I had the urge to dig my pinkie in my ear and search for earwax, because obviously I was having trouble with my hearing and missed most of what he said.

"Sorry." He flushed dark red. "I mean, let's go out Saturday."

"Oh, thanks, but I have tentative plans."

Actually, the plans were all in my head. I had yet to talk to Reggie about going to Lowes with me and pricing tile and gas fireplaces, to start renovations downstairs.

"Can't you cancel?"

"That depends. On my friend, mostly. Why? What were you planning on doing on Saturday?"

"It's a secret." He gave me a kind of trembling, nervous grin.

"You know, Russell, if we had been dating a long time, that might be fun. I've only gone out with you once. Secrets with someone I hardly know, that's a little ... odd." I nearly said "creepy," but the word stuck in my throat.

Russell did strike me as a little creepy. I remembered what his mother had said, and what I overheard between Zach and Gertie. My decision not to go out with him ever again firmed up.

"It'll be fun. I promise." He stepped forward and leaned down to rest both hands on my desk. He made me think of a big, flabby gorilla I had seen in the zoo when I was little, resting on his forearms, kind of drooping, fur patchy and eyes unfocused. I had felt sorry for the gorilla. I didn't feel sorry for Russell.

"Thanks, but I'm going to have to say no."

"It's special. You have to."

"No. I don't want to go out with you. Don't ask me again."

"You have to." He stood up, showing a little of that determination I had seen New Year's Eve.

"No, I don't."

"You have to because we're matched. It's on paper and everything. Scientific."

"What are you talking about?"

The phone rang and I dove to answer it. Emergency number two for the morning, and it was barely nine-thirty. I assured the panicking caller she had made the deadline. We did have rules, and they were even written down, so nobody could argue with them, which certainly made my job a thousand percent easier. She just needed to have a room set up for a Sunday school teachers meeting on Thursday night, but forgot to file her request on Sunday. When I got up to take the message to the custodians' office, Russell moved over in front of me.

"Please get out of my way. I have work to do."

"You have to go out with me." He held out a red spiral-bound notepad, with a thick wad of papers folded up inside it.

I edged past him and took my note to the file cabinet with the request forms, to find the floor plan for the requested room.

Russell unfolded the papers while I marked the places the tables and chairs were supposed to be. I found some comfort in the efficiency of the people before me in this job, to make things like room requests standardized and predictable. Understandable. Logical. Certainly not like Russell.

"You're my perfect match." He waved the papers in my face when I turned to leave.

"What are you talking about?" I knew better than to take those papers. Remembering a self-defense class in college, I moved out into a wider part of the office, so Russell couldn't back me into a corner.

Honestly, what could happen in a church office, with a dozen people within screaming distance? In thirty seconds, someone would come in. That's how much traffic there was, constantly. Then I really looked at Russell's big hands, holding out those papers. Big enough to muffle any scream I let loose. A big guy like Russell, no matter how flabby he might appear, could do a lot of damage in thirty seconds.

All those thoughts flew out of my head when I saw the logo at the top of the page.

A Match Made in Heaven. Surrounded by harps and hearts. All gold and pink. Gertie had been so proud of the new logo last week. She couldn't stop giggling over it.

I snatched the papers from Russell's hands and flipped through them. According to Gertie's printout, Russell Prince and I were a perfect match in nearly two dozen checkpoint areas.

Ain't no way! a voice that sounded like mine, at about age twelve, screamed deep inside of me. The echoes set off a headache that went down into my stomach.

I was relieved to see it didn't spell out specific details, only that we matched in spiritual interests, hobbies, food, entertainment, books, politics. The list went on and on.

"This has to be some mistake. I never signed up for Gertie's matchmaking." I shoved the papers back into Russell's hands. He didn't take them, but I didn't care. They fell to the ground while I beat a hasty retreat for the custodians' office.

Three ladies from the daycare at the other end of the building needed help making copies, when I cautiously returned to my desk. Russell was nowhere in sight. I took my time helping them decipher the instructions on the Space Shuttle/copy machine to put together a little coloring book for their afternoon class.

God answered a continuous stream of desperate prayers, and I was never alone in the office for the rest of the morning. I now considered it a blessing that the bus schedule was just off enough that I had to drive to work. I hopped in my car at lunchtime to head over to Match and clear up this problem.

"Dinah!" Zach was just coming back to the office with a big bucket of chicken when I pulled into the parking lot at Match. His face lit up when he saw me climb out of my car. "You didn't have to come up here, but I'm glad you did. How's it going?"

"Insane. Zach, how did my name and profile get in Gertie's matchmaking computer?"

"How did what?" His smile fell off his face like a broken mirror shattering in a cartoon. Then he got that grim, gritting-his-teeth look, and he turned to the door. "Come on." He tucked that bucket of chicken under his arm like a football. His other hand hit that door like he was deflecting oncoming players.

For about two seconds, I thought about my recurring dream of a white knight rescuing me. Zach didn't need armor. That scowl was armor and sword and lance.

"Gertie!" He looked around the office as he stomped up to her counter and leaned over it. She wasn't there.

"Maybe Russell called ahead and let her know I'd be on the warpath," I said, stopping just inside the door.

"Russell Prince?" Zach nearly dropped the bucket. He put it on the low table in the corner of the office, just as the bathroom door clicked open.

Today Gertie wore chocolate brown with lots of gold beads and bracelets, and a puffy, three-dimensional teddy bear appliqué on her shirt. She lit up when she saw me. Then she stopped short, her mouth open in greeting, when she caught Zach's scowl.

"What did I do now?" Pouting, she stomped over to her desk.

"Gertie, you want to explain how Dinah ended up in your matchmaking files, matched to Russell Prince, of all people?"

"Oh, good, he finally made his move!" She clapped her hands, and bounced into her chair.

"Made his move?" I stomped up to the counter next to Zach. "Gertie, he told me I have no choice, I have to go out with him."

"Well, yes. You're his perfect match. You won't be happy with anybody else. You might as well stop wasting time and get on with planning the wedding."

"Gertie!" Zach slapped both hands flat on the counter, making me and her jump. "It's scientifically impossible to guarantee something like that. Especially when you don't have even half the information necessary to fill out Dinah's profile."

"I do so." She nodded hard for punctuation, lips stuck out in a pout Veruca Salt would have envied. "I asked a lot of people who know her. And people who know her parents, too. It's not that hard filling out a profile when you know who to ask."

"But they're not the answers and information Dinah would have given you. It's her perception of herself that matters." Zach raked both hands through his hair and turned to face me. "Dinah, I'm sorry. If I had known what she was doing --"

"But Russell and Dinah are perfect for each other. And I pray hard over the people I put in the program. I'm positive God uses my program to bring the right people together, who never would have found each other."

"If they can't find each other, it's because they aren't in the same places, they don't run in the same circles, don't have the same friends," I offered.

"Exactly! That's why you need help finding the perfect man. Russell." She grinned again, making me wonder if maybe she had some seriously loose circuits under her crazy, curly hair.

"No, it means we don't have enough in common to be a match in the first place."

"Look, sweetie, Russell adores you. From the moment he first saw you, he knew you were the one for him. My matchmaking program just confirmed it. It's doing its job, because it gave him the guts to ask you out. You had fun on that silly little stargazing trip, didn't you?"

"You went stargazing with Russell Prince?" Zach asked, his voice going sort of soft and raspy, as if he found it horrifying. His eyes got sort of glazed and his mouth went flat.

"And about thirty other people, in public, in the cold," I hurried to say. "I also promised myself I would never go out with him again."

"You don't have to." Gertie crossed her arms. "You two are a perfect match. Stop wasting time and start your happy life together right away."

"No. The last thing I want in my life right now is dating and all the stupidity that comes with it. I have enough to worry about without housebreaking a new man in my life. I don't *need* a man in my life, and I don't *want* a man in my life."

Of course, that was giving Russell Prince the benefit of the doubt, that he even qualified in that category.

"Not ever?" Gertie's eyes immediately got sparkly with tears and her bottom lip trembled.

I muffled a groan of total frustration. Despite my resolve to be less of a doormat, the guilt factor worked on me every time.

"In a year, okay? Give me a year to catch my breath and my balance and figure out what I want in life. And heal. I've been through a lot, breaking up with Thad and switching jobs and all the garbage following me around from my old church and --" I made a concerted effort to stop that before I spilled everything. Mrs. Grant's visit still rankled at the back of my mind.

In that long moment of silence, swallowing my words and trying to remember how to breathe again, it was like my whole world narrowed down and all I could see was Zach's face. Sort of sad. Quiet, like an old dog that's been disappointed yet again, but still won't slink away.

I remembered my speculations after his phone call earlier, the few things he had said weeks ago, and combined them with what I had just said.

Could today's lunchtime talk have been a launching point for ... dare I say it? *Us?* Me, and Zach, going from individuals to an *us*, a *we*, a *couple*?

I had just ruined everything. That much was clear. I had to learn to keep my big mouth shut. Even if I was provoked.

What could I do to fix it?

I would have to give that a lot of thought. I had learned long ago that things broken in the heat of the moment needed to be repaired in the cool of logical thought and planning.

Besides, just how was I going to take Zach aside and tell him that my whole "no more men, ever" vow didn't apply to him? Gertie would hear and twist it around to suit her, just like she had created a profile for me.

Zach scolded Gertie until she promised to leave things alone. Most important, she had to stop insisting that Russell and I should just shut up and give up and get our marriage license.

Like -- ewwww!

He insisted that simply based on the scientific facts, there was no way Russell and I could be compatible. The profile she had put together was invalid. It occurred to me, on my way back to work, that the best way to shut up Gertie was to fill out the profile. The problem? I felt a little nauseous at the thought of voluntarily going into that matchmaking system. Who would it match me with? Did I really want to be hooked up with a guy who tried to take shortcuts by going through a computer program, instead of getting to know me face-to-face, the old-fashioned way?

<><><>

Russell didn't give up. He just shifted into stealth-and-drive-them-crazy mode for the next two weeks. Every time I turned around, he was somewhere, watching me, giving me these pitiful, kicked-puppy looks that would have made me feel guilty if I didn't feel creeped out. It affected my job. Efficiency was difficult while sensing eyes digging holes into my back, and never knowing when I'd return to my desk to find little tokens of affection. Not roses and poetry and jewelry, but chalky candy conversation hearts, and sticky notes with awkward hearts drawn on them and words like, "Destiny."

By Friday afternoon, the beginning of February, I was ready to fling the conversation hearts across the office and set the sticky notes on fire. I had a special bag for disposing of them. I started using it after Russell fished everything out of my waste basket and put them back on my desk. Real nice -- my stalker recycled.

I pulled the bag out of my bottom drawer and tied it up nice and tight, plotting how to get it into the trash compacter room without anyone seeing. I didn't want to know how Russell would react if he knew I had destroyed his love tokens, rather than trying to throw them out.

"Something wrong, Dinah?" Pastor Paulson asked, wringing a shriek out of me.

Fortunately, most of the staff had gone home. Including Russell.

"Russell sure looked depressed when he walked out of here."

He offered a little chuckle and shuffled over to my desk. "I guess you were too busy to notice, but he must have stood here in the door about ten minutes, waiting to say good-bye to you."

I had noticed, and I kept busy to try to block him out. After two weeks of increasing cold shoulders from me, he wasn't getting the message.

For answer, I spilled the contents of my bag on the desk pad. Nine days of candy and notes made a depressing pile.

"Russell won't take no for an answer," I said, as Pastor Paulson bent to pick up a few notes and hearts that had spilled onto the floor.

"Would it hurt to go out with him once? He might be a different person away from work."

"It's getting to feel like he's stalking me."

"Hmm, that's not good. What is he doing besides what I've seen the last few days?"

"Well ..." To be honest, Russell wasn't calling me at home. He wasn't following me when I went shopping. He was just everywhere at church. I finally admitted that and added, "I don't want to be a whiner, but it's a little creepy."

"I'll have a talk with him."

"Would you?" I might have kissed him.

"Russell really isn't that bad. I know he isn't dangerous."

"I don't feel threatened. Exactly. He just ..." I shrugged. If I was totally honest, Russell just generated a *bleah* reaction in me. The more he pushed, the more my knee-jerk reaction was *No way!*

His persistence frightened me -- I was afraid I would eventually give in. One success would encourage him to keep trying the same tactic to wear me down. I shuddered at the thought of Russell putting an engagement ring on my desk every day for months, until I either quit my job or gave in.

"Often in situations like this, you need to take some definitive action. If you give a little, he will have to as well."

"Give a little what?" My sense of gratitude died.

"Make a deal with him. If you give him one chance, and you say no, he'll never ask you out again."

"You think that'll work?" Part of me jumped at the chance of getting Russell to leave me alone. Was it worth the price?

"For the sake of the efficiency of this office, could you try?"

He winked. "I wouldn't cry foul if you made sure both of you had a miserable time. Take the romantic shine from his eyes."

I had to laugh at that.

He picked up a couple conversation hearts, shuffling them between his hands. "I was wondering what was bothering Russell. Usually he's so quiet. Efficient. People have remarked how distracted he's been lately. Then I started watching him, and realized he spends a lot of time watching you."

"I wish he wouldn't. It creeps me out."

"Russell would never hurt you. I'm rather pleased that he has the good taste to be ... well, fixated on you." He chuckled when my face heated up. I could just imagine how red it got. "Show the poor guy some mercy and go out with him at least once. Then you never have to go out with him again."

"Promise? If he won't leave me alone, you'll talk with him?"

"Promise." He crossed his heart. Then he popped two conversation hearts into his mouth. I kind of gagged and wondered how many times those hearts had been handled -- by Russell, by me, sitting on the desk, sitting in that bag, falling on the floor, going into the wastebasket a few times.

Probably not a good idea to tell him.

<><><>

I spent a very hectic Saturday by myself. I kept busy to try to avoid thinking. I ran every errand I could think of, and I didn't get a single thing done. Nothing appealed to me in the hardware stores. None of the tile or electric fireplaces or wallpaper. I toyed with replacing all my dishes. No luck there, either.

I couldn't talk to Reggie. Mostly I was afraid she would laugh. I couldn't call my Dad. His answer to conflict was giving in or running away. Most likely he would offer to find me a job in the Indians organization, and urge me to move to Arizona with him. Then he would try to match me with one of the "young guys" who worked there. Anyone more than ten years younger than Dad was a "young guy." I had heard enough about his work buddies to know I wouldn't want to date one. I was just too tired right now to want to take on a new boyfriend. I was too old, quite frankly, for housebreaking a man.

Essentially, I was in that no-man's land in a woman's life where the only men who might show interest in her were the ones she wanted to avoid. The irony in even silently, secretly labeling those kinds of guys "losers" was the terrifying, painful suspicion that made me a loser too.

No messages waited on my answering machine when I got home around six, after catching a matinee that I didn't even pay attention to. No messages on my cell phone when I turned it on.

Okay, thanks, God. Have You decided to start answering my prayers? Or has the world finally decided to leave me alone?

Of course, I thanked God too quickly.

Russell was waiting for me at the side door by the Singles class Sunday morning. He just watched me with that sad puppy look that made me feel guilty. I was too tired from my miserable Saturday to dredge up any anger at feeling guilty. I stepped inside the door while keeping him at arm's distance.

"Hi, Russell."

"Dinner? Tonight? I swear, just dinner. No secrets." He gave me such a hopeful look, I felt like a puppy-kicker for even thinking of saying no.

"If I go out with you, do you promise that if I say no more dates, you'll leave me alone?"

"Absolutely." He held up his hand in pledge. His smile was so bright, I felt more guilt for putting him off so many times.

He didn't follow me into the Singles class, which was good, because Zach was there in the doorway. He gave me an odd sort of frown, and he opened his mouth like he wanted to ask me something but couldn't decide if he should. On a hunch, I looked back over my shoulder. Zach had a good view of the doorway where I talked with Russell. He had to wonder what made Russell smile so big.

"Hopefully the misery is over," I said, as I walked past him into the classroom. There were very few people there, since it was still early. The coffee was still brewing and the hot water urn's red "ready" light wasn't on, meaning no tea or hot chocolate yet. Most of the people in the room were standing around the snack table, waiting for their drinks and nibbling on pastry.

"Misery?" Zach followed me and sat down in the same row, with two empty seats between us. How was I supposed to interpret that?

"Russell has been bugging me for nearly two weeks to go out

with him. Pastor suggested I go, with the understanding that if I don't want to go again, he won't ask me anymore."

"Uh huh. What happened to that resolution not to have any relationships for a year?" He smiled when he said it, and I prayed that spark I saw was teasing, and not something angry or mocking. Big difference.

"It's worth breaking it to avoid a year of Russell following me around everywhere and leaving love notes on my desk."

Zach whistled. "Poor guy."

"Poor guy?" My voice cracked and seemed to bounce off the ceiling tiles. A few people at the snack table turned to look at us. "What about poor me?"

"Yeah, you have it rough, being the object of desire for dozens of men."

"Yeah, you're just jealous, that's all." I swear, I had to say something. Remarking that I doubted Russell qualified as "men" was too snarky for Sunday. Besides, Thad was leaving me alone, and I didn't see anyone else pursuing me. Unless my speculation about Zach's interest was more than speculation?

He didn't have anything to say to that, but he kind of smirked at me and got up to get something to eat. He brought me a cup of hot chocolate without asking, so maybe he wasn't hurt or offended by what I said.

<><><>

Russell lied.

He said no secrets, but he didn't tell me that dinner didn't mean a restaurant -- it was at his house.

My first mistake was not arguing the moment I realized we weren't going to one of those quaint restaurants in an old house. I was partially paralyzed by a sense of panic and *déjà vu*. Then Russell parked and his mother appeared next to my door and she had the door open and nearly yanked me out of the car. For such a little woman who used a cane to walk, she was strong and had a good sense of leverage.

Well, I had to be polite, and let her drag me into the house. I had the awful feeling she was going on the date with us, as a chaperone. If that was her usual tactic, I wondered if she even knew about the stargazing trip with Russell.

Yes, stupid reasoning, but my brain wasn't firing on all

circuits. Mrs. Prince took advantage of it and got me out of my coat and into the living room before I could catch my breath and start coming up with reasons why I had to get out of there. Like, I was feeling sick and someone at work had exposed me to the Black Plague.

"Oh, this is going to be so fun. I've been so anxious to introduce you to our family," Mrs. Prince gushed as she settled down in an armchair that made me immediately think "throne." One of those big old antique wingback chairs with the tapestry cushions and gilding on the exposed wood of the arms and legs. With a matching footrest, to boot.

"Family?" Beyond her, in the next room, I saw a table just groaning with china and crystal and silverware and lace-edged linen napkins. Definitely not leaving soon for a restaurant. I swallowed hard. "Why?"

"Family is very important. It's so sad you don't have any you want anything to do with. I've heard all the poop on how your father's family treated your mother. Shocking. Terribly sad." She sniffed. "It's so sad your mother is gone. I've heard such lovely things about her." Mrs. Prince bounced in her seat, like a ten-year-old at the amusement park. "But it's so lovely for me. I've always longed to have a daughter and play mother of the bride. And now I get to plan an entire wedding!"

Chapter Thirteen

"Whoa. Wait a minute." I shot to my feet. Not smart, because my legs were wobbly. "What wedding?"

"Yours and Russell's." She giggled, like she thought I was being silly, and patted the chair, gesturing for me to sit. It was on her left hand. Russell settled into the chair on her right hand.

Horror stories I had heard from married friends, about in-laws and power struggles and parents who wouldn't let go and interfered with the marriage -- all flashed through my head.

This was a hundred times worse: a potential mother-in-law who had chosen the bride for her son. A bride who had no choice in the matter.

As if the nightmare couldn't get any worse, Mrs. Prince reached down next to her chair and brought up an enormous knitting bag and spilled it onto the ornate coffee table sitting in front of her. Bridal magazines avalanched across it, knocking the porcelain heart candy dish off the table. It didn't break, but the dusty-looking sourballs spilled across the carpet.

"No wedding," I managed to say, and couldn't get my gaze off all those magazines.

"You can't elope. How would it look?" She giggled again. I wanted to shove a couple of those sourballs in her mouth and stop that sound. It was really getting annoying.

"I'm not marrying Russell. This is only our second date, and a family dinner doesn't even qualify."

"Don't be silly. This is God-ordained. He told me you were sent to marry Russell." Mrs. Prince snatched up a magazine, sending others to the floor and scattering more sourballs. I had the worst urge to step on some and grind them into the carpet.

"I seriously doubt that." All right, not the best comeback, but I wasn't breathing very steadily, and I was feeling a little oxygen-deprived. It short-circuits the brain.

"It is. The match is perfect." She pulled a thick sheaf of papers out of the middle of the magazine, and I saw the Match Made in Heaven logo on the top of the page.

I should have ripped up that printout the first time Russell showed it to me.

"That match is faulty, because the profile isn't legal."

"Gertie Foster promised me --"

"Gertie is a crazy old interfering lunatic!" I snatched those papers out of her hand, and she stared at me, eyes wide and her whole body shaking a few times.

Was she going to have an epileptic fit? Or at least pass out, giving me time to escape while Russell took care of her?

Ohpleaseohpleaseohplease, God?

"Dinah, why don't you sit down, and we'll talk this out? When you see reason --" Russell began.

"You're the one who's not seeing reason." I tore that report in half.

I *tried* to. There were too many sheets of paper in the horrid thing to rip it in half. I settled for ripping half the stack, then the other half. They stared like I was shredding the Constitution.

"We agreed! If I went on this date, and I didn't want to go on any more, you would *leave me alone*."

"Don't be silly." Mrs. Prince regained that indulgent smile. Fortunately, she didn't giggle. She stared as I ripped the papers a third time, and a fourth. "You and Russell are getting married. You're disobeying God if you don't. I've already ordered the invitations. I have an appointment for you to try on bridal gowns next week."

"Cancel! I'm not marrying him and you can't make me!" Then I threw the confetti of the report in her face.

Yeah, real mature.

"Dinah -- honey," Russell blurted, horror making his face paler than usual.

"Don't talk to me ever again, Russell. Don't come near me at work. Don't even look at me!" Then I ran from the room.

For about two seconds I faltered when I couldn't remember which way to the front door and the closet that had my coat and purse. I found them, and I had my coat half on when the front door opened and a horde of people who all looked like Russell came in, calling out cheerfully. Every woman carried a foil-covered casserole. Any other time, the food might have smelled heavenly, but it just made me want to arch my back and heave.

"Oh, hello, honey!" a big, doughy-looking woman cooed. "Are you the bride?"

"No, I am not. Definitely not. Excuse me."

They must have seen something terrifying in my face, because those big people parted like the Red Sea before a furious Moses and let me through to the open door. The storm door clicked shut behind me before I heard Russell calling my name.

My exit would have been better if I could have jumped in a sleek black sports car and sped down the driveway, maybe leaving some tire tracks in the snowy grass. As it was, I slipped and skidded on half a dozen patches of ice and thanked God I had never gone in for high heel shoes. All my footwear was sensible; pumps and loafers and sneakers.

The *déjà vu* stopped there, because Russell didn't follow me in a car like Thad had. I got to the end of the driveway, and it was dark. Well, duh, it was seven on a February evening, with storm clouds rolling in all day. This part of town didn't have streetlights, only driveway lights, sporadic spots of white and gold.

At the first intersection, a large cluster of lights to the left hinted at stores, maybe a gas station, and a visible street sign. I hadn't paid any attention to where Russell drove me. Another mistake. Along with not demanding to know where exactly he was taking me to dinner *before* I got in his car.

Fifteen minutes of walking, wishing I had thought to bring a hat and gloves as the wind picked up, brought me to an intersection with a little strip shopping center. I got the street names and called Reggie to come get me. Then I went into the convenience store and stocked up on some caloric comfort, despite the inflated prices. Maybe my appetite had fled me, but since when did that matter when I had just gone through yet another rough time, courtesy of an oblivious, not-worth-the-powder-it-takes-to-blow-him-up man?

It took until halfway to my house to tell the story.

"Seriously," Reggie said. "You have got to quit that job. Or take out a restraining order on the weirdo."

"It's not Russell. It's his mother. And Gertie." I thought about telling Zach what had happened. Would he laugh? Would he chew out Gertie? Would he hold me, if I started crying?

"Yeah, but until his mother is gone -- like six feet under or in a place without telephones -- she is going to keep pushing him until he gets that ring on your finger."

"More like handcuffs, because I am not entering that house again unless it's under duress."

"Don't tempt fate, honey." She shuddered. Despite her attempt at a cocky, teasing grin, neither of us could laugh.

We got home. My cell phone rang just as we were opening up the ice cream and sugar-coated fruit pies I had bought. I checked it, fully expecting it to be Russell.

Dad. I flipped open the phone, and barely let him get out a cheerful, "Hey, honey, what's up?" before I burst into tears.

Reggie put our provisions away while I bawled and spilled all the sordid details. It took a while, because I kept having to back up the story and explain who people were and what had happened earlier. That would teach me not to keep my Dad updated on all the important details of my life. I could have spent half as much time on the phone, and he wouldn't have asked as many questions, if he already knew about Russell and Mrs. Prince and Gertie's matchmaking service.

Then a thought occurred to me that shut off the waterworks in mid-drip. Maybe I hadn't told Dad, keeping him updated, because he couldn't do much from Arizona? And yes, he had a pretty abysmal track record as a husband, and he forgot to pick me up more times than I wanted to remember in middle school and high school. The thing was, though, he was my *dad,* and he did care, and he had a right to know.

Things had been pretty quiet on his end for a while. At least three, four minutes. I sniffled and knuckled the last tears out of my eyes. Had I made him so angry, by leaving him out of the loop, that he had hung up on me?

"Daddy?"

"Oh, honey. I'm sorry. I feel like a lot of this is my fault."

"Huh?" I would have laughed if my throat and chest hadn't hurt so much from all my sobbing and hiccupping.

"We have a new pastor at our church out here."

I waited, instead of demanding an explanation for what this had to do with my problem and him blaming himself, when he was nowhere around. Some of my friends would probably say I had these problems because my father was absent and not interfering in my life, or running interference with the bozos who showed some interest.

"He's been dealing with me about my ... well, my habit of running away from situations." Dad sighed. "I basically grew up lying down for the sake of peace. I never thought anything was worth fighting over, or fighting for. Which means I didn't know how to fight when there was something worth fighting for. Or someone. Like your mother."

"She knew you loved her," I offered.

"See, my parents were so domineering. Always fighting. It was easier to just do whatever they wanted and let them fight over who would be in control of my life. If they were fighting each other, they left me alone. About the only time I ever defied them was to marry your mother. Pastor has been showing me how I basically betrayed her, day in and day out. Never defending her from my parents. The only woman I ever truly loved." He sighed, and there was a world of weariness in the sound. "When I lost her, I just kept running away, leaving you to deal with all the problems. Like Joyce Rizetti."

"Oh, so you did know she was after you before the explosion?"

"Oh, yeah. Big time. The bowling league had a betting pool on when I would finally give up and marry her." He chuckled. "Buddy and Sy got rich, when I ran for my life."

"So that's why some of the guys wouldn't talk to me for weeks after you left. Should have known."

"Yeah, well, I surprised everybody. The thing is, Pastor showed me that I left you a pretty bad example."

"I kind of figured that part out already, Daddy. I'm a wimp. There must be a sign over my head that says, 'Please walk all over me.' And no matter how hard I'm trying to change that, people still see the sign."

"The hardest part is learning to say no, I guess. No, I know. You have to say no and stick to your guns." He offered a raspy chuckle. "And beat a hasty retreat, like you did tonight. I would have given anything to see you throw those papers in her face."

"Daddy, what am I going to do? Besides keep saying no until people listen?"

"It's gonna be a long, hard haul, sweetheart. Keep telling

yourself that. Maybe keep asking what you really want, and remember the alternatives, if you don't stand up for yourself."

"Marriage to Russell Prince, living in his mother's house, wearing the dress she picks out for me." I shuddered, having visions of *The Dress That Ate New York.*

"It's going to get worse before it gets better. But I think you'll make it, honey. You've got your mother's guts and strength of will. She stayed with me, despite how miserable my family made her, didn't she?"

"Yeah, Daddy. She loved you. And she knew you loved her. That was enough."

When I finally got off the phone, Reggie was gone, I was cried out, and I was too tired to figure out if that quiet place inside of me was just emptiness and exhaustion, or peace and resolution. I caught up on my devotions for the past three days (probably skipping them added to my problem) and wrote six pages in my new journal. A lot of that big entry ended up being a rambling prayer, asking God to help me figure things out. Then I went to bed.

<><><>

Monday, Russell gave me the silent treatment. Pastor Paulson passed me in the hall, nodded toward Russell's closed office door, and waggled his eyebrows at me. Clearly asking how the date went. I shook my head and rolled my eyes. At lunch, he asked me to meet with him and Grace Spagnolli, the head of the ministry to women. We made everything official, and Pastor promised he would have a talk with Russell, to make sure he followed through on his promise. I know he had that talk, because Russell pouted and gave me these looks that clearly said I had betrayed him. Seriously?

Tuesday, Russell left me alone. Still pouting. I relaxed a little. It helped that I was getting to be an old hand with all the fancy-schmancy office equipment. I decided the copy machine was a pretty cool gizmo after all.

Wednesday, I had to hit the grocery store on my way home. I considered doing it after church activities that night, because it would be tight, going from work to groceries to home, unpacking, making dinner, changing my clothes, and heading back to church for the single women's Bible study.

I should have listened to that first idea: groceries *after* church. Making a priority of getting home and into bed by ten resulted in Armageddon in the frozen food aisle of my grocery store.

When I wasn't under stress, I tried to shop healthy. That meant going around the perimeter of the store where all the fresh food was. Depending on how hectic the day had been, I generally ended up circling in toward the frozen foods, the highly processed, sugar- and fat- and preservative-laden stuff that would be (questionably) edible twenty years after civilization ended in global thermonuclear war. Just like cockroaches, radiation wouldn't affect anything made of hydrogenated fats, high-fructose corn syrup, and white sugar.

I saw Gertie toddling along, heading straight for the center of the store. I had been avoiding Match because I didn't want to fight with her over Russell so very much not being my match. I pushed down my craving for ice cream and headed the opposite direction. Fresh fruit mixed with yogurt and drizzled with honey could be just as satisfying. I hoped.

I picked out some tiny clamshell boxes of overpriced raspberries and blueberries and considered pricing bags of frozen fruit. I glided through the salad area, envisioning a gorgeous, multi-colored salad in Mom's huge salad bowl that served twenty. The plan was always to make a big salad on Saturday and then eat off it for the rest of the week. Virtue always sounded wonderful when I was full of energy, or I had just stepped on the bathroom scale. Not so wonderful when I was stressed and had run out of the tasty, spicy, thick, low-cal dressing. My grocery store salad bar always put out interesting things like cranberries and raisins and nuts. Maybe I should stock up on some of those, for variety.

Irony: I was obsessing about food to cover the stress I was feeling, only I was trying to pretend I *wasn't* by obsessing about healthy food. Yeah, and if I binged on all that healthy food, just how healthy was it for me?

I shook off my daze. I had glided completely through the seafood section, heading toward the dairy section, with the bakery dead ahead. I turned around and promised myself a salmon steak if I stayed away from the sticky, sweet, doughy, deep-fried nirvana calling me.

"Dinah." Mrs. Grant blinked, and for a few seconds looked

just as surprised to see me as I was to see her.

Thad's grandmother was a lot of things, but I knew from experience she wasn't a very good actress, so this was entirely an accidental encounter. Mrs. Grant never needed to dissemble or play games to get people to do things her way. She was as straightforward as they came. I still had a soft spot for her, that she took the time to come explain about all the nastiness brewing at church.

"Mrs. Grant." I turned my head a little to see the contents of the basket hanging off her arm. Maybe that was my problem with shopping. I always took a cart, with plenty of room for loading up, while she took a basket and limited herself to the essentials. Smart lady. Would I ever be so smart and controlled and elegant?

"How are you? How is the new job?"

"Long learning curve, but I like it. Thanks." Before I knew it, I had responded to the little swing of her basket, the subtle turning of her body, and we were walking together along the dairy case.

She rested her hand briefly on my arm. "I'm so glad you were able to find work quickly. And not just because it frustrates those simpletons who think if they snap their fingers, you'll come running and take your job back, no need for an apology."

"Somebody wants me back?" That felt good. For about two seconds, I considered it. Seriously. Mostly to escape those mournful looks Russell gave me whenever he passed my desk.

"There have been ... murmurs. And some long overdue earthquakes are finally taking place." Her lips twitched just a little, about as close to a smug smirk as she would ever come. "So, where are you working?"

"Umm, Holy Spirit Independent Alliance."

Mrs. Grant laughed, three short, soft chuckles, and patted my shoulder. "Serves them right."

"You're not mad that I'm --"

"Working for the enemy, so to speak?" She gestured and I stopped to let her step in front of my cart so she could get a block of cheese. It was comforting to see she bought the house brand, rather than the gourmet and imported stuff on the other side of the store.

"I have been around long enough to finally wise up and see the truth. Those who aren't against us are for us. We might have different assignments from the good Lord, and different styles of clothes and music and food and what not. As long as we obey the Bible's teaching and not some idiotic 'new revelation' that contradicts the Bible, we are all Christians. The forces of Hell can only defeat us is if we let ourselves get splintered and divided over simple, silly things like sports and whether to dunk or sprinkle, if guitars and drums are blasphemous, or if wearing blue jeans in church will send your soul straight to Hell." She snorted delicately, and dropped her cheese into her basket for punctuation.

I stopped at the next open refrigerator section to get a carton of eggs. Yogurt was next.

"How is that, anyway?" Mrs. Grant asked, after I put a big tub of vanilla fat-free into my cart.

"You've never eaten yogurt?"

"It always seemed such a fad. My girls were into it, mostly because those gymnasts during the Olympics seemed to live on nothing but, and now my granddaughters..." She shook her head. "What do you do with the stuff?"

When I explained about my trick of fruit, yogurt and honey, she pointed at the flavored cups. I think I impressed her when I explained that no matter how healthy the brands, they added processed sugar or preservatives or gelatin.

She took a smaller carton of vanilla low fat, and we cut through the middle of the store, going between the freezer cases to head back to the produce aisle, for some fresh fruit.

We ran straight into Mrs. Prince and Gertie. Mrs. Grant stopped short and from the flattening of her mouth and the clenching of her hand around the basket handle, I guessed she knew Mrs. Prince and didn't like her. On the other side, Gertie looked positively lost. Mrs. Prince stiffened and snatched her cane off the handle of her cart. Sparks filled her eyes.

"*You*. I should have known you were at the bottom of this," she snarled.

"Bottom of what?" Mrs. Grant chuckled, but it wasn't a nice chuckle. It sounded like a chuckle a very slick movie villain would use while pretending to be a philanthropist who loved children and puppies.

Not an image I had ever entertained about Mrs. Grant,

despite our clashes. It made me curious about her history with Mrs. Prince.

"Pouring poison into the ear of my daughter-in-law." Mrs. Prince was nearly spitting. Amazing, considering that there was only one 's' in the whole sentence. She had a talent for it.

"Daughter-in-law?" Mrs. Grant looked around, trying to find a fifth person. Then everyone looked at me.

"Gertie put my name in her matchmaking program without my permission," I hurried to explain. "It matched me with Mrs. Prince's son, and they insist I have to marry him. But I won't. I refuse. If I'm going to marry anyone, I'd rather marry --" I choked because I wanted to say *Zach*. "Thad," I finished, and stood back, sensing the explosion about to come.

"Who is Thad?" Mrs. Prince demanded.

"My grandson," Mrs. Grant said. "They've been going through some rough patches, but I'm sure they're going to get back together. They've known each other for years."

"You filthy, lying whore!" She raised her cane.

I stood there like an idiot for half a second too long, before I realized she was going to hit me.

Mrs. Grant caught hold of the cane as it swung downward, yanked it from Mrs. Prince's hand, and flung it into the freezer case among the pizzas that were on special.

"You're a fine one to talk." The air temperature dropped about twenty degrees in two seconds. "You know what they say about people in glass houses."

"You!" Mrs. Prince toppled forward.

At least, I assumed it started with a topple, since she didn't have her cane to lean on anymore. Then she lunged at Mrs. Grant, skinny gloved hands bent into claws.

"Gertie, do something!" I tried to get in the way. It was tantamount to sacrilege to treat Mrs. Grant that way. I put up an arm and Mrs. Prince bounced off it.

Mrs. Grant was faster than me, or at least thought faster than me. She stepped around me and slapped Mrs. Prince hard on the cheek, sending her toppling into the side of the freezer bin.

Gertie just stood there, her mouth hanging open, eyes bigger than pop can bottoms, two bright spots of color in her cheeks.

I should have leaped in and tried to separate them, but I was stunned at the words coming out of their mouths. Both of them, snarling about harlots and cheats and liars and delusional manipulators, in between taking swings at each other and digging in the freezer case for ammunition.

Part of it, Mrs. Prince aimed at me. I was betraying Russell. Well, duh, I figured that part already, since she referred to me as her daughter-in-law, instead of *future* daughter-in-law. Excuse me, but I had to actually say, "I do," before I wore that label. As far as Russell Prince was concerned, it would always be "I *don't*." The funny-weird thing was, some of those words were coming out of Mrs. Grant's mouth, thrown at Mrs. Prince while she dodged frozen peas with the grace of a ballet dancer.

Customers gathered around. A couple people in the store's red uniform polo shirts came running. A man in a white shirt and blue tie, with a nametag carrying the store's logo, pushed his way through the crowd. I knew him from high school. He gave me this stunned look like he couldn't believe I was just standing there, watching.

That got me moving. I reached for Mrs. Grant, not sure where I should grab her. He nodded to me and snatched at Mrs. Prince's flailing fist. He got wacked across the face with a bag of broccoli. Lucky for me, as soon as I caught a grip on her sleeve, Mrs. Grant calmed down and let me pull her back out of the whirlwind. Mrs. Prince kept struggling, kicking and spitting and shrieking even louder, to make up for half the fight stepping away.

The manager -- Shaun, I think -- got a couple stomps on his foot, an elbow to his gut that almost made him set Mrs. Prince free, and a few backward slaps at his face. At least he got her away from the freezer case and deprived her of weapons.

"Let's get out of here." I took the risk of letting go of Mrs. Grant's arm to snatch up her dropped basket. I put it in my cart and tugged on her coat. She nodded, looking a little dazed, and we hurried back across the store.

In the coffee and tea aisle, I hooked a left and we headed for the registers. Just before we left that shelter, I stopped us.

"Are you okay? Do you want me to call someone?"

"Oh -- my." Mrs. Grant took a couple deep breaths and pressed her gloved fingers against her cheeks. A shaky little laugh escaped her. "I haven't done -- I've *never* done anything like that before." Then she gave me a little sideways glance as she tried to straighten her hair. It made me think she had indeed had a meltdown like that before. Long ago. In another lifetime.

With Mrs. Prince.

"I bet you're wondering what that's all about," I said, when I actually hoped she would explain to me.

"No. Kayla Heckert-Prince and I go way back. I wouldn't doubt she used the same tactics on you that she used when we were girls."

"Don't fight God's will?"

"If she didn't look so surprised to see me with you, I would have accused her of trying to match you with her toad of a son just to hurt me, by stealing you from Thad."

"She tried to get one of your granddaughters to marry Russell?" I guessed.

That earned a sharp little snort of laughter. She looked out across the open space between the end of the aisles and the row of cash registers. Her color seemed more normal.

"No. First she tried to coerce my brother into marrying her when we were in high school. He was considering the ministry, and she wanted so desperately to be a minister's wife. Reginald went into banking instead. I sometimes blame her for that change of course. Then she decided *my* boyfriend was the one God had sent for her. When he proposed to me, she had a snit and disappeared for a few years. Then when I was a widow, she returned to the Cleveland area. We were never close to begin with, so it amused me when she kept whining about how she missed being bosom pals."

"Then when Mr. Grant showed up, a widower, she decided God had ordained her to be a mother to his children?" I guessed.

"How the feathers flew when he proposed to me after only two dates." Her eyes sparkled for a moment, and that twitch of her lips hinted at something I never would have guessed.

"Why, Mrs. Grant, a whirlwind romance?"

"When you've got it," she said, patting the back of her hair, "you never lose it."

For a few heartbeats, we grinned at each other, and I honestly wished I could be part of her family and have the right to call her Grandma. I never really had a grandmother. Well, I did, obviously, but Dad's family just didn't count.

"Dinah ..." Her color faded a little. All this excitement hadn't been good for her, despite her being a feisty old woman with amazing depths and dimensions.

Chapter Fourteen

"Let's get out of here before she comes anywhere near the door." I aimed my cart toward the registers.

"Indeed." Mrs. Grant brushed her hair smooth one more time, straightened her coat, tipped her head back, and held out her hand. I gave her basket back to her and we crossed to the registers. She waited for me until I paid and took my bags, then looped her arm through mine as we crossed the parking lot. We both needed a little support, even if the parking lot was dry.

Despite all that, I went to church that night. I needed to be with nice people who didn't know most of the stupidity going on in my life. At the door of my classroom, I nearly turned and ran, when it occurred to me that someone from church might have been in the grocery store and seen what happened. The news might be flying around right that moment. I didn't have the safe partial anonymity of being a new attendee. Everyone in church knew me because I was their Gal Friday.

Time to stop running away, Dinah Clydesdale. I straightened my shoulders and walked into the room.

No one said anything. No one raised an eyebrow or blinked when, during the prayer request time, I asked them to pray for a lot of "weirdness" going on in my life. Some of the girls I was still getting to know gave me sympathetic looks. I didn't participate much, but that was all right. I was glad to get my thoughts off me and focus on God for a change.

Maybe that was my problem. Looking at me and not God.

Of course, Mrs. Prince would insist that was indeed my problem, but for entirely different reasons. She would say I had my troubles and difficulties because I wasn't listening to God telling me to marry her precious Russell.

Was that how she had trapped Russell's father? Insisting that God had sent him for her, confusing and exhausting him, until the poor man gave in and married her? Now I could see where Russell got his persistence. Mama trapped Dad by persistence, and he would trap his unwilling bride by persistence. Or driving her crazy until she collapsed, sobbing, and gave in.

Uh … no!

Tabitha walked with me after Bible study ended. She was one of those comfortable people who didn't say much, but when she did speak it was always worth listening to. I had learned to be comfortable in total silence with her. I liked it. Especially after the day I had just had.

"I don't want to be nosy," she said, before we turned down the short hallway to the door. "I noticed you talking with Mrs. Prince and Russell, and the way she looked at you. And then I was in the office a few times and he seemed to be hovering all the time. Are they part of the weirdness?" She offered me one of those wry, sympathetic little smiles.

"Uh, yeah." I couldn't stop myself. "Do they have a track record of ..." How could I phrase it without sounding gossipy?

"Deciding God's will for everyone else?" She rolled her eyes. "If you need support, we have a little survivors' club."

"How many are 'we'?"

"If you go to the pastors to have them get Mrs. Prince off your back, we'll stand with you." She started to walk away.

"You've gone to Pastor about Russell before?" I felt a little chilled at the thought that Pastor Paulson had encouraged me to go out with Russell, knowing his track record.

"Well, no. We figured that was a last resort. Usually we just get a friend from work to pretend to be our boyfriend. You can't do that, since you work with Russell." She shrugged and looked a little more sympathetic. "Anyway, we just hold hands with the guys, and walk around some place where Mrs. Prince can see us. She usually has a tantrum and calls us whores, gets laughed at, and then Russell leaves us alone. Like we're radioactive."

"Okay. Thanks. Good advice."

I played with the idea of asking Zach to pretend to be my boyfriend, to drive Russell and Mrs. Prince away. Would that encourage him to follow through on those hints he had thrown at me? Or just discourage him?

I had the awful feeling Zach would tell me to fill out a profile and run it against Russell, to prove we weren't a match. No, I couldn't. It felt like giving in.

Those thoughts completely fled my mind, when I stepped

outside and headed for my car in the parking lot. Thad sat on my front bumper, arms crossed, obviously waiting for me.

"Is your grandmother all right?" I asked, running up to him.

For about two seconds, it crossed my mind that if I hugged him, where half the church could see, that might get back to Mrs. Prince and really convince her I was the Whore of Babylon. She would order Russell to leave me alone. Problem solved.

The story might get back to Zach. Didn't want that.

"Gran's fine. Thanks." He gave me that dry, pained little smile, and stood up to meet me.

"Considering it was my fault that the whole blow-up occurred..."

"I heard from Shaun at the store." Thad tipped his head to one side and smiled like he used to when we were comfortable together. "Did Gran really have a cat-fight in the middle of the frozen foods?"

"I don't know what to call it. She was amazing. I didn't even know she knew such words."

"Yeah, well, we've heard some things about Mrs. Prince. Granddad always laughed, but I had to wonder sometimes if he wasn't scared to death of her. Gran teased him that he asked her to marry him to escape that woman's plans."

Yeah, just like I had stated in front of witnesses that I would rather marry Thad than Russell. I prayed one of those fast, desperate prayers that no one had reported *that* to him.

Or to Zach.

I gave myself a mental slap. This was not the time or place to get distracted.

"Look, can we talk?" Thad said.

"About?"

"Clearing the air. Settling things." He shrugged. "Apologizing."

"You already did," I pointed out. I had to be fair, right?

"Yeah ... but not enough."

We ended up at Beans and Books. There was always something especially comforting about the smell of fresh cookies, coffee, and old paper. It seemed to me the traffic was equal on the coffee shop side of the store and the used book side. Maybe it wasn't smart to get coffee that late at night, but I suspected with the coiled feeling still in my chest despite the soothing of Bible study, a dose of caffeine might help me relax.

I gave him a few more details of what had happened at the grocery store, and that meant explaining the weirdness with the Princes. Thad apologized for the ambush at Christmas, when I described the family dinner I had fled. That was an improvement -- he saw the connection without any prompting.

"Funny ... maybe not so funny." He tipped his half-empty cup sideways, making the foam at the edges shift. "All of a sudden you're being chased by guys who aren't good enough for you, when you've been ignored for so long."

Me? Chased by guys?

"Maybe I haven't been ... I don't know, ready to consider things like that?"

Was that really as lame as it sounded to me? Sometimes I said things just to have noise in the room, because silence was too painful.

"Do you ever think about what makes a good marriage?" he asked softly.

"Uh ... well, we had that unit on dating and marriage in class a year or so back."

Duh! Yes! Constantly. Or so it seemed to me lately.

"See the thing is, Dinah ... we'd be good together."

"Just because we worked together so well for Singles --"

"I try," he set down his cup and rested his hand on mine, "but I just can't see living the rest of my life without you."

"Thad." I tugged my hand free and put both my hands in my lap. "I'm useful. I pick up after you. And until those hags at church and then your grandmother got you thinking about it ... you didn't think about it. About us. That way. The bottom line is, you don't love me, and I don't love you."

"Well, yeah." He swallowed hard enough I could hear it. "But we like each other. We work together really well. We have a lot in common. That's a good foundation, right? And there's this -- this hole in my life where you used to be."

I struggled for words that wouldn't sound as bitter as the ones poised on my tongue. Words I had wanted to say for a while now. Starting with wishing he had said it was a big, painful hole. I suspected the hole he had just noticed was more like a pinprick letting air out of a balloon.

Finally, the silence got to be a little too long, and I knew he would repeat how well we worked together. That was not what a girl wanted to hear, after she had given a guy the cue of, "You don't love me." The right answer was, "Yes I do, what can I do to prove it?"

So I had to head him off at the pass.

"You can fill that hole with someone else to do all the things I used to do. Lots of people who can work with you in Singles."

"What if I don't want someone else? Why can't we start with what we have and build from there? Why do we have to have roses and violins?"

"I want a guy who wants *me*, first, and not focus on how smoothly we work together. A well-oiled machine doesn't sound all that ..." I shrugged. No way was I going to say "romantic" out loud. "Yeah, partnership is great, but not when it's for the sake of *other* people." I had this horrid fear I would start weeping at any second. Quiet, tired tears. Despite this newer, more thoughtful side of Thad, I refused to cry in front of him, or give him a clue that romance had been lacking between us. It was too late for him to change his tactics and have them mean anything to me.

Romance, I realized with a start like a slap with an ice-crusted rag on my face, was a two-way street. I certainly didn't feel romance for him. More along the lines of, "He's the only one, so hold onto him." Not a good foundation.

"Thad ..." I put my hand back on the table, resting on his now. "I want a guy who feels his life is empty without me, not just a hole to fill. There's a big difference."

"Dinah --"

"Someone who makes *my* life feel empty without him."

"Ouch." He tried to laugh.

"Thad, at Christmas, we were surrounded by mistletoe and you didn't even try to kiss me. Then you gave me that gift certificate. Can you guess how I felt?"

"Ripped off?"

"Like I was the last thing on your mind. Once the mess of the holidays was over, you'd see that, because you're a pretty smart, insightful guy. For a guy."

"Oh, thanks." He managed to smile.

"The thing is, after feeling stupid to hope for more ... I felt relieved to know it'd be over soon."

"Oh." He nodded, tipped his cup and swirled it a moment, then finished the rest of his cooled coffee. Then he looked me in the eye and nodded again. "Okay. I guess ... that makes sense."

<><><>

The following Thursday, after a strangely quiet Valentine's Day (meaning Russell didn't bombard me with candy and notes -- or if he did, my guardian angels in the office whisked them away and had a word with him), Mrs. Grant called me. At work. To come to a meeting at church -- her church -- that night.

"Umm, why?" I looked around the office, having the awful feeling everyone could hear our conversation.

"Well, we need to do some damage control. In some ways, your absence just makes it easier for the lies to dominate. I know you don't care what anyone at our church thinks of you, and you're justified, but ... well, think of what all this is doing to us."

I wanted so much to say it wasn't my concern, they had to deal with their own problems. However … between my morning devotions, and rethinking my conversation with Thad (and a good dose of guilt for being so self-righteous, poor-pitiful-me lately), I suspected it was more than the right thing to do, a debt owed my old church. Maybe I needed it to get some healing.

Maybe refusing to go back there was equal to running away. I had vowed never to do that again, hadn't I?

I agreed. We were to meet with the pastoral staff, deacons and trustees, finance board, and the heads of the ministry boards. I got a little nervous when she said we would be meeting in the parlor. That room could hold about two hundred people, when the chairs were set up right. Too many people to meet in the conference room in the church office?

I should have been more nervous. When I arrived, I saw a lot of cars already there ahead of me, and more pulling in after I parked and got out of my car. Mrs. Grant and Pastor Marcus were waiting for me. They took me into his office.

The change in Pastor Marcus was visible. He had lost weight. There was a new definition to his cheekbones, some darkness under his eyes, and a couple lines around his mouth.

"Dinah, please accept my humblest apology. You have been

wronged. I am ... ashamed to realize I let myself be the tool of enemies of our church. I let them make you a target, and I did not protect you, which was my duty. My only excuse is -- well, I shouldn't have any excuses." He sat down on the front edge of his desk, while Mrs. Grant and I sat in the chairs facing his desk.

"Mrs. Grant explained some of it a while ago. The family-oriented ... extremists, I guess you could call them," I said, after struggling for a few seconds with what exactly I felt and thought about his words. "Their definition of family."

Pastor Marcus had gone through something recently. I wasn't so arrogant to think it was all because of the injustice that had struck at *me*. I wasn't so nice that I didn't feel a tiny thrill at this humbling. Was it wrong to think God had punished him even a teensy bit on my behalf? Or just wrong to want it?

"If our church survives this turmoil, we only have two choices. To be strong, tempered and tested weapons in the hands of our Lord. Or to be a pitiful mockery of what a church needs to be for our time," he said. "I can only hope God allowed these people to infiltrate us to stir us up and make us stronger and purify us, rather than allow the devil to tear us down."

"What does it matter if the result's the same?"

He gave me a sharp stare for a few moments, then that pained look returned. He glanced at his watch and nodded to Mrs. Grant.

"I'm grateful that you're willing to come help us start cleaning up this mess. You're far more gracious and mature as a Christian than many of the people you've had to deal with recently, and I apologize. After all, I'm at the top of that list." He stood up and stepped over to the door and opened it. "Let me also apologize for what you're about to face. We had hoped to keep this a small meeting, only the essential people involved."

I muffled a snort. Small? Enough people to need the parlor?

My exhausted brain hadn't really put things together. Mrs. Grant nudged me from behind and I let Pastor Marcus lead me down the hall and out of the office, to the church parlor.

"When we started calling on people to come and explain themselves, and tried to track down all the gossip, the numbers grew. A vindictive element was under the impression we were putting you on trial," he said, as we headed for the door into the parlor at the small kitchen end. "We did our best to straighten them out. Be assured, no one will be allowed to attack you. Tonight is to begin the healing."

It did feel like I was on trial at first. I sat on the piano bench, next to the door and the short hall of the little kitchen. It wasn't much cover from the glaring, curious eyes of the people jammed into the parlor. Seats were wall to wall, and people stood in the back. At least I didn't have to sit with the church leaders in the row of seats lined up two deep in front of the fireplace.

Mrs. Grant, Pastor Marcus and the others who put this meeting together had invested a lot of thought into it. I didn't have to say or do anything. They started by addressing the rumors, the stories going around about how I had lost my job. Or quit without any justification. Or walked out in the middle of an important job. Several versions were almost laughable. Maybe I would laugh in a couple years.

They started by going through the sequence of events, the decisions made at the board meeting, and the planned timeline for ending my employment. I got a little satisfaction, very short-lived, when they verified Mrs. Rizetti had decided the volunteers would come in a week ahead of time. Two volunteers testified they thought she had a vendetta against me.

"And I could never figure out why. Dinah is such a good girl, and a hard worker."

Interestingly, no one knew who had decided to let me go immediately after receiving my two weeks' notice. No meeting, no discussion. A typed note left on everyone's desk said the decision had been made to terminate me immediately. Mrs. Rizetti was probably the guilty party there, too. I didn't offer my suspicion, because I wanted people to forget I was there. Also, Mrs. Rizetti wasn't there to defend herself.

Yeah, like anyone had ever given me that consideration? She was asked to attend the meeting, and she refused. I was never given the opportunity to speak up for myself.

Mr. Phillips, Pastor Marcus and several others took turns explaining how they had investigated recent events, sensing something wasn't quite right about many new cost-cutting measures. Then Mrs. Grant brought them the information about the family-oriented group that had gained so much power and influence so quickly. It turned out Nolan Peters -- Reggie's Nolan

Peters -- was an investigator for the denomination, and had been tracking the family-oriented extremist group before they landed in our church. He figured out what was what and brought his evidence to Mrs. Grant.

How come Reggie hadn't told me any of that? Of course, the few times she would talk about him, it was to either complain about the children's theater production, or the maneuvering at Rockaway. I should have suspected something right there, that Reggie didn't like to talk about him. Was she the best pal in the world, or was I just a self-focused twit lately?

I heard and saw a lot of murmuring and squirming when Pastor Marcus pointed out how the newcomers gained so much power. Ninety percent of the congregation was content to sit back and let others do the work, and didn't pay attention to decisions being made.

Mr. Phillips had a PowerPoint presentation. On the screen over the fireplace, he went through a chart of all the changes the invaders had made and wanted to make. The cutbacks, the programs to be ended or combined, the shifts in responsibilities and focus -- all aimed at eliminating paid jobs and phasing out ministry to singles, the widowed, and the divorced.

Pastor Steve read aloud from a "manifesto" of the group, condemning the divorced as heretics and rebels who had forfeited their salvation by being divorced. It didn't matter if they were injured party or adulterer. There was similar harsh language for widows and widowers. God punished their sins by taking away their spouses. They needed to purify their lives and get right with God. He would bring a new spouse into their lives as an indication of His favor. As for the singles, we were living in rebellion every day we refused to look for our God-given mates.

That smacked a little too much of Mrs. Prince's theology. I considered escaping about then. The door was only a few steps behind me.

"They believe single women who pursue careers are living immoral lives," Pastor Steve said, finally looking up from the papers. "Which means they had to eliminate Dinah from her very visible position as the nerve center of our church's efficiency. They considered her a bad example to all the single women. Just because she didn't *need* a man to make her life complete," he ended, with a sneer on his face and in his voice.

The silence filling the parlor at that point was a little frightening. Part of me hoped someone would cough, or even laugh, or mutter a protest.

After a few heartbeats, almost deafeningly loud in my ears, Pastor Marcus stood up again and launched into a short sermon. Everyone played an important part in the church body, whether married or single, young or old, office worker, custodian or Sunday school teacher, pastor or kitchen worker. I had to admire his talent for working people up, then smoothly shifting from a sermon back to a church business meeting.

At about the two-hour mark, a resolution passed to examine all decisions and changes made in the last year, where the named family-oriented extremists had been involved. Any change that showed prejudice against the unmarried, or where money was a higher priority than ministry, would be cancelled or reversed.

That was all well and good, but I wanted a resolution tossing those people out of the church. Nobody stood up to defend them through the whole meeting. Nobody protested when they were named. Then again, none of them or their supporters had obeyed the request that they attend.

I hoped -- a little -- they would be given the cold shoulder, scolded, and subtly urged to either turn over a new leaf or leave. Honestly? I wanted them publicly humiliated and excommunicated, more than their keys and passwords taken away. But we didn't do that at our church. (No, wait, *their* church.) There were some things that, in theory, we left for God to punish. The extremists' tactic was to decide who was allowed into Heaven and throw out anyone who disagreed with them. Therefore, it couldn't be our tactic. Not if we wanted to be more spiritually mature and walk more closely in Christ's footsteps.

My brain was still full of this unpleasant self-revelation when I was asked to step forward.

Should have expected that.

Didn't.

Pastor Marcus apologized to me in front of everyone. Nice, since he had already done that in his office.

"You made it possible for more than just the pastoral staff to do their jobs efficiently, without any worry that materials wouldn't be there, equipment wouldn't be in place, and communications might fail. We're helpless without you." He held out his hand. "Dinah, will you forgive us and come back to your old job and put things right in our church office again?"

I swear, the first thought in my mind was that those volunteers had messed things up so badly, everyone had abandoned ship.

And yes, my second thought was to wonder if I was going to get a raise. I had wanted to request one for some time, but didn't. There was always someone carping about how the offering was down and we had to cut back.

Silence spilled through the room. Suddenly, it was a tiny, cramped room, running out of oxygen. I felt the weight of those eyes. I stared at Pastor's hand held out to me, and I didn't want to take it.

There was a difference, I realized in that moment, between running away from problems, and moving on with my life.

Someone coughed. Someone whispered in the front row, only three feet away from me. I looked that woman in the eye. Someone I didn't know. Her lip curled up before she turned back to the woman next to her and whispered more.

"No." I got a cold, empty, falling sensation in my chest when I heard my voice sort of echo through the sound system, picked up by Pastor's microphone.

"No?" He let his hand drop to his side, unshaken. "You mean -- no, you won't forgive --"

"Oh, sure, I think I can forgive all the people who actually *did* something to me, to my face. It's a little hard to forgive the people I don't even know, who give themselves the right to judge me." I pointed at the woman who had sneered at me a moment ago. Her friend nudged her, she looked at me, and she blushed and looked down at her hands in her lap.

"Dinah." Mr. Phillips got up from the end of the row of chairs. "We need you. You're an invaluable part of the team. Our fault is that we didn't recognize that, and you were treated badly. We want you back."

"That's the thing, isn't it?"

My voice cracked. I was going to start crying in another moment, which was utterly stupid. The most important thing right then was not letting anyone see me cry.

"It's always what *you* want. What about what I want? What makes you think I want to come back here, after all the lies and the scheming and the stupidity and -- I have a new job. A great job. At another church. A much nicer church. They don't call me at home, expecting me to fix something that someone else should have done in the first place. They don't assume that because I'm single, I don't have a life. They don't --" My voice cracked. I was going to gush at any moment. "Why should I come back here? I don't owe any of you anything."

"But we're your home," Mrs. Humphries said from the third row. I hadn't even seen her there. "Dinah, honey, you've been here since you were born. We're your family."

"You know what they say -- most murders are committed by family members. Was it fun," I looked at different people sitting there, meeting gazes, feeling this odd thrill of power when they looked away, "stabbing me in the back when I wasn't here to defend myself? Do you honestly think that making a big public apology makes everything right? Oh, sure, Dinah is such a *loser*. She'll just junk her whole new life, abandon her new job and her new church and her new friends and come running back, just because you *say* you're sorry?"

Everything got blurry. I was crying.

I walked out.

Reggie was there, in the hall, when I ran out the door. She looked like I imagined I did -- eyes swollen, fighting not to cry. Somehow, that helped me hold back the waterworks, even after she flung her arms around me. For a second there, I felt this enormous hot, sharp, spiky thing rolling around in my chest. I hadn't even been aware of it until that moment, but I had been terrified Reggie had abandoned me to the inquisition. But no, she had been there, unseen, waiting for me until I needed her.

Reggie followed me home. We watched six episodes of ***Zorro*** and snickered at how easily Diego tricked the evilly stupid Alcalde. Come on, Zorro was six feet tall. The only person in the pueblo that tall was Diego. How oblivious could a guy be? We ate ice cream and freshly baked brownies and didn't talk about what went on at church.

That's what friends are for.

There were five messages on my answering machine, and I didn't see them until Reggie was packing up to go home. She stood with me while I played each one. Every time I heard Mrs. Prince's voice, I hit erase, so she didn't get past the first syllable.

"She's probably giving you more of her 'don't fight God's will' crap," Reggie muttered. Then we both giggled, because she never said "crap," and because even chocolate ice cream and warm brownies couldn't ease all our tension.

"You know, I have a whole new appreciation for how God looks after us," she said, after I erased the last message, unheard.

"In what?"

"That woman could have been my grandmother."

"I'm gonna puke."

We laughed again. A little tired. A little teary. A little headachy. And maybe a little oogy from all the sugar and fat we had consumed. After that fight in the grocery store, Reggie had gotten a refresher course from her grandmother and father on the tribulations Mrs. Prince had put her grandparents through. I felt a little chilled at the thought that Reggie never would have been my best friend, an almost-sister, if she had been Mrs. Prince's granddaughter.

I kept that terrifying thought to myself. Just like I didn't ask about Nolan Peters after the first tentative foray got a brief deer-in-the-headlights look from her. There were some things best friends shouldn't inflict on each other.

<><><>

Hurrah for Friday. I brought the rest of the brownies with me to work. Every time I passed the tray in the common office area, I remembered how Reggie had been there for me last night, and I smiled. I thanked God for best friends. I thanked Him for people who had the ethics and maturity to admit they were wrong, and to apologize, and to try to rectify the situation. I thanked Him for my great new job. I thanked Him that I hadn't really been panicky the whole time about employment. The house was paid for, Dad wouldn't throw me out, and I had money in the bank to cover bills for a few months. I thanked Him for Zach's help in finding a new job. I thanked Him for my great new bosses. I thanked Him for this chance to minister in new ways, and for up-to-date equipment and facilities.

Then about 10:30, I thanked God for Marti Franklin. She had heard about Russell hounding me and called to promise she would stand with me if he started in on me again. She was worse off than me, because Mrs. Prince and Russell regularly hounded her, castigated her as unworthy, left her alone, and then changed their minds and resumed hounding her to marry Russell. Marti was the church workhorse. Everyone turned to her to organize any event. Weddings, bridal showers, Sunday school parties, birthday parties, anniversaries, funerals, and dozens of other activities. She wasn't even full-time staff. People just expected her to know who to talk to and how to get things done. No wonder Mrs. Prince thought she was the perfect daughter-in-law.

I liked Marti, and already felt sorry for her before I heard about what the Princes did to her. It looked like Allen Randall was interested in her, but Marianne Pastorini had targeted him. She was so desperate to be a pastor's wife (shades of Mrs. Prince) she had followed Allen from Central Avenue to Holy Spirit Alliance, just like I had suspected. I had heard things about Marianne that sure sounded like Her Holiness played dirty. Now, knowing what Marti had gone through, and would probably go through again when the Princes gave up on me, we bonded. She agreed, we needed to get the other runaway brides-of-Russell to team up and go to the pastors for some official action.

I just spent the whole morning thanking God, every free moment when I wasn't concentrating on a task. I especially thanked Him that there was no such thing as too much chocolate, when I got back from running errands at lunch and saw one brownie left on the tray. I picked it up for dessert.

Then from the corner of my eye, I saw a familiar black hat ringed with cherries. I froze, the brownie at my lips. Mrs. Prince toddled down the hall and out of the office area. Obviously, Shaun at the grocery store had given her cane back to her.

"Thanks, Lord, that I wasn't here when she walked in. Thank You that she didn't see me on her way out," I whispered. The brownie wasn't dessert anymore. It was medicine.

"Dinah, are you back from lunch?" Pastor Paulson's voice came over the intercom.

"Right here. What can I help you with?" I said, my voice still a little thick with the brownie.

"Could you come down to my office?"

I rubbed brownie crumbs off my lips as I walked the long hallway. No time to repair my lipstick. I passed Russell's office. His door was open. I almost got a cramp in my neck fighting *not* to turn to look at him as I walked past. Whatever he and his mother had been discussing, it was no concern of mine.

Pastor Paulson and Miss Fleming were standing in front of his desk when I tapped on his door and walked in. She coordinated church events and church decorations, interior as well as landscaping. The first time we worked together was coordinating all the Valentine's Day events for different social groups in church, to make sure no one double-booked the same rooms. I thought we got along great, so I was a little puzzled why she looked me over, and a tiny frown wrinkle formed between her eyebrows. What had I done?

"Dinah ... we have a little puzzle here. You asked for the last of March off, didn't you?"

"Yeah, it's kind of a tradition for Dad and me. I fly to Arizona for the end of Indians' spring training. I can cancel, if it's going to cause any problems here," I offered.

"Oh, no, we wouldn't want you to do that. We already agreed that you could go, but ..." He looked at some papers in his hand. "Well, the problem is that we have a wedding scheduled for the weekend you're gone."

"You need me to fill in for the people who work on the weddings?" My thoughts turned to Marti. Good for her, learning to say *no.*

"*Your* wedding."

"I'm not getting married." I wished I hadn't eaten all those brownies. I was hallucinating from my sugar hangover.

"According to this, and the reservation for the sanctuary that Saturday morning, you are." Miss Fleming took the papers from Pastor's hand and held them out to me.

The papers were thick, ivory-colored parchment -- envelope and an embossed wedding invitation.

For my wedding to Russell Prince.

"My middle initial is a J, not an L. And if I was getting married, my dad's name would be on it, don't you think? And I'm going to be in Arizona that day, so this isn't --" I handed it back to her and wiped my hands a couple times on my skirt.

The sympathy on their faces told me they believed me, but it wasn't enough.

"Kayla Prince waltzed in here with that and demanded the date." Pastor Paulson managed a chuckle. "Usually you make sure the date's open for the sanctuary, *then* you order the invitations."

Why hadn't I encouraged Zach? Why hadn't I kept my big mouth shut about wanting a year free of relationships? His presence would have kept Mrs. Prince far away.

"Pastor, you know the situation with the Princes."

"Yes, and I had that talk with Russell. I can see I should have had several people talk to Kayla instead."

"She's never gone this far in inflicting her will on others before," Miss Fleming remarked, her voice soft and dry. "Is she determined, or desperate, to plan the wedding without the bride even knowing?"

"A wedding without a bride!" I thought of Russell. What would I have seen if I had looked in his office when I walked past? Fear? Smugness? Triumph? "Could I have that?" I gestured at the invitation.

Five seconds later, I punched Russell's ajar door open all the way and stomped up to his desk, holding the invitation out. He had the gall to smile like nothing was wrong.

"Russell, I'm only going to tell you this once, and you pass this message on to your mother. There will be no wedding on March 24th. There will be no wedding, period!" I tore the envelope and invitation in half, and then half again. No mean feat, considering how thick that parchment was. Then I tossed the pieces on his desk.

A tiny part of my mind noticed this was getting repetitious.

"You have to," he said, standing up, just as calm as could be. "It's God's will. He sent you to be my wife."

"It is not God's will!" I was close to screaming, and I didn't care how many people came running. I wanted witnesses. "It's Gertie Foster's interference and cheating, and it's your delusional mother trying to force people to do what she wants. Just like she has been trying to do all her life."

"God chose you to be my wife. He told me so." He stepped

around his desk and reached out like he would put his arms around me.

Okay, now he was just as delusional as his mother. Some people should not be allowed to reproduce, or have any contact with children. I retreated to the doorway. If I let him get his hands on me … how long could I keep contradicting him before he snapped and strangled me?

"Well God didn't tell *me* that I'm supposed to be your wife, and it seems to me that's something He'd tell a girl."

"Well, of course not." Russell gave an indulgent chuckle that made me want to slap him. He followed me into the hall.

A good number of people had gathered there, probably drawn by the ruckus. Pastor Paulson was right behind me now, and Russell stopped short in his doorway.

"Of course not?" I shook my head, hating him for being so smug, even amused.

"You're just a woman."

"*Just* a woman?"

It helped me that someone chuckled and several people muttered behind me.

"It takes years of service and marriage and raising children before you're mature enough to hear God's voice."

"Oh, and I suppose you're mature enough to hear Him?"

"Of course. I'm a man. It's only right that God talks to me. You're just a woman."

"Well, I may be *just* a woman." I poked him in the breastbone, punctuating those last three words with a poke for each one. Boy, did I wish I went in for long, thick, pointy, polished nails right then. "But I will never be *your* woman."

Then I slapped him.

Okay, maybe my hand was about half clenched into a fist. I swear the sound was still echoing as I turned and stomped down the hallway.

Chapter Fifteen

When I got to my desk, Pastor Paulson and Miss Fleming and a couple other people were right behind me. I felt like I had when I left the parlor at Central Avenue last night.

The heck with not running away. I couldn't take this anymore. I hated Tabitha for a few seconds. Her and her friends, handling Russell and his mother with tricks. Never reporting them, so they could be stopped once and for all.

"Dinah, I'm so sorry. That never should have happened," Pastor Paulson said. "I've told Russell he's out of here if he doesn't leave you alone."

My shaking stopped immediately, which was a little frightening in itself. "Pastor, I love working here. Everybody -- everybody else is great. But I just can't work here anymore." My voice cracked, and I turned away to search for a bag or box or something, knowing instantly what I had to do. Fortunately, there was a plastic grocery bag in my top drawer. "I hope you won't be too angry that I'm not giving you two weeks' notice."

Then I swept my arm across the side of my desk where I had put a few personal items -- pictures of me and Reggie, me and Dad, the Sportstime Ohio bobblehead desk, a ceramic jar Mom had made with my handprint on it, that I kept candy in, my notebook -- and shoved everything into that grocery bag.

The shaking didn't come back until I took my coat from the closet. A few people followed me out into the hallway and hugged me, refused to accept my resignation, told me to take the weekend to relax, said they were praying for me. Then I was out the door, almost running to my car.

<><><>

I called Reggie with the bare bones: Russell and his mother had struck again and I had quit my new job. She demanded I come to Rockaway, since she couldn't get off work until nine. With all the department heads at other Rockaway locations vying for jobs when their stores closed, she didn't dare take time off. I sat behind the counter, partially hidden from customers by the tall drawers full of makeup, and gave her the ugly details. In between requests for lip gloss and foundation and help choosing a new shade of nail polish. Didn't her customers realize there was a major crisis going on? Bigger than anything in their lives?

There was something bitterly amusing about my ending up there, hiding behind the makeup. I didn't want to go home, and not just because the ice cream and brownies were all gone. If I went home, I'd eventually have to do something to break that silence, like call Dad. I couldn't go to Pastor Paulson for counseling, because really, what was there to say? I had burned the bridge between me and Central Avenue, and couldn't turn there for advice. Kind of ironic, because I really respected and admired Pastor Marcus now. All I had now was Reggie, and our Christmas Day group. I didn't have the phone numbers of anyone in my new Singles group.

I was a woman without a church, without a job, and with very few friends. All I was sure of was that I didn't want to pack up everything and move to Arizona to be with Dad. I would be just as lost and alone there as I was here in Ohio.

During lulls between customers, Reggie and I discussed what I was discovering about myself. She agreed that the whole situation and my epiphany combined to be pretty wretched. Then we made one crazy plan after another for how to get revenge on Russell and his mother. Stupid, juvenile tricks like setting bags of dog poop on fire on their front step, or ordering a couple dozen pizzas to be delivered to them.

"Oh, I got the best idea," she said, after dealing with a group of high school girls. They seemed to base all their decisions in makeup on whether it would get a boy's attention. Those girls thought they had problems? Wait until they got out of college and had to face the real world.

"Is it messy, expensive, and will humiliate them forever?"

"Definitely." She looked around, as if searching for eavesdroppers, then she leaned closer to me and lowered her voice. "Tell Russell you will marry him."

"And how is that supposed to punish *him*?"

"Let me finish!" She giggled. "Tell him you want to make a fresh start, in a new town, just the two of you. Tell him he has to leave home, and go ahead of you to this new town. Tell him it has to be all secret, he can't even tell his mother. If his mother comes to live with you, the deal is off."

"Yeah, like he'll go anywhere without her? She had her name at the top of the invitation, announcing the wedding. Dad was completely cut out, and she put Russell first. Excuse me, but the bride and her family come first."

"Exactly. He's stupid enough to ask his mother for advice. I bet she's just crazy enough to tell him to agree."

"And how is this supposed to help me?"

"Because she'll clear out the house and sell everything and move to the same town, and plan on moving in with the two of you once the honeymoon is over."

"Oh, ugh. I just got this vision of Russell in swim trunks. The idea of living with him was bad enough, but 'honeymoon' means ... sex."

"Yeah. Well, the beauty of my plan is that you won't be there for the honeymoon."

"How do I manage that?" Oddly, I felt a hint of laughter bubbling in my chest. Or maybe that was nausea.

"You tell him you'll meet him in Vegas at a wedding chapel, after he's made the move. But you never show up."

"Not only do I have a psycho wimp and his crazy mother on my case, but he can sue me for breach of promise. No thanks. I'll just find a nice mobster to take a contract out on him."

"No worries. Since you tell him it has to be secret, he won't tell anybody but his mother, so nobody knows what's going on. Nobody will expect you to marry him. He can't sue you. Besides, part of the agreement is that he doesn't tell his mother, but since he *will* tell her, he violates the agreement, so you're free. What's even better is that he's moved out of town. If you're lucky, he and his mother will be too embarrassed to come back here." Reggie stood back, smiling with pride for her nefarious plan.

"That is about the stupidest thing I've ever heard," I finally said.

"I know." She shrugged, and glanced over her shoulder at the customer approaching the counter. "But the thing is, *they're* just nutso enough that it might work."

Reggie proved right there she was my best friend. She loved me. She understood me. And she was just as crazy as ever.

Crazy enough that she called Thad and told him everything, when I left to go home and call Dad. So Thad was in his car, sitting in the street in front of my house when I pulled into the driveway. Funny, but I was glad to see him. It had to be nice to be his own boss, so he could take off whenever he needed.

Maybe I could start my own business? Doing what? I had spent my life working in the background, helping other people get and keep organized, keeping track of other people's lives. It sounded like the work Marti did, as a virtual assistant. Could I do something like that?

"I've been thinking about your problem," Thad said, when he had walked up the driveway and met me by the side door. I was still trying to unlock the door without losing my grip on my bag of personal items salvaged from my desk at church. "The root of it is that matchmaking profile."

"No." I got the door open, pushing hard enough I stumbled across the threshold.

"What do you mean, no?" Thad at least had the grace not to laugh at me.

"You want me to fill out a real profile, and compare it to the one Gertie made and ..." I sighed. "And prove I'm not matched to Russell, so maybe I have some leverage to finally get his mother to leave me alone."

I wondered about that, though, after hearing Russell insist that God had told him I was supposed to marry him. How could substituting a legitimate profile for a faulty one stand up against the supposed voice of God that only Russell could hear?

"It's a start." He held out his hand. "I'll even go with you and hold your hand through the whole thing."

"That'll make it kind of hard to fill out the questionnaire." I wanted so badly to laugh, but I couldn't.

Thad went with me. He didn't hold my hand when I explained to Zach and Gertie what I wanted to do, but he did rest his hand on my shoulder a couple times. That helped, a spot of warmth through all the cold trying to soak into my bones. His no-nonsense stare toned down Gertie's whining, insisting that she *had* got my profile right the first time.

I caught Thad and Zach giving each other that totally indecipherable "guy look," where they seemed to just stare at each other. Whatever communication went on between guys in those moments was beyond me, but they seemed to resolve something. Zach was certainly a little warmer by the time we came to an agreement. Thad shook his hand, which he hadn't done when we first arrived.

Basically, Thad was finally being my white knight. I liked it, and I felt a little sad. Too bad he hadn't been my white knight sooner. Things might have been very different now.

"I just want to make one thing clear," I said, as I sat down to fill out the questionnaire. "I don't want to be matched with anyone."

"Agreed," Zach said, giving Thad another "guy look." "This is just to prove who you're *not* matched to."

Then he left me alone in the conference room with my questionnaire. I heard him and Thad talking for a little bit after he closed the door, but after that all was silent.

Zach had to input all my answers into the computer, so we wouldn't get my profile match until late that evening, or Saturday morning, if he didn't get everything inputted that night. It was going on six when I finished filling out the questionnaire. We agreed to invite Pastor Paulson, Russell, and Mrs. Prince to see the results.

<><><>

Normally, Match wasn't open on Saturday afternoons, so we agreed that would be the perfect time for the "unveiling," without any fear of interruptions. Zach assured me he had spoken with Russell, and my erstwhile groom understood what was being done here. He had been quietly furious when he heard what Russell had said to me about being "just a woman." Zach assured me Russell had agreed to abide by the findings of this match test. If he didn't, Zach promised he would take steps, since the mediation of the pastoral team hadn't helped.

It wasn't Russell who worried me, but his mother and what she would drive him to do.

I drove my car instead of taking advantage of the nice weather and walking from my house to the office. If Mrs. Prince showed up with more ammunition to bend me to her will, badly disguised as God's will, I would just get back in my car. Maybe I wouldn't even go home, but head straight for Daddy and Arizona.

I almost didn't make it to the door Saturday afternoon. I saw five cars sitting in front of the office, and one behind it, with Zach's truck. There was no need for all those cars. Who else had been invited?

My compromise between trust and caution was to peer in through the front door, poised to run away. I had finally learned a thing or two about not walking into any more ambushes. I found Mrs. Prince and Russell sitting by Gertie's desk. I found Zach, leaning against the wall next to the printer stand, his arms crossed, looking calm. Thad and Mrs. Grant sat on the other side of the office. And in the middle were Pastor Marcus and Pastor Paulson, shaking hands slowly, talking, and smiling.

Somehow, the roof hadn't fallen in or caught fire. The meeting of the pastors under friendly circumstances would have disappointed the rabid sports elements in both churches.

Taking a deep breath, I pushed the door open and went in to face the verdict. It occurred to me the safest place in that office was going to be somewhere between Zach and the two pastors, so that was where I headed as soon as I came in the door.

"We all agree, yes?" Zach said, cutting off Mrs. Prince as she opened her mouth. "You will abide by the results of the new match test, comparing your profiles with Dinah's profile."

"Wait a minute? Profiles? Plural?" I got that sinking feeling in my chest and turned to Thad. "That's what you were doing while I was in there."

"I wanted to see how scientific this was." Thad shrugged, but the way his gaze slid away from meeting mine, I knew he wasn't as casual and relaxed as he tried to appear.

"This is a waste of time," Mrs. Prince said. "We already know what the match says about Dinah and Russell."

"That's not Dinah in the profile," Zach said. "That was an image of Dinah made from dozens of impressions."

"Surely what other people think about her is more accurate than how she sees herself?" For just a moment, she actually looked uncertain, maybe even pleading. It didn't last long enough for me to consider feeling sorry for her.

"I've explained the scientific principles. Does anyone have any questions about how we put together the profile and how we compare and analyze the results?" He looked around the room, meeting my gaze last. Everyone shook their heads.

Pastor Marcus rested a hand on my shoulder. "Well, whatever the results are, I hope you find some comfort in knowing you brought us together." He laughed when I gave him a confused look. "We're considering being sister churches instead of rivals."

I just smiled and nodded. I wasn't in any mood to be spiritual and altruistic. They should have been mature enough, spiritually and mentally, to have reached that conclusion a long time ago.

"I want you all to know that I haven't looked at the results of the profiles or matches. I'll be seeing them for the first time with you," Zach said, stepping over to Gertie's computer. She scooted back in her swivel chair and let him get at the keyboard. He tapped a few keys, and the printer started spitting out sheets. Zach took them off the printer one by one and turned them upside down on the stand next to the printer without looking at them.

When the printer stopped, he went back over to the computer and tapped in another order, which I assumed was to print the match for Thad and me. Then he picked up the first packet of papers. He led the way into the conference room and spread the papers on the table so we could see all the results. He had explained the color-coding system to me weeks ago. The male in the analysis was marked with blue, and female with pink. The vertical line between the two parallel lines was color coded to show compatibility. A short green line connecting the pink and blue was ultimate compatibility -- we were close together in our profile on those points. Then it shaded to blue, to purple, to red, and the line got longer, showing increasing distance between us on each point.

I prayed for lots of red on those printouts.

God answered my prayers.

I walked along the table, my arms wrapped around myself, just looking for purple and red. The longer the better. There were a few spots where the lines turned blue, but there was no green whatsoever. That was what I was looking for.

My legs were shaking as I wandered out to the main part of the office and settled down in the waiting area. Zach stayed in the conference room and explained what the charts meant. I found it amusing when Mrs. Prince kept demanding a different interpretation of all that purple and red. The most beautiful sound I had heard in a long time was Zach constantly saying, "Incompatible."

The two pastors came out next, followed close behind by Mrs. Grant. Thad was next. I swear, steam was coming out of Mrs. Prince's ears when she and Russell came out.

"Preposterous," she said, waving her cane in the air. "I refuse to accept these results."

"You promised. You agreed to this," Zach reminded her.

"I don't care. The first profile results are the right ones."

"Kayla." Pastor Paulson stepped over to her and put his hands on her shoulders. He was the bravest man on earth, getting within reach of that cane of hers. "You heard what Zach told us, how this works. The first profile wasn't right about Dinah, and the first match was a lie. You can't change the facts just to suit you."

"How can you stand there and -- and -- encourage those people to steal my son's wife?" She pointed a trembling hand at Mrs. Grant, and Thad standing next to her chair.

"No one is stealing Dinah," he said. "She was never Russell's to begin with."

"And you haven't been paying attention -- which is your standard practice," Mrs. Grant added, her voice softening. "Dinah has turned down Thad on multiple occasions. If she matches up with him in this profile, it will be her choice whether she gets back together with him."

"She shouldn't have that choice. God sent her --"

"No, He didn't," Pastor Paulson said. "You tread on dangerous ground, Kayla, when you presume to claim God's authority to fulfill your private agenda." He looked as stern as I had ever seen him.

"Presume?" She stared up at him, her face pale, two dark feverish spots on her cheeks. Her mouth opened and closed a couple times, like she was trying to speak and couldn't force the words out. Then she glared at me. "You filthy little whore."

"I've had it with your name-calling, you nasty old bat." I stomped over to her. A lot of my trembling went away when she cringed. "I slapped your sexist jerk son, and I'll slap your nasty mouth, too, if you don't shut up and leave me alone!"

The silence rang in the office for about ten seconds. I swore, I could hear everyone's heartbeats, as well as their breathing. I didn't dare look at anyone except that nasty old woman, about to burst into tears because she couldn't get her own way.

"Russell," she whimpered.

"Yes, Mother?"

She held up a trembling hand. "Take me home."

Russell hauled her to her feet and helped put her coat on. Her lower lip trembled, and tears filled her eyes. She didn't say a thing to anyone. It was as if none of us existed.

"What am I going to do?" she wailed as the door hissed closed behind them. "I put a down payment on the perfect wedding dress. What am I going to do with a dress now?"

"Maybe you should buy it from her, Gertie." Zach didn't show any remorse when his aunt gave him a shocked look and pressed a hand over her heart, as if saying, *Who, me?* "She wouldn't have gone on like she did, if you hadn't guaranteed that the match with Russell meant Dinah had to marry him."

"If it had been a real profile," Gertie began, her lower lip sticking out almost as much as Mrs. Prince's. Then her shoulders slumped and she was nothing but a pale, little old lady. "Oh, I'm so sorry, Dinah. I feel like this is all my fault. But that woman -- I don't know why I let her get me into these messes."

I could easily envision the two of them getting into similar problems before this, with Mrs. Prince proclaiming it was God's will and Gertie providing support for her. I glanced around the room and Thad met my eyes. He visibly fought not to grin, and that made me feel better.

"Well, we might have gotten through to her for a change." Pastor Paulson stepped over to me and held out his hands. I let him hold my hands and he looked into my eyes for a few moments. "Dinah, as far as I'm concerned, you were provoked beyond the breaking point yesterday. I would prefer to ignore your resignation. Everyone in the office agrees. We will fire Russell if he comes near you. We'll keep an eye on him and his mother from now on." He squeezed my hands and let go. "Will we see you in church tomorrow? And at work Monday?"

"I'll think about it." That was the best I could do. Right at that moment, the thought of walking into that church made me feel slightly nauseous. Maybe I could do it if Reggie was with me.

"Marcus, it's been a pleasure meeting you. Breakfast Wednesday morning at Denny's?"

"I'll be there. And I'll bring some backup, so we can get started on your plan." Pastor Marcus shook his hand. He stayed standing with me as Pastor Paulson left.

Then it was Thad's turn. I wasn't surprised when most of the match analyses were blue, shading into green. I already knew we were compatible in a lot of things, but like Zach had said, the analysis was only a launching point. At some point, it became the responsibility of the people involved how things worked out, whether employment or romance.

Thad was quiet a long time after we had all studied the printouts and came back to the seating group. I heard a buzzing and looked back into the conference room to see Zach putting both sets of papers in the shredder. Zach was my hero. The less evidence of this whole awful experience, the better.

"Dinah, this only confirms what we all know." Mrs. Grant reached across the small gap between our chairs to take my hand. "Won't you give Thad a second chance?"

"Because *you* want us to try again, or because he does?" I already knew my answer, no matter what Thad said. I was irked that he would do the profile without asking if I minded, if it would make any difference. It did, but how he went about it just underscored my *no*.

Thad let out one of those quiet laughs that was more like a gasp mixed with a sigh. "Doesn't matter, Gran. I should have realized that doing this would be the final straw, huh, Dinah?"

"You understand me a little better than you did two months ago," I said, nodding.

"Why? Why not?" Pastor Marcus sat down in the chair next to me. It was kind of a telling point that Thad hadn't taken that chair. Gertie had gone back to her seat behind the counter, maybe as a defensive measure. Zach stayed standing when he rejoined us in the main room, a neutral party in all this.

I didn't want him to be neutral. I wanted him to follow up on that hint of interest he had given me weeks ago.

"Help us all understand, Dinah. I think it will help me, at least, help other couples with this kind of problem. Yes, I agree, you and Thad have gone too far to be a couple again. At least not without a lot of healing on both your parts. Put it into words for us. It might help you with the healing." Pastor Marcus held my hand, and that sort of gave me strength. I didn't feel trapped.

"Maybe I'm being selfish." My gaze strayed to Zach's, and he offered me one of those little smiles and a nod that told me, I hoped, he didn't think I was being selfish. "But I want a guy -- a husband -- who wants *me*, without any scientific evidence. He wants me for me, because we click, not just because he needs me. A life partner is not a business partner. We've gone too far, Thad. Just like I can't go back to our church after everything that has happened, after the things people said about me. Even if I could grow up enough to forgive them, they won't forgive me. I'll remind them of the ugliness inside them that they didn't want to see, and how it got exposed." I glanced at Pastor Marcus at this point, and he nodded, his mouth a flat, sorrowful smile. "You don't really want me back. Because neither of us can forget."

Silence. I heard Gertie shifting a little in her chair, and the squeaks as it rolled on its plastic floor mat. Finally Thad looked up from his clenched hands and sighed.

"Just do something for me, would you?" He sounded as tired as I felt. "Just promise me that if you haven't found someone in a year, you'll give us a chance again?"

What could I do? I agreed. Saying no would be sour grapes. I should have been angry because Thad assumed in a year, I still wouldn't have found anyone. I was too tired to be angry. Maybe something inside me was afraid that yes, a year from that moment, nobody would have expressed any interest in me.

Or a certain interested person hadn't acted.

When Thad and Mrs. Grant and Pastor Marcus left, Zach took me back into the conference room, to get me away from Gertie. She wriggled in her chair and letting out little sighs. I didn't know if she was really distressed, or just fishing for some pity.

Zach sat me down at the blessedly empty table and came back a moment later with a can of ginger ale for each of us. I choked on a bit of laughter when I saw that.

"What?" He smiled that crooked smile I had grown to love.

"You're one of the few people who've noticed that I like ginger ale, when everybody else drinks cola."

"That's what I do. I notice things."

"It should be a required course in school."

"Hmm, maybe." He took a long sip, meeting my gaze over the can. "Some people are just naturally better at it than others, but it still takes conscious effort. People have to be taught to analyze themselves, notice the little details in their own lives, as well as others. That's the only way we can narrow in on what we're really supposed to do, where we're supposed to be."

"That's why you made the matching program?"

"Pretty much."

"Is your profile in there? For job matching and Gertie's matchmaking?" I took another long drink of my ginger ale, to keep the words from falling off my tongue: How would he match up with me, if he pressed his buttons and commands and did a printout comparing us?

"Job, yes. Not the matchmaking part, though. Why?" He shrugged, turning his can around a few times, studying the condensation rings on the table. "The scientific principles work great for business, but not with the heart and soul, the human element." He lifted his can and paused with it in front of his mouth. "When it comes to romance, I prefer the old-fashioned way. Getting to know them, spending time with them."

"Makes sense." I concentrated on my ginger ale, sipping slowly. The thought of going home and reporting to Reggie everything that happened felt like a heavy weight on my shoulders. She would want to know what I was going to do next, and I had no answer for her.

"Dinah." Zach put down his can and reached across the table to rest his hand on my hand that wasn't playing with the can. "I'm very sure that in a year, when Thad comes looking for you again, you won't be alone or waiting for him."

"Not with my track record." I took another big swallow, to wash down the big lump. Now was the time for Zach to add that he was sure of this because he was interested, he wanted to get to know me. But of course, he didn't say it. So much for Zach being the expert in noticing things.

Chapter Sixteen

Reggie agreed with me only partially. She pointed out that Zach really had listened to everything I said, every time I came into the office -- including when I said I wanted to have a whole year free. That I didn't want to worry about all the complications of relationships until the rest of my life was back on track.

Sometimes, having a guy listen that well wasn't such a great idea.

I went back to work for Holy Spirit Alliance on Monday morning, with the understanding that I would stay until they found someone to take over my job. I didn't have to have any contact with Russell. He had strict orders to stay away from me.

He did, scrupulously. Sometimes I would look up and see him walking slowly past the glass wall separating the office area from the hallway into the rest of the church. Sometimes our eyes would meet, but he would get that pouty look and turn his head and walk away. Quickly. Maybe he thought he was punishing me by giving me the cold shoulder. For all I knew, his mother was counseling him to leave me alone, to give me the silent treatment, and that eventually I would break (under the weight of all her demanding prayers?) and throw myself at his feet and beg him to marry me. Well, that was the scenario Reggie came up with. I felt a little creeped out by the whole idea. All that really mattered was that Russell didn't approach me, in any way, shape, or manner.

I didn't need his help with computer problems. After spending all that time with Thad, I could fix a lot of things for other people. By the middle of March, when Holy Spirit Alliance hired my replacement, many people in the church suggested that I take care of the computer needs, and Russell could be let go. Part of this was because Tabitha and Marti and other targeted brides did file that formal complaint with the church leadership. Mrs. Prince was so infuriated and embarrassed over what she claimed were "lies from jealous little whores, because they couldn't trap a good, decent man," she stopped attending. Russell became hard to work with after that.

He was the product of his environment. Sometimes I think people should have to have licenses, or at least undergo testing, before they're allowed to have children.

I took my computer skills over to Match, and Zach paid me to help install more computers in the office and set up his network. The first collaboration between Central Avenue Christian and Holy Spirit Alliance was to partner in Gertie's matchmaking service. Rather ironic, this focus on forming strong marriages. Central Avenue, with the counseling help and advice of Holy Spirit Alliance, was slowly "guiding" the family-oriented extremists to either change their minds, or leave the church.

Mrs. Rizetti came into Match and tried to get Gertie to make a match for her *on discount*. Gertie knew who she was and refused. Later, Zach told me he might have been tempted to agree to do her profile, and then "tweak" it so she would get stuck with somebody truly horrible. Maybe Russell?

The new policy for A Match Made in Heaven was that Gertie's matches truly couldn't be "made in heaven" unless the couple had spiritual counseling and their profiles and matches were bathed in prayer. There was always at least one member of the pastoral staff of either church on call for Match during business hours. They took turns with a pager and a hotline number, to counsel clients. If those dating matches turned into engagements, the staff would be available for pre-marital counseling as well.

Zach said if the business kept growing, both in the employment side and the matchmaking side, he would have to find new, bigger offices and take on staff. When I came back from spending the last week of spring training with Dad, he asked for my help in finding a new office, setting up the expanded computer system, and especially keeping a tight rein on Gertie.

Did that mean what I thought it meant? Working together?

How did that fit into his hinted interest in having a relationship outside of work?

I was in charge of placing ads in different online sites, the local papers, and the church newsletters in the area. We talked about books and movies, friends and events at church, and yes, baseball. I did computer work and organized the office, and I even enjoyed walking to Match. I spent at least four hours every day there, on a very generous retainer that included health insurance, because Zach insisted. That was the good news. The bad news? Zach didn't move forward away from a strictly working relationship.

What was wrong with the man?

Did I have to do everything in our relationship?

Or maybe we didn't have the relationship I thought we did, or would, or could?

Gradually, I realized some things *had* changed. On Zach's part. When we were at church. Because I did keep attending Holy Spirit Alliance and I got more involved in Singles. Zach glued himself to my side in class and during any social events we had. And not just because, as he claimed, he wanted to make sure he was on the winning team during Bible trivia contests.

Zach and I took a few bike hikes on weekends. I liked those chilly rides, with stops to drink hot chocolate from the biggest Thermos I had ever seen, which Zach cleverly attached to his bike.

I eased my way into helping with the Singles activities. A couple times when they asked about events I had run at Central Avenue, I told them I would give them guidance, but I needed time off. I would help, but I didn't want to run anything. It was hard not to look at Zach when I said I was getting my life back in balance, and I was looking for some personal time and relationships.

Despite the two of us and the church counselors keeping watch on Gertie, near the end of April she resumed making rash promises to matchmaking clients. It was up to us to take her down a few notches.

"I need your help in a big way," Zach told me, when Gertie stomped out of the office after the latest tag-team lecture session. "I think it's time to fall on your mercy and beg you to come on full-time."

"Yeah?" My mouth hurt from the wideness of my grin.

"I know it's the last thing you want to hear, Dinah, after how you got burned before, but I really, really need you."

"I'm glad. There's a big difference, just depends on who's doing the asking."

"Yeah?" That sheepish look vanished, burned out by the brilliance of his smile. "If I had known that, I would have come up with more excuses to keep you around a long time ago."

"Are you sure that isn't guilt talking, because you haven't found me a job yet?"

"No!"

"Then why do I get the feeling you don't really want to offer me a job?"

He shuffled some of the papers Gertie had left scattered across the desk, then finally looked at me. "I'm trying to keep my personal life separate from my business life, okay?"

"Uh huh."

"What do you mean, uh huh?" He started to stand up.

"I've been trying to figure out why -- well, you keep giving me hints -- and I've been trying to give you hints back --"

"You think because I haven't found you a job yet that I'm afraid to date you?"

"Well, aren't you?" I laughed when he scowled at me. A moment later, he grinned. "How about we make a deal? From nine to five, Monday through Friday, you're the boss."

"What about lunch breaks?"

"That depends if we go out for lunch, or eat in."

"So basically, inside these walls, it's all business."

"You're the boss while we're here at work --"

"Yeah? Between you and Gertie, I seriously doubt I'm ever the boss."

I glared at him, but it was hard to hold onto it when he tipped his head back and laughed.

"Okay, okay. It's a deal. Inside these walls, it's business. After business hours, we're dating." Suddenly the laughter left his face. "Seriously dating."

"How seriously?" My heart did a funny kind of flip, pushing on my lungs and my throat.

"We'll figure that out as we go along."

"Sounds fair." I looked at my watch and tried to figure out how to ask him how soon we could leave so we could start figuring things out, without him thinking I was pushing. Or too eager. Or desperate. Or maybe all three.

"Do you mind my asking one personal question, while we're still officially at work?"

"Depends." There went my heart again, hoping that intensity

in his eyes, that crooked smile that kept fading in and out, was a promise of things to come between us.

"How long did you make old Thad wait before he could kiss you?"

I laughed, thinking about that kiss I had hoped for under the mistletoe. "Thad never kissed me."

"He was an idiot."

"Glad you think so."

"Can we get out of here now?" He stood up.

"You're the boss."

"Yeah? Then I'll race you to the door."

I beat him to the door, mostly because he had to find his keys. Then he had to lock up. Zach caught hold of my hand when we stepped outside, and he managed to get the door closed and locked one-handed. He held my hand as we crossed the parking lot, then he kissed my knuckles before he let go so I could get in my car.

All right, I had been hoping he would try to kiss me right there in the parking lot. Timing was just as important as setting. I wasn't worried or disappointed. The real thing was coming.

END

Titles in the Match Girls Series:

A Match (Not) Made in Heaven
Making It All Up (coming)
Uneasy Money (coming)
Go Ask the Widow (coming)
Marti vs. Marianne (coming)
Assisted ~~Living~~ Loving (coming)

About the Author

On the road to publication, Michelle fell into fandom in college and has 40+ stories in various SF and fantasy universes. She has a bunch of useless degrees in theater, English, film/communication, and writing. Even worse, she has over 100 books and novellas with multiple small presses, in science fiction and fantasy, YA, suspense, women's fiction, and sub-genres of romance.

Her official launch into publishing came with winning first place in the Writers of the Future contest in 1990. She was a finalist in the EPIC Awards competition multiple times, winning with ***Lorien*** in 2006 and ***The Meruk Episodes, I-V,*** in 2010, and was a finalist in the Realm Award competition, in conjunction with the Realm Makers convention.

Her training includes the Institute for Children's Literature; proofreading at an advertising agency; and working at a community newspaper. She is a tea snob and freelance edits for a living (MichelleLevigne@gmail.com for info/rates), but only enough to give her time to write. Her newest crime against the literary world is to be co-managing editor at Mt. Zion Ridge Press. Be afraid … be very afraid.

www.Mlevigne.com
www.MichelleLevigne.blogspot.com
@MichelleLevigne

Also by Michelle L. Levigne

Guardians of the Time Stream: 4-book Steampunk series
Tabor Heights: 20-book inspirational small town romance series.
Quarry Hall: 11-book women's fiction/suspense series

For Sale: Wedding Dress. Never Used: inspirational romance

Crooked Creek: Fun Fables About Critters and Kids: Children's short stories.

Killing His Alter-Ego: contemporary romance/suspense, taking place in fandom.

The Commonwealth Universe: SF series, 25 books and growing

The Hunt: 5-book YA fantasy series

Faxinor: Fantasy series, 4 books and growing

Wildvine: Fantasy series, 14 books when all released

Neighborlee: Humorous fantasy series; re-releasing in 2020; 8 books and growing.

Zygradon: 5-book Arthurian fantasy series

www.ingramcontent.com/pod-product-compliance
Lightning Source LLC
Chambersburg PA
CBHW071256190726
48292CB00007B/2558
9781949564747